Love and Fiction

Kate Gaskarth

CRANTHORPE
MILLNER
PUBLISHERS

First published by Cranthorpe Millner Publishers (2026)

ISBN 978-1-803783-3-90 (Paperback)

www.cranthorpemillner.com

Cranthorpe Millner Publishers

Printed and bound by CPI Group (UK) Ltd
Croydon, CR0 4YY

MIX
Paper | Supporting
responsible forestry
FSC
www.fsc.org   FSC® C013604

For the romantics behind dating app screens. May your messages turn into meet-cutes and your meet-cutes into forever.

And to my very own leading man. I love you.

CHAPTER ONE

In the search bar of her slow-speed web browser, Olivia typed the words *'How to write a fictional boyfriend'* and pressed enter.

Do the search yourself, and you'll find a similar, eclectic range of links as she did. *Take this quiz to discover which fictional boyfriend is yours!* Hers was decidedly Draco Malfoy. Olivia was unsure what that said about her choice of men, but after taking the Potterhead quiz and discovering she was a Slytherin herself, it seemed to check out.

The next web search answer was an online news article that was entitled: *Are Fictional Boyfriends Giving Us Unrealistic Expectations for Real-life Relationships?*

The answer is yes, she thought as she brushed a stray strand of hair back from her face. *Yes, they are.*

As a romance author, Olivia had written many steamy, brooding male characters in her career, a long list of men whom she had conjured up in her mind – each one of her novels adhering to completely unrealistic expectations for romantic meet-cutes and swoon worthy heroes. At first, that was the point. To write someone so much more impressive than the boys who she had spent most of her twenties swiping right on. But long ago were the days when she had dolled herself up and dressed to the nines just to try and actually impress someone. Let alone a man.

No, rather than spending her time attempting to flirt with guys who advertised themselves by holding a dead fish or deer slung over one shoulder, she decided to flirt with something much more interesting: fiction.

Unlike real life, in fiction chivalry was not dead.

Instead, it was thriving, as though the pages were the soil, the ink was its water and the reader its much-needed sunshine. Romance stories, including Olivia's soon-to-be fourth novel, were conceptualised with one aim in mind: to give the reader hope that out there, in the city of London and beyond, some of these seemingly unrealistic men did, in fact, exist. As Olivia sat in her literary agent's spacious office the next morning, fingers nervously picking at her cuticles, she hoped her agent could read between the lines of text and see it. To say she dreaded these meetings, where they shared how well things were going, would be a royal understatement. Because this time, it wasn't going. For what seemed like forever, Olivia had tried, failed, tried and failed again to write any more words.

Since her world came crumbling down, since she lost *him*, her dazzling hero who taught her how to love madly and freely she hadn't been able to write a single pick-up line, love scene or intimate moment. She had begun to question if she understood what love is at all.

In her novels she wrote about happily ever after because she thought she knew them, she thought she'd found hers.

Keyword: *thought*.

"I don't know them." Olivia sighed, staring at the landscape oil painting on the grey office wall behind the desk where her agent sat, rifling through the precious pages. The smooth green lines forming the rolling hills of the English countryside seemed to move together, merging in one big blob of brown and khaki green as she distracted herself by focusing intently on the landscape, anything really, other than the elephant in the room.

Writing her first novel had been easy; the premise of her first bestseller was based on the disappointments from her youth – terrible boyfriends and learning to love herself as a twenty-something female in a world of men. A romance that held the deeper meaning of what it meant to feel feminine and in control of her dating and love life.

It spent six consecutive weeks at number one on the New York Times Bestseller list. She had published her books as though they were her diary. Writing broken characters that all had happy endings felt like an emotional release. To Olivia, it was euphoric. She guessed it was that different kind of success you got when you said *fuck you* to your ex-boyfriend by writing his name in a bestselling novel. Karma was sitting on her living room bookshelf in the form of a shiny gold literary award.

Her second book was a cheesy Christmas romance, with mulled wine and fairy lights alongside the exchange of provocative presents and a fake dating trope. It was her second successful work, and she was officially on the radar.

Hearing the fluttering of paper folding, Olivia looked up at her agent with the inside of her cheek firmly bitten between her teeth.

"You'll get to know them; you don't have any other choice." Hannah Pierce, literary agent, forthright and uncompromising in all her dealings, sat against the corner of her desk, a few pages of Olivia's latest manuscript open in her hands. Furrowing her brows, she plonked the papers before Olivia and smacked her ruby lips. "This is good, but we both know you can do better."

"It's complete and utter rubbish," Olivia blurted, her fingers halting their attack on her cuticles. Crossing her legs, she tried to stop their nervous jiggling. It had been over a year since the accident, and she had found it difficult to pick up a pen and write ever since.

Hannah gave her a sympathetic look, "Look, you're one of my good friends. I understand you've been through a lot in the past year, but there's a deadline. It is creeping up faster than anticipated, and the head office is starting to breathe down my neck"

"I'll finish it; I just need to get back into the swing of things."

"You've had three months to get back into the swing of things. I need more than this." Hannah flicked her manicured fingers towards the measly stack of papers. "At the moment, I'm not sure we can use any of these pages…"

Olivia's heart deflated. It had taken her months to write those measly twenty-something pages – and she had yet to get to the desired meet-cute. She kept going over it, rewriting it and rewriting it, never happy.

Hannah sighed, looking at her client with a tough love stare. "I'm just wondering where the award-winning, bestselling author we invested in is?"

Olivia struggled to find the words; she couldn't answer the question because she simply didn't know. Where had her bestselling writing gone?

Biting her lip, Olivia gnawed on the flesh in the same anxious manner she did whenever the cursor blinked on an empty document. "They normally speak to me, but this time around, I don't know… I feel like I'm trying to force the characters to come forward."

Licking her finger, Hannah sifted through a large pile of papers on her desk. "I'll never understand this 'the character speaks to me' lingo that authors go on about. It honestly sounds a bit insane to me." She was fiddling. Something Olivia knew was Hannah's small and subtle signal that this meeting was coming to a hard close.

Olivia sighed and glanced down at the watch strapped to her wrist by thin brown leather. Noting the time, she let her gaze fall forward again, swinging her arm back into her lap with a small thump of leather against linen. "If characters don't want to be written, they're not written. That's just how it works. Maybe this female character is supposed to be a nun and live a life of celibacy."

Hannah threw her head back and let out a snort laugh. "Three-quarters of your books are purely R-rated sex, Liv. Celibacy isn't in your vocabulary."

She was right. The bulk of Olivia's writing was uncensored, illicit passion between characters. Emotional or otherwise. It's what got readers interested. Steam is what had helped her market her novels online before she got professionally published. Sex sells. It always had and always will.

Olivia groaned, her blonde curls curtaining her cheeks as she leaned forward, elbows on knees and head laid heavily in her slightly sweaty palms. With the brainstorming hour ending and lacking inspiration, she felt as though this meeting had been utterly useless. Nothing had changed. She was in the exact same position she had been a month ago. Rather than forwarding the story with mediocre words – something writers did just to get the story out of their head and down onto paper – Olivia had just edited, again and again, meticulously refining the same chapters over and over.

Correction, something had changed.

Hannah made her way around the desk and sat in the plush leather chair. She seemed to be running out of patience and, Olivia supposed, time.

Leaning forward with her navy skirt bunching around her knees, Olivia snatched the manuscript off the hardwood desk and smoothed over the pages before looking up at Hannah with a determined glint in her eyes. "I'll think of something." She nodded her head as if to convince herself that her inspiration wasn't completely dead and gone.

Hannah stood from her chair, smoothing her grey pencil skirt down before placing her hands on her hips. "Just, whatever you think of and *whoever* you think of, do it fast. The deadline is quickly approaching, and we need our leading man. ASAP." She gave a tight-lipped smile.

Nodding again, Olivia took the silent meeting eviction notice and began to gather her things before giving Hannah a small, unconvincing smile. "August 15th, right?"

Hannah's eyebrows pulled down low on her face. "Fabian moved it up a few months. Didn't you get my email?"

Olivia was seventy-five per cent sure that Hannah had not, in fact, emailed her. Realisation sparking, she asked the dreaded question. "How long do I have, then?"

Hannah took the brutally honest approach Olivia held

ambiguous feelings for. "You have until the end of June."

Two months? Her brow brimmed with sweat. *Is she insane?* Did she have a vendetta against her? Was Ashton Kutcher about to jump out and yell, "*Punk'd?*"

"June!" Olivia cringed. How was she supposed to sort and dissect all her notes, scribbles and thoughts into a compelling story in as little as two months?

She had the bones, sure, but she needed the meat.

She couldn't even write steamy sex between two characters who were still strangers to her because she had yet to decide the characters were dominant and sensual or loving and submissive. How was she supposed to write a perfect male protagonist when every time she thought of romance, she felt sick to her stomach? The concept of writing two characters in love was almost alien to her. If the past year had taught her anything, it was that love was time-sensitive and didn't last forever. She had the worst kind of writer's block a romance author could ever possibly have.

"End of June," Hannah stated as if adding the emphasis of a whole thirty-day month made it better. News flash, it didn't.

Olivia shook her head in disbelief, looking out of the floor-to-ceiling windows to her left at the sun slowly setting over the London skyline. It had been a sunny day for the capital city, and Olivia felt incredibly silly when she remembered about how she had woken thinking the words: *Today will be a good day.* Oh, boy. How wrong she was.

First, she had knocked her coffee all over the kitchen floor approximately fifteen minutes after that very affirmation, and now she had two months left to work on her fourth official manuscript.

Hannah settled back into her black leather seat and began shuffling some papers. "Look, it's doable. You just need to hustle down and focus on the deadline."

Olivia scoffed, gathering her own things and pulling the bag over her shoulder.

"Go people-watching or something," Hannah continued. "I don't know. Just go find him, and when you do, don't call me. Write."

Chapter Two

Olivia lived in a shabby one-bedroom apartment north-west of the Hammersmith line. Adorned with various mismatched colours and textures, the boho chic apartment looked like an old fabric store. Fluffy pillows, dark oak, and mustard yellow splattered on the walls in frames and woven through the old woollen living room rug gave it warmth, while her exposed kitchen shelves housed copious amounts of cacti and tacky handmade mugs. It was small and filled to the brim with far more knickknacks than any girl would need, but it suited her perfectly fine.

With large windows overlooking the London cityscape and situated down the street from a Tesco Metro, she had everything she needed at her fingertips to write a bestselling novel.

Yeah, sure, she scoffed. *If only I could think of a leading man...*

"You know what would look amazing in here?" Danielle interrupted her thoughts, opening the plastic supermarket bag on the dining table, reaching in and grabbing out a bottle of rosé. With a cling of glass, she placed the bottle down on the kitchen worktop. If they stood side by side, the two women would encompass the entire length of her small and semi-improvised kitchen set-up. An old wooden sideboard acted as an island, with second-hand round-top stools far too tall for it shoved on the other side.

Olivia hummed, "Enlighten me." She dragged herself away from her thoughts and instead grabbed two generous wine glasses down from her glass cabinet.

Danielle flung the rest of the shopping bags on the creaky island with a heavy thump.

"Roses," her friend continued, her arms spreading out as if she pictured the flower upon the mantle in front of her. "Pink roses."

Her best friend, Danielle, owned a small boutique flower shop down the way, where they had spent hours discussing arrangements for her small living room, eventually settling on buying a little bunch of peonies to sit on the white wooden mantel above her fireplace.

She had known Danielle since high school, both moving to London from the south-west for big city life and to chase their dreams. Not even two years after their big move, Danielle had met John at some swanky hotel bar in central London. Flash forwards a few years, and they were now happily married and even more in love than they had been when they first met each other. It was sickening. In all the lovey-dovey 'please stop reminding me I'm cripplingly single' romantic ways.

From the very start of their love story, Olivia partially blamed them for her unrealistic expectations of love. After all, meeting your soulmate in a random hotel bar, in 2024, while asking for directions seemed too easy. Too simple. When, for the rest of us twenty-something folk, it was near impossible.

When Danielle met her husband, she had vowed nothing

would change between her and Olivia. That the two of them would gossip to the heavens without his presence once a week whether he liked it or not. She had even written it into her premarital clause (a totally fake document that she had made up, the type of thing Danielle always did) and made him sign on the dotted line before sealing the deal with little more than a kiss. Olivia didn't need the details. But she got them anyway. As best friends did, she knew far too well that her best friend was getting laid on the regular.

It made Olivia's interactions with men look completely complex, even if she was just asking them to help get some ready-salted Pringles down from the top shelf at the supermarket.

Until she met *him*.

Olivia paced her apartment with anxious strides, shoving the thought of *him* deep into the archives of her mind and locking them away with a mental key. Tonight is not the night to remember *him*.

She looked around her autumnal-coloured apartment, from the mustard pillows to the rust-orange throw crumpled up on the edge of the two-seater sofa. Then at the peonies they had only just purchased but which didn't really match her decor. "Roses. Are you sure?"

The evening was cool, rain pelting the windows in typical British fashion. She had made the room feel cosy, turning on only her fairy lights and warm white lamps, something she preferred over switching on the harsh overhead lights.

It was their weekly ritual to buy the cheapest bottle of wine, turn on trash TV and gossip. They had done it for years, and after the meeting with her literary agent earlier that day, Olivia was in desperate need of some girl time. And a ginormous glass of rosé.

Danielle nodded her head, "Oh yeah, I'm sure. With the orange, it would look like a beautiful clash of retro colours." She popped the bottle's cork and began to pour generously into the wine glasses.. "It would totally amplify the vibe you've got going on here."

Olivia looked around the small apartment once more. Her vibe was second-hand, thrifted and comfy fabrics. It looked a mess and didn't match at all.

"I'll go to the shop early next week for a fresh bunch then." Olivia took a deep slug of her wine, humming in delight.

Making their way to her small sofa, they both kicked their shoes off and sat down.

"Anyway, how's the writing going? Still got a huge red stop sign flashing in your brain, or does green finally mean go?"

"Currently in the orange. I've written a little bit, but nothing noteworthy." Olivia sighed heavily. "I don't know what's wrong with me. It's like I've just lost the ability to write."

Normally, Olivia would settle herself in the corner of the closest coffee shop – her favourite being Caffè Nero as of late – and hunker down with her laptop and a latte, listening to the conversations of those around her. There was a sort of magic about taking in the variety of London fashions and accents it had to offer. She would sit there all day making countless notes, writing descriptions of peculiar people or unique wardrobe choices that sparked ideas for her.

But this time, she had tried that.

She had even tried travelling to the Cotswolds, taking a

week to go on country walks, and having baths with lavender-scented soaps. Something that was a luxury for her. She'd thought that a getaway was what she needed to refuel and hit the writing hole at top speed.

She had also tried to find inspiration in other places. By trying new things like tennis or a yoga class she would definitely not be returning to.

Nothing. Nada.

Absolutely bugger all came to her. She had no ideas, no bursts of inspiration, and for a while, she had thought her career as an author was over. She would never write again. This was the writer's block she would never recover from. She was sure it would be her downfall.

Olivia's fifteen minutes of fame was over, and what did she have for it? A trilogy of soppy romance novels with her name plastered on the front of them, and a mother who didn't approve of her career no matter how many bestseller lists she got on.

"Livvy, you're the best writer I know. You've been through a lot; give yourself a break. I know you'll think of something. Whatever it is, it will be nothing short of amazing."

"Your optimism is appreciated." Olivia took a heady gulp of her wine, basking in the warm berry notes.

"It better be," Danielle joked, nibbling on a row of chocolate before swinging her feet up under her and turning towards her friend. "Let's brainstorm then. What are you stuck on?"

"Oh, just everything. The meet-cute, the love story, the leading male character. I have no idea who he is or who he will be."

Danielle hummed in thought, glancing mindlessly at the television. "Okay, hear me out then. The best ideas are always constructed under the influence of cheap rosé."

Olivia nodded, slumping her head back against the sofa hard and sinking further into the soft seat.

"Coffee shop meet?" Danielle suggested. "Cliché, but I'm a sucker for them."

Olivia shook her head. "Overused."

"Best friend's brother?"

"Already done."

Danielle quirked an eyebrow. "Mafia boss?"

A possibility… but Diana Weisman, another romance author, had recently topped the charts with the third instalment of her Mafia romance series, and her publisher had asked for something fresh. Something no one had done in a hot minute.

"No," Olivia quipped, reaching over and nabbing some chocolate from the bowl of sweet treats laid before them..

"What about enemies to lovers? He could be a vampire?" Danielle suggested. "Maybe there could be a blood kink; I heard that's popular with the kids nowadays."

"No. Not vampires. My novel is a romance, not a tween fantasy about iron deficient boys who don't age." Olivia cringed. "And don't use the words kids and kinks in the same sentence, please."

Danielle hummed. "CEO?"

"Did that last time."

"Werewolf?"

Olivia felt like doing the biggest facepalm of all time. It wasn't that the ideas lacked substance. Though they did. But for her fourth novel, the meet-cute was a pivotal moment. It needed to be fresh. New. The ideas suggested were missing something. They didn't seem to fit with where she wanted to go with the story.

At least *that* was something she knew.

Danielle shrugged her shoulders. "You're right. Silly suggestion."

"I feel like I've exhausted all avenues."

Her friend glanced at Olivia and muttered into the rim of her large wine glass. "Not... all avenues."

Olivia laughed, her hair flicking over her shoulder as she turned and faced Danielle with a defeated smile. "What else could I possibly try?"

"Well, it's been a year since the accident, and you haven't been on a date since..." Danielle spoke carefully. Olivia had been through a whirlpool of emotion and trauma in the past twelve months, and Danielle had been there by her side the whole way. She helped her more than she knew. Olivia could see that glint in her friend's eye, and before she even said it, she knew exactly what her friend was about to say.

"Are you suggesting I date? Because you're giving me that look, the one you get when you're about to say something wild, so if you are, then my answer is a hard, definite no." Olivia shook her head. "No way."

"It's been a year, Liv. You need to get out again and have fun."

"I'm well aware of how much time has passed." *Not long enough*, she thought. It would feel wrong. The past twelve months had all felt so wrong.

"Look, there's heaps of apps nowadays where you can meet

people, not even for dating. Just community. Maybe that's what you need. To find your people. Your heroine's man. This could be it. A few online dates, and you could have your leading man before you even open your laptop."

Olivia gnawed on her lip as she thought. Her fingers had grown numb from the ice-filled glass of Rosé, and like her memories of *him*, she felt the numbness wind up her arm and clutch her heart in the same icy grip she'd had to endure many times before. The same icy pain that stabbed her heart when she realised he was never coming back. No, she couldn't date. Not when it had only been a year. A measly twelve months. Some said that it would go away, the numbness, but when she looked around and saw reminders of *him*, it still felt too raw. She was scared and hated to admit it, but Danielle was right. She *could* have her novel's leading man before even sitting down to write. That excited her and sparked something that hadn't touched her mind for a while. The itch to write, the incredible possibility of opening a blank Word document and writing whatever she wanted.

Three hours, two bottles of wine and nothing but an empty food container next to her later, Olivia glanced down at her phone, which lay on the coffee table. Her eyes shifted back and forth between the device and the sad lack of writing on the Word document tab open on her dinosaur of a laptop. Danielle had left a half hour prior with some final words of inspiration, a rushed "Good luck" before she blew her a kiss and piled herself into the back of her husband's car.

How bad could it be? She would only do it for research. Some would even call it science. She would download the apps, swipe to her heart's content and see where it went. She'd done it before, in university. Hell, she'd even walked halfway across Oxford to meet with a guy in a shabby Starbucks. Didn't even tell her mum or friends. No location tracking. Nothing. She'd lived on dating apps once. Existed in the realm of early adulthood hook-ups and online dating. She could do it again.

Think of the book. Think of him. Whoever he is. He's obviously not going to write himself.

With a sigh of defeat, Olivia snatched her phone off the table and resigned herself to downloading every single dating app available.

"I cannot believe it's come to this," she admitted to herself in the dim yellow light of her living room, watching as her photos uploaded and the first possible leading man in her area appeared on her cell phone screen.

Then, she began swiping.

Chapter Three

"So, tell me about yourself," the golden-haired man sitting before her asked.

They had been on this so-called date for all of five minutes and Olivia already felt like rolling her eyes. It was a Saturday, and after a week of scrolling and swiping, she had humoured Danielle's idea of getting online and meeting men.

All in the name of research. She had been surprised when she woke the next morning to find a string of matches waiting in her inbox. Her swiping session had been more successful than she realised. Knowing that over ninety-nine men in her surrounding area had 'liked' her made her stomach churn with a guilty plummet. After two coffees, one for the caffeine, and one for the taste, she'd opened the first message and taken a deep breath. *This is research*, she'd convinced herself as she aimlessly swiped. *Sad and debilitating research.*

She chose a suitable Italian bistro with a promising menu of small appetisers and decent wine where she would be content to stay for several hours. The restaurant and bar with its unlimited breadsticks was the perfect spot to meet the men, fishermen, farmers and suits alike that she had reluctantly swiped on. *It's all for the greater good*, she had thought last night while huddled on the Sherpa rug on her living room floor between her sofa and the small glass coffee table, this time with a glass of Merlot in hand. *It's not unethical at all, even if it's only been a year. A year since him.*

The first man arrived fifteen minutes late and with an apparent ruby-red smear of lipstick on the side of his collar. Classy.

Was Olivia in the game for finding real authentic love with Jim from south London, whose hobbies, according to his dating profile bio, were: *doing you *winky face**? Olivia visibly cringed at the memory. No. Absolutely not.

So how could she blame him for arriving at their mechanical-seeming date, completely unashamed of his adulterous nature, when he clearly wasn't interested in committed, authentic love either? In all honesty, she had to give him some props. At least he'd got some. *And...* she needed a vice. Something to help her dig herself out of this writing rut and back on track to writing an unforgettable male lead. That wasn't in question. Hannah never failed to drive the threat of the deadline deep under Olivia's skin every time she opened her emails. She had to meet it, and this was the quickest, and least morally grey way to do so. She was willing to try almost anything to help her cause.

Almost. Note the keyword there.

Glancing at the man now sitting before her, all dishevelled and lanky, with thick-rimmed glasses hanging low on his nose, she politely smiled before recalling the brief and to-the-point monologue she had prepared in response to this very particular and standard question. "Well, I'm an author—"

"Wow! That's amazing," the man interrupted, leaning back in his chair and puffing out his chest. His buggy blue eyes met hers in unsettling eye contact.

Olivia blushed at the compliment, tucking a strand of her hair away from her face. It was not often she received such positive feedback about her career path. The kind words allowed her to brush over the interruption. "Thank you, I—"

"You know, when I was younger, I used to want to be a karate sensei." The man, whose name she had already forgotten, reached up and adjusted his glasses with bony fingers.

Olivia's eyebrows shot up in surprise. "Really?"

"Oh yeah, I loved the idea of it. Seemed badass." He paused, taking a long swig of the drink before him. The ice cubes sloshed and clanged obnoxiously in the small glass as he sipped.

After a few moments, Olivia smiled once more, unsure if he was going to continue speaking or if that was the end of that topic. "How did you get into karate then?"

This conversation was about as interesting as yesterday's pop culture news. Aka, tedious. Worse, in fact, than the third man she had met, an hour ago, who kept rambling about moving to Germany to become a farmer. The curly-haired ginger had gone on and on about earning enough money to afford a combine harvester. At least he had goals.

A few more beats of silence were shared. Olivia glanced at her date before reaching over and grabbing a breadstick from the wicker basket to the left side of the table and nibbling on the crust. "Did you ever—?"

"Oh, God no," he interrupted once again. "I've never set foot in a dojo in my life."

Olivia pursed her lips with irritation. That was that. She

decided she couldn't take any more. She liked to think of herself as a patient person, but one could only put up with so much. With a deep sigh, she leaned down and pulled out her shamrock notebook, clicking the top of her pen.

When she had contacted Hannah the previous night regarding her speed dating mission, she had said three things. *"Be brave. Be ruthless. Write that man."*

It fuelled Olivia's mission. Find her leading man. Just write *him*.

Olivia felt remorseful for crossing their names out of her notebook, but why take up any more precious time? With June only two months away, it was a precious and holy commodity she couldn't bear to waste. Her leading man simply could not wait.

"What's that?" the man asked, eyes coming together in confusion.

Olivia interrupted him by drawing a sharp, emphasised line through his name on the paper. Looking up, she gestured to the waiter and asked for another generous glass of red. "I'm so sorry, Jake…"

"Jett."

"Jett." Olivia gave him an apologetic smile. "But we seem to be out of time."

"Out of time?" His confusion was bundled up into three lines on his forehead.

She held up a palm, pausing his objection. Yes, it was rude. But at this point, she didn't care. "Yes. Out of time." She leaned forward and placed a hand on his. "Look, I'm not here to waste my time or yours. So, I'll cut to the chase."

Be ruthless. Olivia prepared herself with another deep

breath. *Just do it. Like ripping off a plaster.*

Jett let out a disbelieving laugh, dragging a hand down his face and scratching the small scruff along his jaw. "But—"

"No buts. We've been sitting here for all of fifteen minutes, and you've interrupted me every time I've spoken. I'm very thankful you made the journey, but this will never work."

He began to protest, his hand curling up to tug on his tie, "You can't just—"

Be brave, be ruthless. The only way she would get through the ethics of the night was to take off her cloak of caution and instead adorn the armour Hannah had provided.

"Oh, but I can, Jett." Olivia lifted her hand up and gestured towards the door. "Have a safe journey home."

His eyes flitted around the restaurant in embarrassment, cheeks reddening at her candour. Mouth opening and closing like a goldfish. God. You would think that she'd just broken his heart.

Olivia folded her napkin, smiling as the waiter returned with the bottle of red, filling her glass as requested.

Shaking his head in disbelief, Jett stood, pushing away from the crisp white linen table and out of the plush blue velvet seat before making his way out of the establishment with some murmurs that she knew were derogatory and offensive remarks about her.

She had been as ruthless as she could be and would be lying if she said there wasn't something powerful about watching a fully grown man stomp out of a dining establishment like a toddler throwing a tantrum in the playground because she had told him no.

After all, that's what this Italian bistro was, for the next few hours. Her playground. She had come on this speed dating mission with intent. And Lord help her if she let a five-foot-five man with no social awareness ruin that for her.

"So, I told him, you haven't seen anything yet!"

Meet Brad. Thirty-one years old. Can often be found sneaking alcohol to minors at music festivals and pretending he's still twenty-one.

Aka, a real catch.

Olivia had swiped on him in an attempt to broaden her search net.

He was nowhere near what she considered her type. No, hers was tall, dark and handsome.

Instead, Brad reminded her of her best friend's ex.

Blond and with a questionable intelligence quotient.

Olivia had hypothesised that to achieve her goal of finding her leading man, she'd have to go on a few questionable drink dates. Maybe even kiss a few frogs. And she was prepared. With breadsticks and peppermint chewing gum from the Tesco Metro around the corner.

"What happened next?" Olivia feigned enthusiasm, humouring the man-boy sitting across from her.

"I fucking KO-D him, man!" Brad leaned back, slapping his hand heavily on the table.

Olivia felt the knock on her forearms and winced as the sound of cutlery rattling echoed around the small bistro. If no one had been looking at their table before, they sure were now.

Olivia picked up the shaken metal utensils, realigning the knife on her napkin.

Did he just call me man? She let out her own laugh, one of disbelief and, dare she admit it, a little embarrassment.

Man. Olivia was unsure if she had just been unconsciously friend-zoned or if it was just a strange, surfer-slang thing he had going on.

London was nowhere near the sea, and on the coast, deep-water fishermen were the closest thing you'd find to California-esque surfers.

There was most likely only a small group of surfers who would brave the English Channel or sea. At the very least, not many would be caught dead wearing the fluorescent Hawaiian printed shirt that loudly adorned Brad's slight beer belly and hairy chest.

Still laughing, Olivia leaned down and grabbed the notebook once more. "Oh, Brad…"

From the outside you might have glanced Olivia's way and thought one of two things.

One: that poor girl. That poor and desperate girl. She must be so lonely. How utterly insane to be going on multiple dates back-to-back over the course of one night, ordering way too many glasses of Pinot Noir and breadsticks.

Two: (if someone stuck around long enough to see her reach into her satchel bag and retrieve the dreaded green book) What a rude, unforgiving woman. A woman who held such little – or no – regard for someone else's feelings. How could she? The sheer audacity of women these days…

Mario did not see the notebook coming. How could he when they had been having a pleasant time so far? Olivia even had high hopes for him. He was charming, respectful, ambitious. He was her type and had a ridiculously sexy Italian accent.

It was all going so well until he told her what he was passionate about and where that ambition was directed.

"I want to race cars."

She pursed her lips, eyes examining the dark Italian features, floppy hair and thick moustache adorning his top lip.

"You want to race cars?" She had to bite her bottom lip to contain her amusement. *Don't laugh, Livvy. You're better than this. Don't laugh, don't laugh, don't laugh…*

Nodding her head, her eyes met Mario's. "What type of cars?" she finally asked, intrigued to see if he was doing a bit or not. Surely, he was doing a bit. He was even wearing a red shirt, for crying out loud.

"Go-karts."

That was it. Olivia burst out laughing. It was the first time that night she had genuinely laughed. "Go-karts!"

"Uh… yeah, go-karts." Mario looked at her, his eyebrows coming together. "Is… is there a problem with that?"

Olivia wasn't even embarrassed when she snorted, eyes filling with water as she continued laughing. She swore she had never laughed so hard on a date before. Real OR fake. This time, it was her turn to slam her hand against the crisp cloth.

"Excuse me," Mario spoke, his voice lined with offence.

"Just because I race cars—"

"Oh. Come. On," she interrupted, wheezing slightly. "You cannot be serious."

Olivia smiled, looking across at Mario. She watched as his expression remained stoic, and she felt her smile freeze.

Oh God. This man, who was named Mario, who liked to race go-karts and whose favourite colour was red… Was *serious.*

"Oh…" Olivia cleared her throat before whispering, "You're serious."

He stood up, stomping past the bar muttering a small but poignant "*Bitch*" under his breath, and left the restaurant with swift footsteps.

This time, once she had retrieved her notebook, she wrote her own name at the bottom of the lined page, right under his, and with two strikes, both were gone.

He's troubled, she thought. *No. He's too much work. That's what he is.*

Regan.

He was number nine. His online dating profile had shown a picture of him at an indie pop concert wearing an open, white linen top and a thin silver chain around his neck. She'd appreciated it with a firm right swipe. Confidence is key, she had thought, and lo and behold, she had matched with him. She had no idea how but was happy about the fact, nonetheless.

He had an Austin Butler look to him: sandy blond hair

gelled and fluffed just right, eyes blue that glinted with mystery and smoulder. He had a sleeve of tattoos decorating his right arm, the curling patterns peeking out from beneath the cuff of his leather jacket.

He was undeniably sexy –? It was still a mystery how had she even managed to match the dreamboat in front of her. But though this attraction pulled her in, and was the reason she hadn't crossed his name out yet, the other more important question swirling around in her head remained: what was wrong with him?

She made a mental note to check her app settings once she returned home later that night. He exuded stereotypical 'bad boy heartthrob' energy. The kind of guy who owned a motorcycle, and your mother warned you against seeing. The kind of guy you would climb out your bedroom window after midnight as a teenager just to watch him smoke a cigarette.

He was sexy, sure. But Olivia had to momentarily check in and ensure she was being realistic. She didn't want a bad boy. She had long since gone through that phase. Numerous escapades in high school and university of the 'let's just go with the flow' type, which had of course led to casual sex. They had meant nothing to her. They were not real love, but instead a string of young infatuations.

So, she couldn't help but sigh as Regan continued nattering his exciting, thrilling, maybe even dangerous tale. He was captivating. There was no denying that. It was just a shame bad boys were a breed she no longer had any interest in. And, sadly, neither did the heroine of her novel. No, this book would be different from the others lining the shelves. No, it was out with the boys, out with the Jetts and Brads and

Marios and Regans, and in with the real men.

The dependable kind.

The kind who fell in love hard and fast. Like passionate, spontaneous sex. The kind where you're both so consumed with one another that before you even blink, it's happening. You're pressed up against the door with your skirt hitched up around your hips, moaning in pleasure.

Her male lead needed to be in control but also be able to recognise a woman's ownership of her sexuality and feelings. He needed to love like Olivia's leading character was his religion and her hips their god.

Regan was, unfortunately, not that man.

After Regan had left the table, furrowed brow and all, muttering the exact curse words and names she had heard numerous times that night, she no longer felt any guilt in crossing his name out harshly with black biro.

In fact, she pressed so hard the pen formed a small hole where his name was on the cream paper, rendering it decipherable after his melodramatic exit.

Olivia had had enough. Nine terrible dates, and she felt the enthusiasm of Danielle's speed dating research proposal drain out of her.

Now, all she longed for was her fluffy slippers and the comfort of a *Friends* rerun. She was ready to give up, delete the apps entirely and throw her phone in the furnace. Or out the window. Either one would do.

She—

"Sorry I'm late," a voice interrupted, before the familiar drag of the velvet chair sounded. "I believe you've been waiting for me?"

CHAPTER FOUR

Theo twirled the cocktail stick around the bulky glass in his hand. The jingle of ice cubes colliding filled his ears, muting his friend's elaborate monologue.

"Come on, man. Stop looking so sullen." Finn slapped a forgiving hand on his friend's back before lifting the empty glass from the bar top and slinging back the remnants of his Guinness.

Clicking his fingers towards a waiter with black slacks, Finn continued, "We'll find someone for you."

Theo rubbed a hand across his forehead. His friend's words made him feel like a man hopeless at love, but that wasn't the reason for them sitting in the bistro with a strong drink in each of their hands.

His sister was getting married. What should have been an exciting time of planning and celebration had come to a halt when Theo announced he had broken up with his girlfriend of three years – eight months ago. He knew he should have told his family, but in all fairness, they had only met her a handful of times. It had taken him five months to build up the courage to introduce them, and he could count on one hand how many times since their first introduction that they had met again. Theo could still hear his sister's words from the weekend prior, her voice high-pitched and laced with evident worry over the phone.

"Theodore, we need your RSVP. Are you bringing Annika? I think she would make a beautiful bridesmaid. Becky's grandmother just died, poor thing, so a bridesmaid spot has opened up. It would make me so happy."

"Yeah, about that..." Theo had said hesitantly., *earning an irritated sigh in response.*

The problem was, Theo's ex was, quite frankly, a horrible person.

Theo had discovered that she cheated multiple times throughout their relationship. It was all rather unfortunate. Theo had never thought this would happen to him. It had taken his best mate to show him a shady online dating profile and some scandalous comments on her Instagram to determine that she was playing him. Well, that and him getting home to their flat only to find her legs swung over some other man's hips and the haunting sight of their bare skin.

Denial was the first and the last step for him. Acceptance came all too quickly. Forgiveness was simply not in Theo's vocabulary.

Not when Annika had decided to cheat on him with some businessman from an accounting firm downtown. The businessman in question had also been in a relationship at the time.

His about-to-be-ex-girlfriend's feelings for him (or lack thereof) now starkly obvious, he'd promptly ended the relationship feeling like a complete and utter dipshit.

"Annika and I decided to part ways." He didn't want to beat

around the bush.

Georgia scoffed. "That's the polite way of saying you dumped her."

Theo decided to stop avoiding the elephant. "That's the polite way of saying I wasn't the only one she was seeing, Gee."

Georgia let out a gasp. "I swear to God, Teddy, if I get my hands on her—"

He was glad to know she had his back in the situation. "Calm down, Georgie, it's not a big deal. It just means that my RSVP is just me."

She laughed disbelievingly. "Oh, no, you don't. I'm not having my wedding photos look uneven. We need an equal groom and bridal party. You need to find someone."

The line cut out a bit, leaving Theo wondering if it were the cogs in his mind making the silence seem louder or it was just the shitty reception from across the Irish channel.

"Really, it's not a big deal. I'll just come by myself and dance with Mum…"

"No. Please. You have to find someone. For me, pretty please? You would hate to let your baby sister down so close to her wedding, wouldn't you?" Georgia pulled the baby sister card, and Theo groaned, knowing he wouldn't win this war.

She was taking full advantage of the fact he would do anything for her. Including finding a stupid plus-one for her wedding day. Strings or no strings attached.

"Please, please, pleeeease."

Theo moved the phone away from his ear and sighed into the darkness of his empty apartment. "Fine."

Georgia squealed on the other end of the line. "Thank you, thank you, thank you!"

"But I get to choose who I take," he interrupted her celebratory squeals. "No involving Mum, understand?" Theo stood firm on his condition.

He knew if his mother were involved, he'd be taking Janet from Zumba class or Stacy-from-bridge's granddaughter.

Silence filled the line for a few beats before Georgia sighed. "I accept your conditions only if you promise you won't bring Finn. He doesn't count. You need to bring someone who would look good in the cowl-neck silk dresses I ordered."

"You don't think Finn could pull off a blue silk dress?" he teased.

His sister and best friend of ten years had a strange relationship. They had known each other forever, but every time they were in a room together, it was like watching a WWE match fought with words. Insults were fired everywhere, and there was no protective gear to stop them from spitting blood. Theo thought 'relationship' because, amidst the quarrels and not-so-subtle jabs at each other, the two would sit and smile nicely in holiday photos or laugh at the same crude joke made by one or the other.

Georgia scoffed in annoyance. "Not funny. You have two weeks to RSVP with a plus-one."

"I'll see you in June, Georgie."

"Okay, see you, big bro."

"Love you."

"Yeah, yeah." Georgia spoke hurriedly before clicking off, the thrumming dial tone resounding in Theo's ears.

So here he was now, sitting alongside Finn at the bar of a small Italian bistro in central London.

"On the hunt," Finn had said during their overpriced taxi ride. Theo had given his bachelor friend the side-eye and a

disapproving shake of the head before he had even finished the comment. Propping themselves on two bar stools, overlooking two sturdy wooden slabs holding liquor, and illuminated by blue neon lights, Theo and Finn had ordered drink after drink.

Gazing over the restaurant every now and then, they eyed up the middle-aged women sitting lonesome at the bar down from them and the sickeningly happy couples at the square white linen tables, holding hands and eating spaghetti Bolognese far too elegantly. Theo regarded the women with a watchful but respectful gaze, admitting defeat at the fact there were no women here who were single, emotionally available, or crazy enough to agree to a random wedding invite to Ireland.

"Look, we've been here for over an hour now. There's no one here." Theo took another swig of his drink.

The sound of a chair scraping back harshly got the pair's attention; they watched a short, dark-haired man storming off with a pointed "*Bitch*" thrown over his shoulder. Theo lowered his glass from his lips and frowned, turning on his stool and facing the small dining area, finding where the man had come from, eventually landing on a small table on the far side of the restaurant. There sat the most beautiful woman he had ever seen.

Golden locks, curled at the ends and shining under the dull lights of the bistro, adorned the edges of a heart-shaped face. Bright blue eyes, which he noticed flickered with something humorous, before his attention was drawn down her button nose to her bottom lip. Painted a daring red and tucked into her mouth in a look of contempt. She wore a tight black dress, the neckline teasing him with a small glimpse of voluptuous cleavage. He wondered what it would feel like in his hands, what it would be like to kiss down her throat and down her décolletage, paying special attention to those pale soft mounds.

The woman, who had at this point captivated every cell in Theo's body, leaned down and scribbled something in a small, A5 green notebook. Something sparked deep in Theo's mind, a glint of curiosity beaming across his face.

"Oh no," Finn resounded.

"Oh no, what?" Theo asked, still looking towards the woman, who was now shaking hands with another man. He watched as the other man sat down, noting their polite meeting, the way her lips curled up seductively. The shift of her eyes over the figure in front of her. This second man, wearing a worn leather jacket and with slicked-back dirty blond hair, seemed to get her attention enough. Even Theo had to admit the man in front of her was one his own sister would probably swoon over. The ladies often called that style the bad boy look.

They appeared to be enjoying each other's company. The woman licked her lips before wrapping them around the end of a breadstick far too suggestively, more so than she probably knew. He had no doubt the man had picked up on the action and noted how he shifted in his seat not so subtly. The woman leaned back and shook her head with laughter.

It looked as though she was having a nice time, laughing at jokes and sipping red wine. It was only when she leaned over the table and placed her delicate hand on the man's sitting across from her that Theo noted how his smile dropped, eyes narrowing at her. The corner of Theo's lips quirked in interest as he watched her ruby-red mouth form words too far away to decipher before Leather Jacket pushed the same velvet chair back and stormed past him and Finn, muttering "Fucking bitch" in the same degrading and offensive manner as the last.

Clicking his tongue, Theo shifted his eyes back to the woman, who, to his surprise, exhaled loudly before pulling that same notebook out from her bag and making an aggressive stroke across the page.

"You've got that look."

"What look?"

"The look." Finn followed Theo's gaze and began to shake his head. "No way, man. No way. Her?"

Theo grinned.

"Her."

CHAPTER FIVE

"I believe you've been waiting for me?"

"Excuse me?" Olivia glanced up from her attack on the page, neck craning to see a broad figure standing before her.

Wide palms and long fingers holding the back of the chair adjacent to her were linked to strong, taut, muscular arms leading up to wide-set shoulders. Her mouth opened and closed as she took in the firm chest clad in a crisp white shirt and brown jacket.

Olivia could tell from her seat he had to be at least six feet two. Her eyes continued to make their way down the man's body, taking in the strong thighs clad in dark-washed jeans before trailing back up to his head of dark wavy hair and piercing brown eyes.

"I'm sorry I'm late; I had another engagement. I hope you haven't been waiting long," he said, and gosh, Olivia felt a ping in her lower stomach at the low baritone.

Pulling out the same chair nine others had sat on that night, he sat down. The old navy seat seemed more fitting for him than it had for the others. His broad frame filled it in an almost regal manner. The soft-cushioned frame swallowed his shoulders; however, he still sat with a perfectly relaxed posture.

Olivia frowned, staring down at the list of struck out names before her. James, Reuben, Jett, Brad, Mario, Regan...

Was she expecting someone? She was sure her evening was due to draw to an end, the long list of names teetering off into thin blue lines and empty paper.

"Uh..." Olivia was baffled. She glanced at the list once more before confirming that she had, in fact, not forgotten another date. She simply did not have another one planned. "I think you've got the wrong—"

"I'm at the right table." He said with a confident smirk.

Theo had considered leaving after his third whiskey, but after she had caught his eye, he knew he was staying. Despite his friend's tempting offer of bar hopping down the street to the Royal Oak, he had declined, instead noting the compelling way she had leaned back in her chair and let out snorting laughter at a man wearing a terrible red button shirt.

He couldn't help but be fascinated by the small green book and the names she had crossed out within. He was intrigued. He wanted to know what she was up to.

"You are at the right table?" she asked sceptically.

Theo leaned back and stared at Olivia with unfeigned interest. Up close she was a sight to see, bright blue eyes staring back at his with sparks of passion and curiosity that matched his own. There was no denying the woman before him was beautiful. Now that he was sitting before her, he could see the light freckles that were scattered over the bridge of her nose, and the smooth, plump curve of her cupid's bow, forcing his eyes to take in the deep pink flush of her lips. This woman, he swore, could bring any man to his knees with a mere glance.

Theo was going to find out what was written in that book, and what this woman was doing speed dating on a Saturday night, when it was apparent from the lustful glances of the other men in the room that she didn't need to do so. If she just looked up, she would see that the last thing she had to do was to search for men. They were right there.

"Most definitely," he said.

"Okay," she humoured him. "Name?"

"Theo." He gave his most disarming smile. "Now, tell me – what's in the book."

She pulled the notebook towards her chest, suddenly protective. "It's confidential."

Theo quirked an eyebrow, hoping it made him look attractive, charming. His eyes beamed with curiosity, telling her he wasn't going to let up. He was determined.

"Listen, you're attractive," she started. "I get it. You've got that whole 'I'm the guy you'd take home to your parents, but they'd hate me if they found out what I'm like in the bedroom' look."

He grinned, two dimples finding a home on his stubbled cheeks and tipped his head down at her suggestive words.

Theo was more captivated by her than she knew. For the past hour, he had waited for an opening, wanting to be one of the men she talked to and flirted with, laughing at their terrible jokes. He had watched her gulp back her wine like it was water and glance towards the exit as though placing her own personal hex on each date that stormed out with a huff.

She had waited a few minutes each time until the door had swung shut, and the men had left with their dignity in shreds, before reapplying her dangerous red lipstick and placing that damn green book back in her bag. Oh, how fascinated he was by that bloody A5 notepad.

Theo felt the corners of his lips curl up as she called him attractive and watched as her polished nails clutched the book, applying pressure and fidgeting with the elastic strap.

"But," she continued, "you're not what I'm looking for. You're not who... Naomi is looking for."

"Naomi?" Theo was caught off guard. So, this was not for her. Maybe a sister, friend, oh god – her mother? She was going on dates to find someone suitable for someone else. She was either incredibly loyal or incredibly stupid.

What perplexed him, however, was why had she dressed up. Who would lather on a seductive red lip lipstick and squeeze into a little black dress to find a suit or for someone else? "Who is Naomi?"

"My main character," she stated.

Theo felt his eyebrows pull together in question. Her eyes flickered across his face, before she let out a small sigh and brought her gaze away from his jawline and back to his eyes.

"So, you're a writer?" he asked after a moment of consideration.

"Yes." She blinked. "And... and you are not what I... I mean, what *she* is looking for." She spoke with such determination. Such intelligence.

"Enlighten me." Theo leaned forward, his curiosity through the roof. "What is she looking for?"

She was stumped. The whole point of this evening was to shine a spotlight on the answer to that very question. However, after the long record of bad dates, she was reluctant, but not too prideful to admit it had been a failure. Instead of receiving clarity about what she wanted, she found herself stuck further in the grey zone. More dark corners were lurking, and she had many, many more questions. She still had no idea what she was looking for. With this admission at the forefront of her mind, she felt doubt and fear creep in once again. How stupid was this idea? How silly was it for her to have gone ahead with such an evening? Her best friend was amazing and incredible, but this time Olivia was starting to think she had been wrong.

At this rate, she was never going to meet her deadline for the manuscript, and her leading man would remain unwritten. She felt the same numbness begin to make her fingers jolt with pins and needles, the heaviness in her heart growing with her doubt.

"I-I … don't know," Olivia admitted. Slumping back in her seat, she let her guard down for the first time that night, kicking off her heels underneath the table and slapping the notebook alongside the crumb-covered side plate.

Theo eyed her. Her shoulders had slumped, her eyes felt heavy. It had been a long night. She grabbed a breadstick and bit the end off irritably.

In a brave voice, he asked, "May I?"

She paused nibbling and stared at him. *What's his prerogative?* She allowed her eyes to drift down, following the small and hesitant gesture of his left hand towards the book that lay between them. Blinking, she shoved the bonded paper across the crisp tablecloth towards his awaiting fingers.

What had she got to lose? All her dignity had already been thrown out the window that night. Surely a stranger reading her notes wouldn't damage her self-esteem much more than date number eight had.

The man made haste, flipping through the pages, eyes hungrily scanning what she knew was her barely legible writing. Silence seemed to settle between them; the only sound was him running his finger down the page, caressing it slightly, before using his pointer finger to flick the page over. Olivia swore she had never been so turned on at this simple movement. Who knew sifting through the pages of a book could be an art of seduction? Finishing off the breadstick, she licked her butter-covered fingers and reached for the remainder of her wine.

"Jett…" He suddenly spoke, making her pause in her pursuit of alcohol, if only for a moment. "Karate kid wannabe. Kept interrupting me." Reaching a hand up, he dragged his long, limber fingers through his dark waves, messing up his hair in an irritatingly perfect manner. She couldn't help but follow the small, almost unconscious gesture. Coughing under her breath, Olivia crossed her legs under the table and pulled the hem of her dress down. Her cheeks were flushed much more than they were supposed to be, and if he had the audacity to ask why, she would have no problem blaming the wine instead of her raging hormones.

It had absolutely nothing to do with the fact she had not had sex in over a year, or how she had not even entertained the idea of diving back into the dating pool since *him*.

"Reuben…" Theo continued. "Asked to see my feet… Mario, was too much of a video game weirdo. Called me a bitch." He paused, remembering the red shirt who had cursed as he left the restaurant. Clenching his jaw, he moved on quickly, trying not to focus on how nice it would've been to punch him.

"Dan… bad breath… Richard, dick." Theo glanced up at the woman in front of him, his eyebrow lifted in question. She gave him a knowing glance that made him quirk the side of his mouth.

"He was a dick. Rude and self-centred. I took inspiration for the insult from his name, so what?" She shrugged, leaning forward and flashing Theo a small strip of creamy skin. He looked away, which she found endearing.

"Kian," he continued. "Made a comment about how many breadsticks I have eaten." Theo glanced up, this time glancing between the near-empty wicker basket on the table and the gorgeous woman before him. "How many?" he asked.

She sighed again, lifting her glass, "Not enough to soak up the two bottles of red I've consumed."

Theo laughed. "Fair. I'm sure I'd be the same if I'd had your evening." He looked thoughtful for a moment. Then, "I'll help you," he stated finally, still holding the notebook.

"What?" Olivia spluttered.

"I'll help you," Theo repeated as if it was simple. "You want a leading man, well, here I am." Reaching over the table, he grabbed her pen and wrote his name at the bottom of the list, before passing the book back to her with a snap of the elastic. "When do you need him?"

"Uh." Olivia was stunned. This stranger… who was he,

42

and why was he willing to help her?

"I'm assuming you have a deadline to meet of some kind?"

Despite the questions circulating her brain, she answered him almost immediately. "By the end of June."

"Two months." Theo pondered the timeframe for a moment before speaking once again. "Okay, that's possible. We can do that."

We.

He said 'we', as though they were going to work together. That by the end of June, she would have her leading man.

"I'm free most evenings, except for every second Sunday." He reached over and grabbed himself a breadstick.

"You're going to help me?" Olivia stuttered, placing her glass down at the table. Suddenly she felt sober. As if she hadn't just drunk two bottles of Pinot and started a Merlot 2023. She couldn't help the surprise she felt.

"I'm going to help you," he confirmed. "If you want me to."

Olivia continued to stare at this man who had willingly added his name to her notebook of questionable men. "Why would you do that? You don't even know me."

He reached out a strong hand, veins prominent and disappearing underneath the sleeve of his jacket. She could only imagine what his forearms looked like. Placing her sweaty palm in his, she hated how firm his grip was, and how her own small hand was oh-so perfectly engulfed by his.

"Well, you know my name." He smiled, showing a row of perfectly straight teeth, two dimples on either side of his cheeks. He raised an eyebrow enquiringly. "And you are?"

She felt red heat travel up from her chest and settle in her cheeks. "Olivia."

His smile widened, before she felt him give her hand a gentle squeeze. "It's a pleasure to meet you, Olivia."

Her eyes had travelled down and zoomed in on his plush lips, noting the way they curled, and how his tongue clicked and moved as he said the word *pleasure.*

"See," he continued, their hands still joined. "Now we're not strangers."

Narrowing her eyes with curious excitement, she thought, *who is this man?* Before asking, "And what if it doesn't work? What if it gets to June, and I still have no leading man?"

"You will." He shrugged confidently.

"How can you be so sure?"

"Look, you're in control. If you're not happy, you get to do what you've done to every poor bugger who has been fortunate enough to hear you laugh, smile and simply be in your company tonight." He let go of her hand and picked up the notebook once more, before placing it between her fingers. "You get to take your pen and strike out my name. No clauses, no questions, no explanations. At any moment."

"What's in it for you?" Olivia considered. "How do you benefit from this?"

He dragged his hand through his hair one more time, before looking intently at Olivia. "My sister's getting married in June. Small ceremony, but she's been bugging me about finding a plus-one. If this works, and I help you find your leading man, then all I ask is for you to take a night off and watch two sickeningly in love people get hitched in Ireland with me."

He sounded in earnest, and for some reason Olivia trusted

he wasn't going to lie to her. To add weight to his story, he took his phone out of his pocket and showed her the sheer volume of messages from his sister and mother asking if he had found someone yet.

"I've got to tell them next week who I'm bringing and frankly I've been putting it off. But if you said yes…"

She was aware of the pit growing in her stomach over how transactional this interaction was but knowing he was open to such a ludicrous idea without expecting romance in return gave her immediate ethical relief.

And he said she could cancel the arrangement at any time, right? She's in control.

With a devilish gleam in his eyes, Theo lifted his whiskey towards her. "So," he asked. "Do we have a deal?"

Chapter Six

"Mysterious Theo." Danielle shoved Olivia's shoulder with her own. "Sounds like a nineties romcom, you know? When you told me about him on the phone the other day, I was almost jealous."

The two best friends had decided on some late-night shopping on Oxford Street, their shoulders bare and white legs left free beneath maxi summer dresses, as they tried to enjoy the false summer breeze that had surprised the capital. The street was bustling as usual, but the girls loved it. Picking up a basket, they headed into the department store with absolutely no particular reason except for smelling some candles and perusing the multiple-level building.

"Are you kidding?" Olivia gazed around the cream lino-floored store, the bright lights leading them straight to the expensive perfume and make-up counters. "You literally have an ex-army lover waiting at home to ravish you as soon as you step through the door. He can't keep his hands off of you, and you're jealous of me meeting a random guy at a restaurant?"

"Hey, I said, almost jealous." Danielle's heeled shoes clacked against the floor with each of her steps. "You know I wouldn't trade my six-pack hunk for anything." Turning towards Olivia, she had that same, dangerous glint in her eyes. "Speaking of which, did I tell you about what he did with his tongue a few nights back."

"I don't need to know. Please spare me." Olivia cringed, picking up a glass bottle and giving the scent a whiff. The smell attacked her senses, and she immediately placed the bottle back with a firm shake of her head. Too musky.

"Are you sure you don't want to know? I literally died and went to heaven."

"I'm sure." Olivia looked at her best friend. "You keep your crazy sex life out of our conversations, please."

"Come on, who am I supposed to tell this stuff to, my mother? No, thank you. You're my best friend. You can even use it for one of your steamy scenes." Danielle's voice sang out.

"John is a great guy and by the sounds of it, a *very* generous lover. But no, I don't want to hear about your sexual escapades. I'm conducting my own research."

Olivia knew far too much about how well-endowed her friend's husband was. So much so that for the first few weeks that the pair dating, whenever they went out to dinner together or bumped into each other at the florist, Olivia couldn't look him in the eyes.

"Your own…" Danielle leaned down close to her friend, "*sex* research?" She whispered the second half of her sentence as though the word *sex* was some kind of swear word her parents had forbidden her to use, eyes sifting the counter to make sure the attendant wasn't eavesdropping.

"*Dating* research." Olivia lifted up another perfume before scrunching her nose at the putrid smell of too much vanilla and put it down, turning sharply away from the display. "I went on what feels like one hundred horrible dates before Theo sat down. He wasn't even on my list."

"Yeah, but he's helping you, right?" Danielle ran her hand along the fabric of a few hanging tops before following her friend to the elevator.

"I'm meeting him on Thursday to suss things out, see what this agreement looks like in practice, not just on paper."

"Tell him I'm his biggest fan," Danielle murmured. She hadn't even met the man, but she was already so invested in the whole leading man agreement. "He sounds dreamy."

"You don't even know him." Olivia pressed the up button twice just to be sure. "Hell, I don't even know him."

An elderly woman entered the elevator with them, pulling a trolly basket with her. Sending the woman a polite smile, Danielle continued. "Yes, but I like him already. He clearly thought you were interesting enough to approach you. That gives him a head start in the approval process."

"Approval process for what? I won't date him; he's just helping me out. In what capacity, I'm not sure yet, but still. Just helping." The older woman glanced at the two friends before looking up at the numbers and arrows. Second floor. With the sharp ding of the elevator and monotone announcement, the two friends wandered out and into the clothing department. Crisp white mannequins posed precariously around the floor with draped necklaces, low neckline tops and big hats on their figures.

"What did Hannah say to the idea?" Danielle asked, making a beeline for a floral dress a few rows in.

Hannah had emailed another deadline reminder with the words *'Manuscript due in T-minus two months and three weeks.*

Send chapters one through five to my desk by Monday, and I won't heckle you until next the Monday.'

Olivia had responded with the news of her research and sent through the rough chapters a few days afterwards. It was only when she had emailed the draft chapters that she got her agent's opinion regarding the unorthodox research method she had chosen.

"She said, 'Well done for putting yourself out there, go get 'em tiger'," Olivia muttered while sifting through linen fabrics. "And that I was also absolutely batshit crazy for agreeing to let a stranger help me."

Danielle laughed, pressing a new floral dress up to her frame. "Do you think I could pull this off?"

Olivia looked at the thin cotton fabric clutched in her friend's hands and the busy design, before curving her eyebrows down. "I liked the other one better."

Danielle hummed in agreement as she placed the dress back on the rack and continued her search. "I'm surprised Hannah didn't pull out the 'remember to make him wrap it before he taps it' line. She can be a real Amy Poehler in *Mean Girls* sometimes."

"I just said I had downloaded those stupid apps, and now I've got the assistance of a good-looking, six-foot-three man."

"So, you admit it. He's good-looking." Danielle grinned.

Olivia thought back to when Theo had first sat down opposite her in the bistro and looked at her with that determined, focused gaze that had set all her nerve endings abuzz. "I never denied it."

Objectively and subjectively, Theo was a handsome man. He had the classic Hollywood-type look to him, all sharp lines and dark broody features. His browneyes had twirls of gold, which Olivia felt almost embarrassed to know about after staring in them for far too long and the swooping dark locks that had slight curls at the ends, made him look like he had just stepped out of a Giorgio Armani advertisement. She would almost bet her life that in the summer his olive skin turned golden in the sun, and the thought made her bite her lip while wincing at her Irish heritage. She was all white. Some would even say translucent, and in summer tanning was something foreign to her. Instead, she just turned a beetroot red and burned like a seasoned lobster.

Beside them, a mother pushing a double pram squeezed between two clothes racks, her child grasping the hem of a hanging women's summer top with desperation. She sent Olivia a struggling smile before prying the fabric from her toddler's sticky fingers and moving further down the aisle. Olivia smiled back, moving out of the mother's way with a small wave to the child, who was now fussing over his seat buckle.

Danielle nudged Olivia's shoulder, breaking her out of deep thought as she watched the mother push her child towards the elevators, and shot Olivia a smug grin. "Hey, who knows? Maybe he'll end up being your leading man…"

CHAPTER SEVEN

"So, what kind of things do you write?" Theo twirled his teaspoon around, mixing a sachet of sugar into his coffee before tapping the edge of his mug three sharp times. He had met up with Olivia at the local Caffè Nero around the corner from his flat that Friday afternoon.

The two of them had dusted off the sprinklings of spring rain from their jackets when they arrived and hunkered down in the worn brown leather chairs by the big bay window. The air was thick with the scent of warm cocoa and coffee, and the soft buzz of the coffee machine burring in the background created a welcoming ambience for their first meeting. Although he had shared her company before, he still felt nerves pool in his stomach as he ordered their coffees. The jumper he had picked out to wear felt tight around the collar. He was *nervous*.

If this arrangement went well, not only would she write a bestseller, but he would finally get to make that call to his sister and confirm the plus-one to her wedding. He could practically feel the buzzing excitement that she would have when he told her he had found someone to attend her wedding and that her bridal party and groomsmen would be of equal number. His mother, who had made it explicitly clear how eager she was for him to settle down and start giving her grandchildren, would also be off his back. There was no downside to this agreement; he had nothing to lose and almost everything to gain.

Olivia, whom he'd watched break the hearts and dignity of a procession of men last Saturday night, the blonde bombshell sitting before him, was the only one who had something legitimate to lose. And something more than just a fickle wedding date to gain.

"I write a lot of things. Poetry, short stories, articles…" Olivia said half-heartedly, picking the blueberry muffin he had ordered with their drinks up off the white ceramic plate. She was wearing a fluffy cream cardigan and a thin gold necklace that hung down the V of her top, accentuating the same gentle slope of creamy skin he had been staring at from across the bar last week. After a once-over of her petite but curvaceous figure, he'd had to shove down the desire to find out if the supple ivory of her chest was as soft as it looked and put it out of his mind quickly.

"But ultimately, I write romance novels. At least that's what my book deal is contracted for." Olivia let out a small laugh, and that's when he realised that she was nervous, too. Nervous, perhaps, about how he would react to the kind of romance she wrote. He would never make her feel uncomfortable talking about her work; not when she was so passionate about it, not when her eyes captured the golden light from the hanging bulbs overhead so perfectly, in a bright twinkle like a fire had started in her eyes, flames of crystal blue shining and shooting rays of sunshine through her eyes and into the air that clung to each of her words.

Staring at the petite woman in front of him, he wondered if she wrote the slow burn, holding hands type of romance or the hot and heavy smut that he had seen an ex-girlfriend carry around everywhere she went.

"Do you enjoy it?" he asked, despite already knowing the answer. The twinkle in her eyes as she spoke about it was answer enough; he just selfishly wanted to see that damn sparkle once more. "Writing love stories?"

Olivia placed the muffin down on the side plate before clearing her throat. Her gold necklace swung in the space between her breasts. Theo forced himself to ignore the movement.

"I love the idea of love. About constructing ways people could meet someone, take chances, fall in love. For instance, that girl over there wearing the pink hoodie and tight jeans?" She turned her body slightly and pointed to a young woman to the right of their table. "Maybe she's had a bad day and decided to come here for an afternoon pick-me-up, order a caramel macchiato... something sweet like she is. However, the barista across the counter remembered her choice of beverage and made it without her ordering."

Theo glanced at the barista, then back to the woman in the hoodie. He felt Olivia lean closer to him, the waft of floral perfume welcome to his senses. Rose and vanilla. He hoped he was subtle as he took a long, deep breath, making note of the faint scent.

"He's been taking her order for years," she continued, "and despite him pouring her coffee every day, taking it from his hand, reading the cute notes he leaves on the side of the cups, she barely looks up."

Theo shook his head and quipped teasingly, "What a missed opportunity."

"Completely," Olivia agreed. "But don't you think that we all lose out on opportunities like that? Looking down at our phones? Not leaving the house? Not meeting new people?"

"So that's it then? She ignores the barista's notes and nothing comes of it?" Theo asked.

Olivia tilted her head, glancing back at the woman in the hoodie and made a small sound of question. "That's one possibility. But for a writer like me? Their story has only just begun."

Theo was invested; her voice lulled him and he became captivated by the made-up tale. He turned back to Olivia, leaning closer towards her slight figure. Their forearms were millimetres away from each other on the small table between them, their foreheads nearly pushed together like teenagers telling each other secrets they didn't want anyone else to hear.

"Then what happens, what's their story?" he whispered. The café door swung open and a gust of cool evening air brushed against their sides, but he hardly noticed it, not when their bodies were huddled this close, both on the edge of their armchairs, hands wrapped around warm coffee mugs and nestled in the cosy corner of the small shop.

Olivia drew a breath, tilting her head to the side and gazing over his broad shoulder. "Normally she doesn't read the notes." Her tone matched his, a breathy whisper shared between them. "But today, she notices, and suddenly they're talking. She's thanking him for making coffee and then he's telling her a joke so terrible that it makes a smile appear despite her having an utterly crap day."

"And that's it?" Theo asked. "That's the meeting."

Olivia pushed back in the small armchair, her voice a normal volume and sipped her forgotten coffee. "But it was never the beginning."

They sat together in silence for a few beats, breathing quietly and taking tentative sips of their coffees and bites of the now crumbled muffin on the mismatched plate.

The bell above the coffee shop door dinged again as the door swung open again. again with another breeze of cool air, this time causing the brown paper napkins to fly wildly across the tiled floor. A burly man walked in, a gym bag swung over his shoulder, his thin vest doing little to cover his bulging muscles. Theo had to wonder if he was the kind of man who Olivia found attractive. The kind that chugged protein shakes and lifted heavy weights every day. Then, the man walked across the narrow shop with purpose.

"And cue the boyfriend," Olivia whispered.

"She's taken?"

"Of course she is." Olivia's hand reached up and began to fiddle with the necklace pendant. "Look at her, she's gorgeous."

Yes, she is, he thought, looking over at her golden hair against the beige background of the evening, shining like strands of pure gold. His eyes flickered down to where her hands curled around that goddamn necklace. *She is gorgeous.*

The gym bag smacked heavily into the back of an empty wooden chair ten feet in front of them, causing the flimsy wood to scrape painfully along the floor. The sound snapped Theo out of his thoughts and back to the café. Back towards the hoodie girl and gym stranger.

Theo frowned, watching as the burly guy leaned in and gave the girl a puckered kiss on the lips. Slinging his arm around her, the burly man shot a condescending smirk at the barista. With a huff, the poor coffee shop worker turned and stomped off behind the swinging staff door.

Theo knew what the man had done. He had claimed the girl. He had made it clear to everyone in that café, himself included, that the girl was his. No one else's.

"The girl and the barista." Olivia let the necklace fall from her soft grasp and leaned in once again, watching the couple out of the corner of her eyes as they wandered closer to where he and Olivia were seated. "Let's say they dated. For, I don't know, five months. He fell madly in love with her. But she didn't fall as hard, or at all. To her it was just an exciting, illustrious affair. A way to pass time, keep her bed warm and her mind busy until the next man."

"So, she's a casual kind of girl?"

"More like a 'keeping my options open' kind of girl."

"Okay, so they break up, or were they ever really together?" Theo asked. "Because, depending on the relationship definition, the outcome is variable."

"Just because they weren't 'officially dating' doesn't mean the barista hasn't been completely infatuated with her from day one. From the second she walked through those black double doors." Olivia gestured her hands towards the café's entrance and sighed. "Unrequited love can break just as many hearts as infidelity does. If not more."

Theo looked at Olivia carefully. Taking another sip of her presumably now cold coffee, she continued. "What the barista didn't know was that after her morning coffee, after their morning kisses and cute conversations, she was going to Pilates and getting railed in the gym bathroom by that hunk…"

Suddenly Theo had the answer to what kind of romance she wrote, and he couldn't stop the rush of heat that crawled up the sides of his neck and settled in his cheeks. Hearing her construct this elaborate story about strangers was like watching a master painter splash paint expertly across a canvas.

"… who, naturally, would be called something like… Zac. Bryson. Something that sounds foreign and exciting to her." Olivia huffed.

Theo frowned. "That's it? She just never loved him. That's not a happy ending."

Olivia let out a small cynical laugh. "Yeah, well I've learned that not every love story has a happy ending."

The comment pulled at something in his chest and made him sit back in his chair and consider her once more. If someone could make up such elaborate storylines for complete strangers in the span of five minutes, then he had no idea why she had failed to think up a leading man. So, why did she have writer's block? Why couldn't she conjure up one of those stories and write something as captivating as this one she had just elaborately told? Happy ending or not.

"You don't seem to be lacking creativity. So, humour me. Why do you need my help?" Theo found himself asking.

Olivia pulled the sleeves of her cardigan down past her wrists and gazed into her half empty coffee cup. She rubbed the circular stain the mug had left on the wooden table with her cardigan. Theo passed her a semi-crumpled napkin and silently waited for her answer.

She muttered a small "thank you" and wiped up the spilled caffeine.

She sighed, finally. "Honestly? I've written the burly Mafia king; I've written the best friend's brother. I've written about her enemy realising that he loved her all along. If it's published, sitting on a shelf in a bookstore, then I've done it, and so has everyone else. I'm looking for something different. Something that bridges the line between a fictional boyfriend and real-life 'this is the type of man I want'."

"You want to write about a man who could be real?"

"I don't want to conceptualise all the fluffy stuff anymore. Those men are not realistic. It's not logical—" Olivia stopped, looking out into the sparkling lights of the London Street through the wall of windows to their side. "Sometimes fantasising about fictitious men is great and all, but not everyone meets a hot fisherman on a trip to the coast and falls madly in love... or suddenly gets a second chance with their first love." She looked down for a moment, a wash of sadness filtering across her face and disappearing again before he could register.

He had seen the stories that his ex, Annika, had read. Smutty romance books about a brother's best friend. He used to listen as she commented on which tropes she liked better than others. Theo grew up surrounded by women, their reading preferences a clear thrill compared to the more boring books men read. These romance stories, the ones his sister had piled up in her living room, and the ones he used to buy his ex for her birthday were plain dirty. Hot. Steamy. Spicy. Filth.

Some of the language used in those books reminded him of the scandalous Mills & Boon romance books his mother had read in the late nineties and early two thousands.

"I want to write a character who exhibits both fantasy and reality. A leading man that meets the bare minimum of showing respect for a woman. Who opens doors and kisses them goodbye and hello. And says, 'I love you', without being afraid of coming across as too emotional. The problem is, I just don't believe they exist anymore, so how do I write him?"

Theo wanted that for her. Oh, how he wanted to wield a pen himself and write the part for her, but if he did, he knew it wouldn't be as good as it would be coming from her.

Polishing off their coffees happened faster than Theo would have liked. He walked her home across the busy streets of London, and onto the Elizabeth Line, and all the way until she was safely inside the battered navy-blue door of her apartment building. He was miles from his own home, which was a forty-five-minute tube journey in the other direction, but he didn't care.

Tucking his hands in the pockets of his jacket, he walked to the station in the light drizzly rain. His mind was clearer now. He had a better picture of what the next two months would look like with Oliva in it. He also knew that he needed to get her out of his head for a while. The way she flipped her hair over her shoulder and revealed her long slender neck to him. The way she puckered her lips around the rim of the steaming mug, taking elegant sips of her drink, and every now and then licking a stray drop that threatened to run down the porcelain. He needed a cold shower. A beer out of the fridge, and the football final.

In that exact order.

Theo wanted her to write that man, and even more, he wanted to prove he existed. That there were men out there that were faithful to their partners, and loyal, and kind. That men, real men, weren't afraid of declaring their love so freely. Not when it came to the right person. Making his way down the bustling street, thoughts swirling in his mind, he came to the realisation that Olivia knew what she wanted in her leading man.

Now, his only mission was to try and help her find him.

CHAPTER EIGHT

"Hannah."

Olivia had called her agent despite the clear instruction the previous week

"Just go find him, and when you do: don't call me. Write."

And she was. And she did.

She was sitting on her sofa, her phone tucked under her ear, the older style landline cord wrapped around her fingers. She had spent the majority of the day writing at a café in Brixton, and the early afternoon doing a small grocery shop before settling back into her flat for a relaxing night of bubbly and watching cheesy romance movies. Another form of research.

Somewhere during the mid-morning, between the obscene coffee consumption and spending far too long in Sainsbury's biscuit aisle toying between Digestives or Hobnobs, she had finally brushed the cobwebs off her laptop and had the guts to begin typing. Nimble fingers flitting quickly over black keys, she was finally getting somewhere. Finally dotting i's and crossing t's. After rambling and sharing a blueberry muffin with the handsome man who promised to help her, Olivia had officially written two more chapters.

Although not much, it was still something. For the first time since the meeting in her literary agent's, she swore she could see an inkling of light at the end of this tunnel. A rope had slowly lowered into the pit of despair and the small voice in her head told her to hold on tight as it heaved her up out of the dark writer's block that she had fallen into all those months ago.

"Olivia." Hannah's voice filtered through the phone receiver. "How's the writing going?"

"How's the writing going?" Olivia spoke as though it were a rhetorical question. "I'm writing. I have written. That's how it's going." The words fell out of her in a waterfall of excitement.

"Oh, thank God." Hannah let out an exaggerated sigh of relief.

Despite being her literary agent for the past three years, she was also one of Olivia's closest friends. As an author, one's social life could often become a shell of what it was, unless you actively made the decision to integrate yourself into the world of those with the same passions, the same interest in creative endeavours, the same goal-orientated mentality. Together, Olivia, Hannah and Danielle were three peas in a pod. They shared similar pastimes, and although they all had schedules reflecting their extreme girl boss energy, they still got together and laughed.

Hannah had always encouraged Olivia, and it wasn't for the pay cheque.

It was for the late-night-over-wine therapy she had given throughout Olivia's previous break-up, or the random text messages saying she had met an actor on the subway and how integral it had been for her to ask the B-list celebrity for a photo.

Her job title firmly out the window as soon as it reached 5:00 p.m. on a Friday, Hannah swapped from business to party mode and had no problem dragging Olivia along to the hip new clubs and drag queen shows that the London nightlife had to offer.

"Seriously?" Olivia felt like Hannah should have been a bit more enthusiastic about the fact that she was writing, but then again, this was Hannah. Her support was delivered like her advice. Abruptly and with brutal honesty. "I tell you I'm writing again, and the first thing you say is 'thank God'?"

No longer was she sitting alone in her apartment and wallowing over the thought that her writing was mediocre and unrelatable. That her characters were all made of utter fluff and façade. No depth or authenticity in their descriptions or actions. Nothing solid to connect them to the readers as they should. Writer's block sucked. Majorly.

"Need I remind you of the urgent, impending deadline you have creeping up? The more words you pump out, the less likely I am to get fired. So yeah, hallelujah." Hannah breathed. "Anyway, how's the research going? Has your leading man spoken to you yet?"

Olivia had a dirty big grin on her face at the thought of Theo. How she had gone home and written something for the first time in a long time. "He's spoken to me."

"Come on, I need a little more than that." Hannah muttered. "How's it all really? The research, I mean. It must have helped something because you sent those pages pretty darn fast."

Olivia kicked her sock-clad feet up onto her coffee table and grinned as she curled further into her plush sofa cushions.

"It means Danielle told me to download every dating app that has ever existed, and I ended up meeting a stranger who has agreed to help me find my leading man."

"A stranger on an app?"

Olivia frowned. " A stranger as a result of the app."

"What?"

"The app was the catalyst, but I met Theo…" Quite randomly, really. He had just waltzed up to her table and sat down like it was his. "By chance."

"By chance?"

"Yes." Olivia couldn't fight the new smile that had begun to turn up her lips at the thought of Theo. "It was all rather serendipitous really. He just kind of showed up."

"That sounds like the beginning of a horror film, Liv."

"I've met him, obviously, and he's agreed to help me. He's going to set me up—"

Combining online dating with the dates Theo was setting her up on, she felt as though she had been constantly swiping, talking and deleting men. It might sound cold-hearted and completely unlike her bubbly, friendly self, but Olivia now had no shame after speaking to some of the shocker men on the sites.

"Wait, he's setting you up?" Hannah asked, her voice distant on the phone. "Why doesn't he just do it?"

"That's what Danielle said too, but I'll tell you what I told her." Olivia rolled her eyes. "He helps me find my leading man through dates, and I step in as his plus-one at his sister's wedding. Simple."

"Okay," Hannah replied sceptically. "As long as I get the chapters required by Monday I am excited for you."

"Hannah, that means so much to me, you don't even know—"

"Yeah, yeah. Go write a masterpiece and I'll see you soon." Hannah let out a chuckle before hanging up.

Olivia was sitting in a shabby chic armchair in the back of one of her favourite coffee shops in Soho. Artisan Aroma sat in the space between the local Chinese takeaway and a small London souvenir gift shop. She sat with her green notebook in front of her, highlighter poised at the ready. For a writer, she was what you called a walking contradiction. When she was in the middle stages of writing, she hated it. When she wasn't in the depths of a novel and didn't have the itch to write – the moments where she would wake up randomly at 2 a.m. and hurriedly scribble words onto a page under the blinding white light of her phone's torch before rolling back over, reading the mysterious notes she had written in her half-dream state the next morning – she missed it. The spontaneous side of writing, the unpredictability of getting the best ideas at the most inconvenient of times.

To finish this manuscript in time, Olivia had set herself a strict word goal. Achieve it, and her novel would be finished with time to plan a second and write a first draft of it within the end of a year: her Virgo brain required everything to read through perfectly before she even considered it a semi-reasonable final draft. She had roughly fifteen hundred words left to write before the weekend, but her brain still felt fuzzy from yesterday's meeting with Theo, and every word on the page in front of her seemed to mush together into a whole lot of jumbled nonsense.

She was still waiting for his text – eager to know when they would meet again. To say she was excited was an understatement. Olivia had enjoyed the man's company far more than she thought she would have. Theo had huddled close to her in the coffee shop, listening to her ramble. Something that few men had had the guts to do and even fewer able to remain attentive enough to ask questions as he had.

Olivia came to the conclusion that she needed to up her standards for men. If she were to meet her ideal goal of being married with one point five kids by the time she got to thirty-five, a goal that she had pushed back year after year, she had to find one fast. But now she was an established career woman. The goal had never seemed achievable when her economic success had so heavily relied on the, at the time, new writing venture. On this creative outlet that she had been fortunate enough to undertake full time as of last year after quitting her tutoring job.

Although her savings account was far from starving, there was always room for a gooey chocolatey dessert with extra whipped cream. Aka, the additional extra on top.

Looking up from her notebook, Olivia watched the busybodies enter and exit the coffee shop, eyes focusing on a group of girls at the front, thin strips of their stomachs showing over the top of their low-rise jeans. Apparently, those nightmares were back in fashion.

Olivia cringed as she thought of her classic 2008 mid-washed jeans and tight T-shirts that were the same style and shook her head. Nope. Never again. She refused to go backwards in the realms of fashion. It had taken her a few decent years to filter down her colourful and sometimes unique style to a sustainable amount of clothing. Let alone be able to look back at pictures of her teen years without cringing.

Olivia liked to call her wardrobe a capsule wardrobe. If capsule wardrobes looked like a rainbow threw up in them and came with crochet cardigans. Even if they did hit the pages of *Vogue* in the near future, Olivia swore at that moment that she would never again submit herself to such a crime of fashion as the low-rise denim. She'd rather wear a bootleg.

Biting the end of her highlighter, she reread the scribbled dialogue she had written on the small page. Adjusting her earphones, she pressed skip on the song that was playing and finally put pen to paper, scribbling notes in the thin margins and squeezing them between the lines of her already mediocre writing. Finally making headway, her phone buzzed, the music dimming enough for her train of thought to fly out the window and never return. With a sigh, she flipped over her phone on top of the table, her heart thudding as she read the message notification.

Theo

Are you free tonight?

Dragging the pen through some dialogue, Olivia stared hopelessly at the rest of the passage. Jotting down another random sentence on the side, she hoped the words would materialise into something, some scene or pivotal moment between the two leads. Olivia cried internally as she continued to skim-read, realising that it made absolutely no sense and that she might as well cross out the whole paragraph. Retrieving her phone, she replied.

> Me
>
> Sorry, not quite at my word limit for today. My brain is fried, but I really need to get this done.

> Theo
>
> You're writing?

> Me
>
> Attempting to, yes.

> Theo
>
> Look at you, bestselling author.

Olivia watched as the three dots remained on her screen.

> So, there's no chance of convincing you to go to Robbie's and grab a beer with a potential suitor?

Clicking on the phone app, she pressed the call icon. Theo picked up almost immediately. She had barely been able to register the shock of his one ring answer when the smooth baritone of his voice came through the phone in a hurried breath. "Hey."

She could hear the station announcement system in the background behind him. "You could've started with *I've got a potential suitor for you, Olivia.*"

"I could have, but I wanted to know if you were free first."

In the background there was a swift click, and the distinct swipe of his card before metal dividers turned. "So, what do you say? Robbie's at 6:30?"

Olivia sighed, glancing pitifully at her notebook, accepting the knowledge that she was not going to be able to write any more that evening. This was her first mission. The first set-up. Feeling the twist of her stomach, Olivia didn't know if it was the tuna sandwich she'd had for lunch, or the nervous energy of potentially meeting her leading man this evening. "Details first: who's the potential suitor?"

"His name is Taylor. He works in human resources at my mate Finn's company, and is, potentially, your leading man." Theo's voice filtered hastily through the line. He was out and about, the sounds of bustling London alive and thrumming behind him.

Olivia couldn't help the smile that began to tug at the corner of her mouth. "Taylor. Okay." Taylor was a nice name. Strong. Unisex.

"I've digitally vetted him, and you have my number if it all goes south." Even the thought of Theo stalking this Taylor guy on the internet gave Olivia a sense of peace.

After their meeting a few days prior, she felt more confident in their ability to work together. To find a leading man in just under two months she had to start taking chances now.

"Uh, alright. Robbie's Bar did you say?" Olivia uncapped her pen and scribbled the address down on her small notepad. "Perfect. Be prepared for some potential drunken texts afterwards though, if it's the Robbie's I'm thinking about, their Apple Martinis are my weakness."

Theo's deep laugh was like music to her ears, the sound

making her lower stomach pull in a way that made her squirm in the plush chair.

"So I'll tell him you'll meet him there?" Theo asked, making Olivia glance down at the time on her watch. It was already 5:30. If she packed up now, she could make it to Waterloo just in time.

"Sounds good. Cheers," she said in a faraway voice.

"Olivia?"

"Yes." She blinked.

His voice softened, his reassuring words swarming the anxious muscle in her chest. "It won't go south."

Chapter Nine

Not having time to go home and change, Olivia buttoned her long jacket and adjusted her soft navy blouse as she walked down the dirtied cream steps and into the underground station. She had briefly stopped in front of a high street store window and stole a glance at her dishevelled figure. With a sharp tug at the scrunchie in her hair, she shook out her blonde locks and bit her bottom lip, praying some blood would rush in and make them look slightly plumper and pinker than when they were pursed in thought all afternoon.

It was cold outside, the May sun still not making itself known, much to everyone's disappointment. For Olivia, last year's spring had been colder than this, just not in the Celsius. Walking through the barrier and trying desperately to rush through the murky scent of oil and underground, she couldn't believe it. She was doing it. Dating.

Please forgive me, she thought, remembering him sitting on the worn sofa of her apartment, his hands clasped over his face just how he had done whenever he was in deep consideration of something. *It's for my writing, nothing more. You knew — know how important my writing is to me.*

Olivia trudged along the station platform, making her way into the small carriage and settled on to a spare blue seat.

In theory, while the train screeched to a halt at each stop before hers, she could have taken her notebook out and tried to make her word limit a reality. Instead, she sat crammed on the train carriage trying to calm her racing heart. Who knew you could still carry such guilt for something you hadn't even done yet? All in worry of hurting someone's feelings who wasn't even there. For someone in your past.

Instead, she sat there and mentally prepared herself to see the man Theo had set her up with. Phase one of finding her leading man had ended with her meeting Theo, and now with his promise to help her, phase two was well underway.

Olivia got to the pub first. It was always her worst nightmare to arrive at a date or meeting late. She had no idea what Taylor looked like, and at 6:30p.m. on a Thursday in a London pub, there were plenty of men between the ages of twenty and seventy to choose from. On the overhead screens, a rugby game played, showing burly men in tight shorts tackle each other with the same determination Olivia had for finding her leading man.

Robbie's sat on the corner of a cobbled street, directly diagonal to an old stone bridge that led into town. With rose-flushed cheeks, Olivia pushed open the stained-glass door, stepping out of the chilly evening and into the building. The pub was sturdy, with thick brick walls and solid wood floors that creaked with every step you took. The rumble of people talking, glasses clinking and the sound of laughter, young and old, reinforced the fact that pubs were places for all generations. Growing up, Olivia had loved visiting the local pub with family. The lingering smell of cigarettes, beer and dust mites somehow felt like a warm hug. Alongside her mother and father, back when they were still married and happy, the three of them would take shelter in one of the mahogany booths and eat their weekly Sunday roast.

Taking a deep breath in, Olivia felt her shoulders relax as she took in the familiar smell. This nostalgia might be just what she needed to get through the evening with success.

She could picture it now. Her dad in the corner playing darts, her mother sitting by her side, colouring in the page printed on the back of the menu while they awaited their meal.

"Olivia?" A deep voice severed her from her thoughts.

Olivia turned around to see a tall man with slick, dirty blond hair standing behind. His hair was wet from the rain and pushed back as if he had raked his fingers through the ends too many times.

"Hi, I'm Taylor, it's nice to meet you." He let out a small, unsure laugh.

"Of course, sorry. Hi. It's been a long day." Olivia shuffled her feet before turning around and scanning the thrumming pub filled with activity.

Taylor tugged his red cashmere scarf off from around his neck. "Shall we get a booth?"

Nodding absent-mindedly, Olivia turned and headed towards a small booth on the far side of the pub, the scuffed fabric seats facing two small poker tables to their left.

The pub was quaint, with low-lying green and red chandeliers filled with small warm lightbulbs. A fake fireplace crackled in the far wall that had mismatched portraits and eclectic art decorating the peeling wallpaper. It looked like it hadn't been renovated in well over twenty years, but then again, what good pub did? The worn-in atmosphere of the space made it feel as if the new high-rise buildings around it had been constructed to make the unique establishment stand out like a rare gem alongside the walls of grey and glass.

"Would you like something to eat?" Taylor asked. His posh accent came out in a smooth and unscathed drawl. Folding his grey trench coat neatly and placing it down on the matted fabric of the booth, he sent a polite smile Olivia's way.

Olivia was starving, after all she had been living off large lattes and the odd muffin all day at the café. However, she always made sure to remember Danielle's dating advice: "Don't commit to food, otherwise you'll be three hours in and listening to how his mother irons his trousers." Small talk was supposed to be the only conversation on a first date. Refined and elusive small talk. She wanted to give enough about herself, so he would be interested to know more, but not too much that he decided to chug his drink and make a runner.

"I'll just have an Apple Martini please," Olivia responded curtly. She would eat later. He took note of her order, and she watched as he approached the bar, politely waving over the bartender and paying for their drinks. Taylor seemed nice and proper. He exuded an Oxford-educated air, his accent one that was not common in this area of London, rolled and refined like a fine chocolate.

Placing one questionable-looking drink on the table, as well as her nuclear green Apple Martini, Taylor spoke.

"So," he began. "Theo tells me you're a writer."

Theo.

Theo had told this man things about her. Oh, God.

Suddenly dread filled her lungs, and she felt her breath shorten. What had he told him?

Taylor must have seen the panicked look splayed across her face as he leaned over and placed a hand over hers. "Don't worry, everything he told me was good. Promise."

It better be, she thought. *Or that wedding date to Ireland in June? Yeah, that promise can be flushed right down the loo.*

"Good. I'm glad." Olivia gave a small smile. "I'm sorry, he didn't tell me about you at all."

Taylor laughed, taking a sip of his drink. His eyes drifted behind her for a brief moment, before flicking back to hers. "Well, I'm an HR manager working on Bond Street. It sounds boring, but it's more interesting than you'd think."

"I'm sure it is." Olivia took a tentative sip of her beverage, her shoulders slumping as the tangy apple hit the tip of her tongue.

There were a few things in the world that made Olivia completely melt with pleasure. And sadly, it wasn't men anymore. Not since *him*. It was a Robbie's Bar Apple Martini.

"Wow." Taylor coughed, watching Olivia moan in pleasure at the taste of the drink. "You, uh, you sure like that drink."

"God, nothing tastes better than an Apple Martini after a long day at work," Olivia moaned.

"So, what do you do exactly?"

Olivia straightened in her chair. She found the question unexpected, but warranted. "What do you mean?" There was plenty that a writer did other than sit at a laptop and type all day. They researched, conducted experiments, interviewed. Authors were essentially the journalists of the literary world. Books were laced with personal and fictional happenings; to

Olivia they held the author's soul, gave her little nuggets of various perspectives of life. They were so much more than just ink stamped words on paper.

"When you're not writing, I mean. Theo told me you were going through some bouts of writer's block." Taylor clicked his tongue and reached forward to grab some of the peanuts that sat in a small blue ceramic bowl in between them.

"Uh, well. When I'm not writing I try to find inspiration to write." She gave him an awkward smile.

A few beats of silence were shared between them.

Behind them, the television roared with the crowd's joy at the game's first try. The door had not closed since they had arrived, a steady stream of office and construction workers and elderly men had been trooping through the door with their sights solely on a cool glass of beer. Happy hour was certainly popular here in London.

Especially when the drinks were on a two-for-one deal.

Theo had bought her coffee the other day at the café, no option of her even considering doing it. She took a mental note that Taylor had done a similar thing.

Tugging on the sleeves of her jumper, she covered her palms and curled the soft fabric into her fists. "So, how long have you known Theo?"

Taylor was staring over her shoulder. "Uh, Theo. Yes. Sorry."

Olivia turned her head. She was aware there was a league game on but come on.

"Well, uh, not long. We're more acquaintances really."

"Ah, alright then." Another sip of apple goodness.

Another look over the shoulder. Another lapse of silence.

The conversation was completely standard, but this felt awkward, even for a first date. Sure, first dates were supposed to be awkward and messy. But was it her who was making this as awkward as it was? Not counting the other night, she hadn't done this for years.

Maybe that was why her high school boyfriend, Jack, had told her to 'lighten up' and to let her hair down every once in a while, and go to a party every now and then instead of curling up in her room with a book. She wasn't boring, was she?

For the third time he glanced over her shoulder, a glazed look in his eye. *Three strikes, and you're out.*

"What is so interesting over my shoulder?" Olivia turned her body, hair flipping as she glanced behind her. It took all but two seconds for her stomach to plummet and an acidic taste to fill her mouth. Standing directly behind her, and leaning over one of the wooden booth tables, was a waitress wearing a short, incredibly tight work skirt. "Are you serious?" Olivia blanched.

"Pardon?" Taylor's eyes flickered back to hers for a second, the glazed look refocusing as if he had just realised he was still in her company.

"Have you seriously been staring at that waitress's ass the whole time we've been sat here?"

Taylor leaned back and took a long sip of his drink, his shoulders shrugging as the tips of his lips pulled up slightly. Olivia knew that move. Her exes had done it all the time.

Were you really out of town that weekend?
Are you sleeping with her?
Are you lying to me?

She would always get the same response.

"You're crazy." Taylor laughed. "Of course I haven't."

Olivia licked her lips before picking up the Martini and sculling it. If this date was over, she was getting her evening's worth of alcohol. Stuff being polite when he was basically groping the woman behind them with his eyes. His beady, blue eyes.

Slinging her jacket over her arm, she got out of the booth. "Little word of advice, Taylor." She leaned down slightly, rolling her eyes as his flickered towards her cleavage. "Next time you tell a lady you're on a date with that you're not staring at another woman's ass, try not to look directly at it as you do so."

Placing her phone against her ear in a huff, she took out her trusty notebook and struck out *Taylor* from the list of names Theo had added to the bottom after his.

Strike. The sound of the pen scraping against paper was music to her ears.

Taylor was most definitely not her leading man.

CHAPTER TEN

The phone rang two times before he answered. Olivia didn't even wait for him to finish greeting her before unleashing her wrath.

"Theo, I swear to God if you set me up with another Taylor I'm going to throttle you." She shoved her scarf deep into her bag with a huff. She had called him as soon as she had turned onto the next street. It was raining now, and her jacket did little to stop the spray from completely drenching her. A typical evening for springtime in London.

"Well, hello to you too, sunshine."

"Don't you 'sunshine' me. I have a bone to pick with you. That..." Olivia stepped on the train platform with a pained look on her face. "That complete and utter prick."

"What happened?" His breath rattled through the receiver with a firm tone. Could she be imagining it, or did he sound concerned about her? Worried. There was a rustling of fabric on the other end of the line before a series of distant laughter.

"He was a *total* prick. At first, I thought it was going well. He ordered our drinks and paid without even asking. But then... instead of focusing on me, he decided his time would be better spent focusing on the waitress's backside." She let out a small huff as she gazed upon the station map. Noting where her train was coming in, she began walking up another flight of stairs to the east side of the platform.

"Oh." Theo sounded surprised.

Olivia continued her ramble. "Poor woman, she didn't even know she was being objectified right then and there by that weirdo." She paused on the steps, slightly out of breath and turned around, glancing back at the busy street that led back to the pub. "Oh no, I should have warned her. She's probably being harassed by the corporate lawyer dickhead as we speak."

"So, this date didn't go well, and he was a prick. That's okay."

Olivia continued walking. "It is?"

"Not every date goes well, Olivia," Theo said softly.

"I know that." She rolled her eyes. "Believe it or not my dating life is not as sad as I make it sound." The low droning of a TV came through the receiver, followed by the sound of other men's laughter in the background. "Are you busy?"

"What?"

"T, get off the phone, you're missing it!" She heard a man's voice yell through the phone.

"Shut up, man," Theo yelled back, before sighing. "Sorry about that."

"I can call you later. I'm sorry."

"What? No, it's just game night at Finn's. We're watching the rugby." "He sounded as if he was popping another bottle of beer open, the pang of pressure being released and the cling of glass ringing out.

"Of course. The game. You're probably missing it. I should let you go; you're with your friends." Olivia shook her head, making her way down the second steps and onto the concrete platform, her hair now completely drenched from the misty rain. The rumblings of another train zooming past at top speed sent the realisation slapping across her face. "Oh, my goodness, I totally forgot. It's Sunday. I shouldn't have called. I'm so, so sorry."

"Don't be ridiculous, Liv," Theo muttered. "You can call me anytime." She heard him shuffle in the background, as if he was moving away from the loud noise of Rugby League and shouting men. The sharp click of a lock, then she heard the echo of his voice resound in what she assumed was a bathroom. "Now tell me about the date."

"John, please tell me I'm not going crazy." Olivia was perusing the small interior of her friend's florist shop. Picking up a fresh, light pink rose, she gathered it in her hands before twirling the flower and picking up another. After a day of sitting in the city library, she had successfully outlined three more chapters, pulling paragraphs from her numerous notebooks and slotting them together like a jigsaw puzzle until the beginning of a pivotal scene began to play out on the paper before her.

She had arrived at Danielle's flower shop at two in afternoon, stepping in from the unseasonably warm spring day and into the cool air-conditioned storefront.

Danielle's husband had just wandered out of the back room carrying a box of scented candles ready to stock up the shop walls when Olivia hit him with the question.

"Are we talking about the fact that you like pineapple on your pizza? Cause the answer in that case is no." The burly man looked so comedic carrying the pink logoed cardboard box, the heavy scent of peony soy wax candles wafting in the air as he passed her.

His wife rolled her eyes, turning to her friend and handing her another flower. "Ignore him. You're not crazy. That dickwad Taylor never should have said that. He was clearly a weirdo."

"Did Liv go on a date?" John sputtered, placing the heavy box down beside Danielle.

"Yes. She did."

John's eyebrows shot up, glancing at his wife with surprise.

Olivia took note of the look of disbelief on his face. "Yes, John. I went on a date. I know, hard to believe, right?"

"You just have never showed any interest in dating since... If I had known, I would have set you up with one of my brothers from the army." John picked up some pliers and began clipping off the sharp prickles on the rose stems. It was a job he demanded he do, claiming he didn't want Danielle to hurt herself.

Another reason Olivia felt like puking any time she was around the couple. They were too cute.

"I'm not interested in dating."

John frowned. "Then why did you go on a date."

Danielle reached forward and squeezed his bicep as she moved past him to grab the de-thorned flowers. "Honey, it's for her new novel, remember?"

"It's all in the name of research." Olivia hummed, grabbing one final rose and placing in on the wooden table before him.

A dozen pink roses. Just like Danielle had suggested a week prior. Her living room would look refreshed and retro. They weren't Olivia's favourite flower, but she could tolerate them if they made her apartment look and feel like something out of a home and style magazine. If it didn't, well she'd donate the flowers back to the florist shop. If they were still alive by then. Olivia swore keeping plants alive was harder than keeping a puppy or even a child alive.

John gave a low chuckle as he made his way towards the back room. "Yeah, sure. *Research.*"

"Quit it, you." Danielle's hand reached out and smacked his backside. "Besides, I already made that joke."

Olivia averted her eyes at the movement, instead occupying her time by fiddling with the rolls of silk ribbon in front of the till. It hadn't been so long ago that she would have found the act romantic. Now all she felt was envy. Green, ugly envy. Twirling a thread of inch thick bright orange around her fingers she pushed down the jealousy seeping from her bones.

"I swear to the florist heavens, Danielle, it is just research. He's doing me a favour. I had a date with that schmuck, Taylor, and that's okay. Theo said he'd be more attentive to who he picks next time, and that he potentially has another date for me. I'm just waiting for him to send me the details."

"Another date?" Danielle asked. "Already?"

"Yes, already. What did you think? That my leading man would just write himself? I've got Hannah breathing down my neck whenever I even think of opening my emails." Olivia hummed, watching as her friend wrapped the roses up in plush paper and that orange ribbon. "I need quick turnarounds. If the date doesn't go well, find me another. I made that pretty clear to Theo."

"Let's hope this one is better than the last one," John noted, wiping his hands on the pink apron tied around his waist. The things he did for Danielle were truly inspiring, including wearing a neon pink apron and helping his wife at her store on his day off.

"How much do I owe you?" Olivia asked, pulling out her wallet, she was eager to get home, crack open her laptop and finally make a picture out of those jigsaw pieces.

Danielle winked. "Girl, put your money away. This one's on me. You can repay me by giving me all the details about your next 'research' session."

Chapter Eleven

"You promise this guy is better than the last?"

Theo sighed, passing her a warm cardboard coffee cup. "I promise, sunshine. He's a decent lad. His name is Mason Ducrot. Twenty-nine years old, has three sisters and is currently practising medicine as an A&E doctor. Ambitious and goal-orientated, right? Those were on the list." Theo walked beside her on the wide Oxford Street pavement.

Along with noting the names of her previous dates, Theo had taken a keen interest in the list of attributes she wanted her leading man to have. Ambition being only one of the main characteristics that were important to her – as well as for her novel's leading lady.

The two of them were out looking for a dress, which Theo said she'd need after asking her if she had something suited for a Michelin starred restaurant in Soho. "So, he cares for people, that's a check. I like that. But why are we here again? I have clothes."

The pair stopped in front of a designer store and glanced at the perfectly lit display window. These were the types of shops she stared into and dared herself to dream about entering. Let alone purchasing the perfectly stitched garments inside.

She had the black dress she had worn the first night she

and Theo met, the low-cut wrap dress that never failed to drive men wild with its show and tell of two of her best assets. As much as Olivia had dreamed of fancy dresses and matching purses when she was younger, she didn't need any of that. She was old enough to know that if a guy liked her, he wouldn't care what she was wearing, whether it was from a designer store, or the TK Maxx down the road.

"We're here to shop." Theo grinned.

Olivia rolled her eyes. "Again, I have clothes."

"Yes, and you looked beautiful in that black mini at the bistro, but we're here for your pretty woman moment. Go in there and pick something that your leading lady would choose. She's from a rich family, isn't she?"

Olivia frowned. Her leading lady was from a rich family, a detail she didn't think was important, but had shared with him anyway. Her book outline had been sent to his email in a crisp PDF format from Hannah once she had noted his involvement in the project; Olivia was just surprised he had actually bothered to read it. "Well, yes but…"

"You want help finding your leading man? Well, who knows what she wants more than the leading lady?" Theo suggested, pulling the wide glass door open.

Olivia glanced at the lush interior of the store. Individually lit rows of garments and bags lined the walls, a broad security guard standing in each corner of the room. . Two art decor bean-shaped seats were situated in the middle of the shop, their crisp white fabric something she would be worried to go near for fear of staining it with the blue dye of her jeans.

Taking a deep breath, she stepped into the store. "Theo, you have strange but wonderful ideas."

"Thank you, sunshine. Now get inside, you're letting all the warm air out."

The dress she had picked was a vibrant red. The sweetheart neckline was something out of a dream, and its soft fabric floated down to just above her knees, a slit teasing the glowing, freshly waxed flesh of her thighs, her heels completing the look. When she had come out of the dressing room, she swore Theo gulped, turning away from her with maroon-tinted cheeks. From his reaction, she knew it was the one. The dress she would wear to charm the butt off Mason Ducrot. She had almost had a heart attack at the register, however. Theo brushed it off as though it were pocket money, when in reality she had made less money than the price of the dress during the first print run of her first novel, and that had hit number one of the literary charts for six consecutive weeks.

Now, as she sat in Veritas, the fanciest restaurant she had stepped foot in in a long time, across from her next potential leading man, she couldn't help but notice how her shoulders were pulled back, smile wider than normal as she felt herself embody her heroine. Not only was the dress practically a million bucks, but it made her feel that way too.

"I'll have a bottle of your finest red, please." Mason spoke politely to the waiter.

They had come to the restaurant a mere twenty minutes prior, and he was already checking things off her list. Holding the door open for her? Check. Kissing her cheek in welcome? Check.

"Whenever I come to these places, I like to splurge a bit," Mason said, his eyes shining as the waiter retreated from the table.

"When in Rome, right?" Olivia laughed. "Or should I say, when in Veritas."

Mason let out a laugh at her poor joke, tucking his napkin beneath the table.

"So, Theo tells me you're a doctor."

"That would be correct. I work as an ED doctor, so it's very unpredictable."

"I can imagine."

"It's also very rewarding though. I get to help people every day, and although some don't make it, I try my best to provide the best care I can to everyone who comes through the ED doors."

"What made you want to be a doctor?"

He didn't respond and she was about to repeat the question when the waiter approached their table once more, a bottle of red in his hand and a pearl white cloth hanging over his forearm.

They watched as the waiter poured both of their glasses, before he placed the bottle between them and asked for their food orders.

She opened the menu, scanning the cuisine. Mason's dismissal of her question did not go unnoticed but she put it down to the interruption of the wait staff.

Salmon. Caviar. Steak. It all seemed luxurious, and utterly out of her budget. Various French dishes lined the page, the descriptions giving little idea to what the dishes contained. Deciding on her meal, she turned towards her date.

"She'll have the salad, and I'll have the steak, please," Mason interjected.

If there was one thing Olivia hated more than a well-done steak, it was a man ordering for her at a restaurant. For some, sure it could be seen as a romantic gesture, but to her, it screamed misogyny.

"Actually," Olivia turned to the waiter and gave a small smile. "Could I have the salmon, please, with a side of broccoli."

"She'll have the salad," Mason repeated to the waiter before sending another smile her way. "You'll have the salad."

The waiter shuffled from one foot to another.

"I'm sure the salad is really nice; however, I will be having the salmon." Olivia gave a thankful glance at the waiter and watched as the poor guy skittered away faster than any waiter had before.

Mason scoffed, picking up his glass of wine. "A chef in *Cook's Gazette* said in an interview that this place has the best steak in north London. I've tried a few in my time so I'm curious to see how it is. The best was in New York."

Olivia swerved the conversation around her dinner selection by instead jumping at the side topic of travelling. She had never been to New York. From the few pictures of the large skyscrapers and huge billboards she'd seen, she was sure it would feel similar to being a speck of dust on the windowsill. Everything was larger in America, that's what Hannah had said when she'd tried to convince Olivia to expand to a US audience during her younger author years. Now she had her books on sale and proudly distributed across the United States of America as well as the United Kingdom.

"So, have you travelled quite a lot then?"

Mason hummed. His mousy brown hair falling over his eyes in thinning strands. "I wouldn't say I've travelled a *lot*. My family moved over from the US, so I have some ties there. I have ventured over to Tokyo, though, it's amazing there. The culture is so rich, and the sushi is, as expected, next level."

"I love sushi, give me some good ol' sashimi and I'm a happy gal," Olivia joked.

After that, the evening went smoothly. Mason ate his steak, offering her a bloody piece of the raw meat for her to try halfway through the meal, to which she politely declined. Olivia ate her salmon, and they shared a sticky toffee pudding for dessert. Everything was going really well.

He held the door open for her, and she clasped her hands over the tie of her coat as they entered the cool evening air of London's nightlife. The restaurant they had gone to was fancy – much fancier than any other she had been to in quite a while, and when the waiter handed the bill over to Mason in a smooth leather booklet, she noted how his eyebrows rose slightly as he sighed and placed his credit card in the reader.

"Well, I had a lovely evening, Rachel. Thank you for a magical night." Mason spoke confidently, giving her a small smile. At first, she thought he was thanking the wait staff, but once she clocked that he was looking directly at her, she was unsure how to continue. Surely he remembered her name; they had been within each other's company for the past two hours. Olivia decided to brush it off with a sharp smile.

"You too, Mason." She spoke politely.

"Would you like to do it again sometime?" Man, he really was trying his luck.

"I'll call you." She made the empty promise without a single thought.

"Wow, I'll have to message Theo and say thanks. You're definitely a ten. Any chance I could get a goodbye kiss?"

The thought of kissing his lips made her stomach churn. If there was one thing her leading man needed to be it was courteous enough to remember his date's name. Kissing was not something she wanted to do. This was just research, and like her novels, completely fiction.

"I have to get home, but it was great to meet you."

"Ah, not the type to kiss on the first date?"

"Well, I've got to keep some kind of mystery, don't I?"

"Night, then Rachel, it was a pleasure to meet you." Mason turned and walked towards a row of taxis lining the street. Opening the door of the first one, he slipped into the car without even so much as a last glance.

"Yeah, night." *My name's not Rachel*, Olivia thought, as she tightened her grip on her purse before turning and walking down the rain-covered street.

CHAPTER TWELVE

"So, you said you'd call him?"

"Yeah." Olivia tapped her fingers on the lino table. It was the night after her date with Mason, and Olivia had invited Theo out for a date debrief, that, or she just wanted an excuse to see him. She was still reluctant to admit the scale was tipping towards the latter.

They had decided on Five Guys, and after squeezing themselves into a small corner booth, with its shiny red rubber cushions and hard cream seats, ordered the greasiest burgers they could find to tuck into in celebration of her writing a further measly nine pages.

"But I'm not going to call him." She sighed.

"And if he tries to call me in hopes of a second date with you...?"

Well *shit*. Olivia hadn't thought of that possibility. Surely he wouldn't do that. She glanced hungrily at her burger and shrugged. "I dunno. Be creative."

Theo laughed. "He's probably waiting by his phone hoping you'll call."

"Well, he should have thought about that before he called me Rachel." Olivia peeled the tomatoes off her burger and put them on the side of her plate.

"He called you Rachel?" Theo frowned. "Even in that red dress?"

Olivia sighed. "Even in that red dress."

"Oh man, he fucked up. How could he forget your name? You're the least forgettable person I know."

Olivia had an air about her, something that left a sharp zing in his chest whenever she was near. At first, he thought it was just because she was drop dead gorgeous. Any man, Taylor and Mason included, must be blind and dumb to not recognise the beauty they had just been out with. Olivia was what you would call a blonde bombshell. Her hair, no matter how windswept it was, always seemed to fall gracefully across her shoulder in waves of gold. Her eyes, no matter how wired on caffeine, were always sparkling with cerulean-blue mischief.

Theo let his eyes drift over her soft knit top and sighed as the V-neck cut of her jumper made her creamy skin look softer than silk. He wondered what it would be like to trace his calloused finger from the soft edge of her jaw, down her décolletage and down further until he was caressing her chest with his hand.

He gulped. "If he calls me then I'll say you lost his number and couldn't find it. Or that you were injured in a shark attack or something." Leaning over, he swiped up the tomatoes and added them to his burger before giving her his gherkins.

Theo watched as she didn't hesitate before grabbing the pickle slices and placing them in her mouth, biting down on the crunchy vegetable. "Thank you," she said to the pickles. Or the date excuse. Or both. She lifted up the small container of sauce, pushing it his way. "Ketchup?"

Theo hummed into his burger, as she also swapped their condiments. "Where did he take you anyway?"

"Veritas." Olivia dipped some hot chips into the aioli he had traded and stuffed them into her mouth as gracefully as she could. "It was nice, and he organised everything. The food was delicious." She grabbed another pickle slice. "The venue was far too extravagant for a blind date, but hey, he paid so I can't really complain about much."

Theo cracked a grin, looking over his half-eaten burger at her. "Other than the fact he called you Rachel instead of your actual name."

"Yeah, that's about it though, that and the fact he insisted on me getting the salad."

Theo snorted. "What did you get instead?"

"I ordered the salmon." Olivia leaned forward in the small booth and swiped a hot chip off his makeshift wrapper plate. "Ten out of ten, by the way."

Theo pushed the remaining chips into the centre of the table and shot her another grin. "I'm glad you didn't starve with a salad."

Theo took a moment to gaze over her. She looked fresh, face bare of make-up, hair pulled up in a high ponytail, loose tendrils of blonde framing her face where the pieces were too short to be pulled back. The light blue jumper she wore over her summer dress brought the colour of her eyes out.

She was elegant, far too pretty to be sitting in a small red lino booth, on a plastic bench, eating a greasy Five Guys burger and chips with her bare hands.

He liked this side of her. The untamed, messy side where she ate her weight in red meat and cheese with no care about

94

her figure, or whether she was being ladylike.

"You know, maybe I should set you up with someone."

Her words drew him out of his thoughts with a sharp tug.

Not going to happen, he thought. *The only person I want to see is you.* He shook the revelation off with a booming laugh. "I'm fine thanks."

"Why not?" Olivia glanced at him, her bottom lip pouting slightly. He drew in a sharp breath and forced himself to look anywhere other than her lips.

Their eyes met as he picked up his drink. "I'm perfectly content being single."

"You're a good-looking guy. You've got that tall, dark and handsome mystery thing going for you. Surely you don't have trouble getting women."

"Is that a compliment?" Theo chuckled.

The burger joint was thrumming with activity, a long line of people, young and old, all queuing up for one of the delicious, greasy meals they were both tucking into shamelessly.

"Oh, come on. You know you're handsome. You can't pretend not to see it, that's just ego seeking. But yes, it was a compliment."

Theo looked bashful for a moment, before he grabbed a napkin, and reached over to dab the corner of her lips, where a small blob of sauce had lingered. "You have some sauce..."

Olivia reached up quickly and swiped her thumb across her bottom lip, placing her thumb into her mouth and licking the sauce off the pad.

Theo cleared his throat, eyes dragging themselves away from her lips.

"My… My last break-up was messy," he admitted, slumping back on his side of the booth. "What was it you said about unrequited love and infidelity again?"

"I think I know what you mean," Olivia muttered, burger long forgotten. "I'm sorry, Theo."

"It's okay. I just don't want to rush into anything right now, and dating seems like a whole lot of effort and energy I'd rather be giving you. And…uh, your leading lady."

Was he blushing? Her own heart fluttered at his words, at his dedication to helping her find her mystery man, though she still couldn't help the curiosity that budded at the corner of her mind. Who had caused him to have such distrust or reluctance to start over? Theo was one of the most confident people she knew, and for him to say he wasn't ready to date after being single for a while, although not unusual, still baffled her. The man was gorgeous, with his brooding looks and height, all the women in this Five Guys joint had at least sneaked one glance at him at some point during their dinner.

She hadn't heard much about Theo's past dating life, or his current affairs for that matter. He was incredibly elusive when it came to his relationships, whether that be romantic, familial or friendships. It was one of the reasons she had thought he was keeping her at arm's length. That this was all merely business for him rather than a potential friendship.

He was only helping her finish her novel, nothing else. They were not friends.

It was cowardice to encourage him to jump back into

dating when she could barely entertain the idea herself, afraid to land on two solid feet.

Though he gave minimal details, the soft frown upon his forehead, small shake in his fingers and tense lift of his shoulders told her everything she needed to know about his break-up. "Whoever she is, I'll send her one of those threatening notes using letter cut out of a magazine or something."

Theo let out a booming laugh, shaking his head. The idea was absurd. Olivia was far too nice to do anything of the sort. He knew it, and she knew it. "No, you wouldn't."

Olivia couldn't help but return his infectious grin. "Yeah, you're probably right. I wouldn't, but you know what I mean."

"So, how's the novel coming?"

"My leading lady is still on the hunt for a leading man. I've outlined some chapters, and I'm getting there. I only have an outline of him, he's like a black and white sketch and I'm trying to dig further and look for the colour, ya know? Depth." Olivia snagged another chip before continuing. "For instance, is he blue, or green? What's his eye colour, or the colour of his favourite T-shirt? I'm still trying to figure that out."

She toyed with the discarded remains of her meal. She leaned back in her chair as she spoke, looking up at the ceiling as she tried to articulate her crazy thought process. She didn't need to explain it, though, she knew Theo understood perfectly. He understood *her* perfectly. Although she had a quirky way of describing it, her words made perfect sense to him. She was searching for all the things that made someone a man. His being. His aura, or however you want to describe it. She didn't want to write just a handsome man; no, she wanted someone who was kind, and this was reflected in the scribbled attributes she'd put in her green notebook from the very beginning.

A list that she was revising with each disaster date.

"You'll find his colours, , it's only been a few weeks. There's still time."

Olivia scoffed. But he saw the glint of optimism in her eye all the same.

CHAPTER THIRTEEN

Theo sat next to Olivia in their usual coffee shop. Between them on the small table was her laptop, the back of the screen littered with meme stickers, beneath the keyboard a series of pink and yellow sticky notes, scribbled scrawl in blue ink noting down comments and words she would use later in her writing.

It was midday, and after receiving a 'we need to talk' text from Olivia at lunchtime, he had taken an early lunch to meet her at her writing spot.

He saw her cheeks blossom with red when she noticed his glance move upwards. It was only then that he realised her chest heaved with heavier breaths than moments before. "I just need to start choosing better guys for you. Has your criteria changed since you started the research?"

Olivia folded her laptop closed and reached down into her bag to bring out that green notebook. Flipping it open, she secured the page with the elastic and passed it over to Theo.

Leading Man Attributes:
*(The first four are non-negotiable, the others subject to change.)**
   1. Respectable.

2. *Ambitious.*

3. *Chivalrous.*

4. *Kind.*

5. *Tall.*

6. *Romantic.*

7. *Interested. (NOT looking at the bloody waitress behind me.)*

8. *Remembers small details, most importantly my <u>name</u>. (I'M NOT RACHEL!)*

*Correction. All are non-negotiable.

Believe it or not, the list was not crazy demanding. Olivia just wanted a nice, decent guy to be her leading man. Someone who would respect her, and her leading character. One thing Theo knew as a man in his early thirties was that what she was asking for, what she expected, was a lot harder to find than she might think.

The men he had set her up with so far, he had thought were all right. Obviously, he was wrong, and that fact left a sour taste in his mouth.

"This doesn't seem like a lot to ask for." Theo passed the book back after taking a long glance. "How's the writing going anyway?"

The café was busier than normal, with office workers seeking a quick midday caffeine and lunch break away from the cold outside.

"Despite being on one bad date, and one mediocre date, at least I'm writing. Given, it's not good, but it's something."

Theo admired how optimistic she was. If he had a

deadline for a novel fast approaching and had gone on the dates she had, he wasn't so sure he'd have the same pep in his step as she did. He would almost certainly begin to look at other ventures, including other ways of helping. His friend, Finn, worked as a business analyst not too far from here and Theo had learned a thing or two from him in regard to fixing problems, and Theo liked fixing problems.

Call it selfish, but that might have been the reason he wanted to help her in the first place. He wanted to fix her writer's block. Allow the gorgeous woman before him to have another bestseller. But she also intrigued him.

Her books were good, great even. Strong characters and solid storylines with erotic love scenes that had made him blush the first time he read them. He had been on the underground, huddled on an end seat, reading filthy words that had come straight from her mind. A young woman wearing a daisy sundress had glanced at him from across the train carriage, eyes moving down to the book and back up at him with a wink, and had quipped a flirtatious, "You up to page 160 yet?"

Oh boy, he had passed page one hundred and sixty moments before, and he felt himself grow even more uncomfortable in his extremely public location. He had slapped the book closed and shoved it back in his bag before promptly getting off the train at the next stop.

Embarrassment had never been a problem for Theo, but that woman had clearly read the same book and knew how the two characters hadn't even managed to make it out of the car park of the diner before they were getting sweaty and naked in the back of the main character's truck. The way both characters licked whipped cream off each other's bodes slowly and sensually behind the tinted windows, excited by the prospect of being caught at any moment.

Olivia's writing, however, had a way of meshing important messages with a comforting amount of romance and class. These books were nothing like the Mills & Boon books his mum used to read, no. These were stories about more than passion and true love. Stories that encouraged you to empathise with the characters, who had all gone through something difficult in their lives, whether it be strict parents, anxiety or other limitations and disadvantages. She didn't shy away from political topics or what her characters thought was right and wrong, and with each book he read of hers – and other authors in the same genre – he appreciated her candour even more.

Her mind is brilliant, he thought as he watched her looking up at the café lights before grabbing her pen and scribbling down notes: different adjectives she had found and thought were interesting new words, and lines of dialogue, which he knew would soon become something meatier once her nimble fingers got to typing.

"You have such an interesting way of writing." He couldn't help but say it out loud, his eyes yet to stray from her form.

Olivia halted her notes, looking up at him through those ridiculously long lashes. "What do you mean?"

"You have notes everywhere, scribbles and doodles. It's a complete mess but it seems to make perfect sense to you. As if you write your own little code."

"Oh." Olivia blushed once more. She seemed to do that a lot more around Theo than anyone else. "Well, I kind of do have a code. Do you want to see?"

She leaned forward on the table, showing him a small set of symbols. A triangle, a heart, a double forward slash and an asterisk.

"The triangle is for when I need to change something. Could be grammar, general formatting or just a rewrite. The heart, obviously, is a love scene, or any moment that there's a romantic aspect of the story. Such as foreshadowing what is going to go down against the character's bedroom door, or in the hotel down the street; the double slash is that I need to add dialogue or expand, and, well, the asterisk leads to my other notebook..." Olivia paused and reached into her bag, pulling out a small red binder. "... where I have series of ideas ranging from small colour wheel details to my chapter-planning and inspiration pictures. It all helps me write more cohesively. I know it makes no sense—"

"It makes sense," Theo interrupted her. "It makes perfect sense. It's your method."

Olivia's cheeks pulled up into a blinding smile, her top teeth showing as the corners of her eyes crinkled slightly. "Exactly," she breathed. "It's my method."

Their coffees had gone cold by now, and Theo knew his lunch hour was almost over. The warmth of her smile, combined with the gentle heat being pushed out by the radiator next to them made him want to stay and talk with her forever.

Closing the notebook in her hand, she leaned forward even further. "Tell me about your sister's wedding. Her name is Georgia, right?"

Theo took a sip of his coffee, his eyes squinting in disgust over the cooled liquid. "Yeah, she's five years younger than me. Marrying a guy she met in Dublin. He's a businessman, something to do with property development." Theo paused, glancing at her before shifting in his seat. "I actually wanted to talk to you about that. We're having a get-together at Finn's next weekend. Georgia is coming to visit, and I thought it would be a good time to introduce you."

Olivia nodded slowly, her tongue flickering out and licking her bottom lip before she pulled it between her teeth. "Okay, yeah that sounds good. Would we be going as friends or—?"

Theo coughed. "I, um, my family is under the impression the date I am taking to the wedding is something more than a friend."

"Like a girlfriend?"

"Yeah," Theo said. "I doubt my sister would let me bring a complete stranger to her wedding. Hence, the agreement."

"Yeah, no problem. Send me the details and I'll meet you—"

"I'll come pick you up, Liv."

"You don't have to, it's quite far."

"I'm not going to let my date arrive before me, and I am well aware of how much you like to be on time to things, if not at least seven minutes early."

Olivia flushed once more. She hadn't been aware that he'd picked up on her tendency to be far too early to everything. She'd rather be early than late. Coffee meet-up or dentist appointment, it didn't matter. She was there long before she needed to be.

"What's the rules then?" she asked.

"Rules?" Theo's long legs stretched beneath the table,

knocking against her smooth, tights-clad legs. When she'd got up for a glass of water twenty minutes beforehand, he'd almost had a heart attack at the way her mini corduroy skirt perfectly hugged her backside. As his pant leg brushed against the sheer fabric clinging to her shapely legs, he took in a breath. She began speaking.

"Can I touch you?" Olivia blurted. "I mean, at the get together. What are the rules around public displays of affection. Do we have to kiss?"

Theo let out a booming laugh. "If you want to kiss me, Olivia, believe me, I have no objection."

Olivia opened and closed her mouth, unsure what to say next. He decided right there that he loved making her speechless.

His eyes burned into hers with an unconcealed fire. "To sell the whole relationship thing, don't get freaked out if I give you a kiss on the cheek, or hold your hand. Subtle touches are what people most often look for. For example, the way your body reacts to mine when we sit next to one another."

"What do you mean?"

"Well, since I stretched my legs out beneath the table, your leg has been gently pushing against mine. We've essentially been playing footsie for the past ten minutes."

Olivia glanced down to where his calf rested against her leg, at the subtle sway they had been doing without noticing. Correction, she had not noticed she had been doing. With every gentle nudge, he would retaliate.

"You already react to me, which is good. It will help us sell that we are in a relationship," Theo stated, bumping her leg once more with a small grin.

Olivia gulped. "You said your sister met him in Dublin, what lead her there?"

Theo picked up one of the loose sticky notes off the table and flipped it between his long fingers. "A teaching conference. She teaches the reception year at a primary school."

"She must be very caring and patient. If I had to wrangle thirty four-year-olds, I think I would go insane."

"She's definitely one of the most caring people I know. Which is why I don't want to hurt her feelings with this." Theo took a deep breath. "I neglected to tell her about my break-up 'til recently… it was messy, and I kept it from my family. Not my brightest hour, but it seemed like the best thing to do. My family, especially my mother and sister, seem to always get attached to my partners quickly. My mother will most definitely bring up grandchildren with you when you meet her, and don't be surprised if my sister throws her bouquet directly to you at the wedding. It's their mission to get me settled down as soon as humanly possible."

"Do you mind me asking what happened with your ex-girlfriend?"

Theo swallowed the thick lump in his throat and found a happy distraction in glancing towards the rainy London Street outside the large glass windows to their left. Considering it was nearly the beginning of summer, the sun was nowhere to be seen. The cloak of rain falling heavily over London for the second week in a row had put a damper on summer plans.

"I was dating her for three years, we were living together and if I'm completely honest, I was out looking for engagement rings on the weekends like a lovesick puppy. After two years she made a comment about me proposing, but I hadn't even considered marriage before then. Before her it seemed like a crazy idea my mum had for me, but once we moved in with each other and did everything normal couples did – go on weekend walks, make breakfast in bed, go grocery shopping together, fight over what cushions we wanted on the sofa – it all became real. I was ready to commit to her. But then, towards the end of last year, just after my company Christmas party, I found her with her legs wrapped around another man's waist in our bed, yelling a name that definitely was not mine."

"Oh God, that's awful," Olivia exclaimed.

Theo considered it. "After that, I came to the conclusion I hadn't ever really wanted to marry her, I think I just felt the pressure. I had just turned thirty and my mum was making comments about us; my sister got engaged and was planning her wedding. It seemed like the right thing to do. But underneath it all I think I knew it wasn't meant to be."

"How can you be so nonchalant about it?" Olivia asked. "If that happened to me, I would swear off of love altogether. Probably buy five cats and live my days out as a proud spinster."

Sitting quietly for a moment, Olivia regarded Theo with a questioning gaze. *If it happened to me, I would swear off love all together.* It took that small, innocent sentence to realise that she had done exactly that. That after the accident she had sworn off love forever. Because that's how long she felt it would take her to get over *him*.

The dim café lights shone streaks of gold into his eyes, the curls around his ears looked soft to touch, falling perfectly around his defined jaw and handsome features. Theo chuckled. "Well, I've had nearly nine months to think it over. Plus, it's not too different to your leading man situation."

How can you be so nonchalant about it? she thought again. *When I am burning from the inside out with grief.* Its hot scorch left nothing but ash over her heart when she thought of loving another. Giving her heart, her hand and her mind to someone other than the one who was supposed to her leading man forever seemed impossible.

Her eyebrows drew low on her face. "Nine months isn't a long time when you put it into the perspective of three years. You dedicated years of your life to her, and she just cheats on you? People are terrible."

"At least we weren't married." He hummed. His lunch hour was up, and standing from the small wooden chair seemed like the hardest thing he had to do in his life. Theo shrugged on his coat, leaned over and kissed Olivia on the cheek. "And at least, we can organise another date for you. One that better suits the attributes you've written down."

"Hmm." The corners of her lips turned up as the heat from his lips tingled against her cheek with much more meaning than just a goodbye.

CHAPTER FOURTEEN

Naomi slid her hands up his arms, feeling the corded veins and hard muscle. She sighed, her head tipping back as he kissed her neck giving it firm licks and bites.

"You have no idea what you're doing to me, Naomi..." he breathed, brushing her hair back from her face, and laying another passionate kiss along the curve of her throat. The club lights flashed overhead, sending beams of purple and red flickering in her view. She knew this was dangerous, dancing with the enemy. But she couldn't help it; he was addictive. His presence filled the room, his tall figure looming over her like her greatest fantasy and worst nightmare rolled into one. All of her doubts faded away in his firm hold and with the promise of privacy in the form of his shoulder's shadow. She sighed, pressing her body further into his, looking up into his bright...

"Urgh!" Olivia bashed her fingers on the top of her keyboard, panicking when the words she had just written disappeared right before her eyes. "No, no, no! Please have auto saved..."

Hitting CTRL-Z, the mediocre words reappeared, allowing her temper to calm a little at the sight of what she had typed. Despite writing all day and having her leading man in the back of her mind, she still couldn't even make simple decisions such as what colour his eyes were.

Blue? Green? Brown? Hazel?

Olivia sighed, rereading the passage with uncertainty, pressing the backspace and deleting half of the words she had just written. After a few moments, she panicked, clicked undo again and watched the lacklustre script reappear.

She repeated the motion numerous times before just accepting the words for what they were. Words. And words were progress; however shitty they were. She would revise them after she finished this first draft. For now, she just needed to write.

This is only one of many drafts, she thought, lifting up an old Christmas mug her mother had got her in New York last winter, and taking a painful swig of her now cool tea.

Blue? Green? Brown? Hazel? What colour was her leading man's eyes? There was almost too much choice.

Why was she finding it so difficult to come up with a character description when there were plenty of options; she should just choose one and stop being so picky. Her femme fatale wouldn't care if she was dating someone with blue or brown eyes, so why should it matter to Olivia?

But she was stumped. With her word count creeping up, she had somehow managed to plan and write around the leading man character, placing capitalised words, such as INSERT NAME HERE and THINK OF IT LATER, as temporary placeholders for what she had failed to come up with.

Maybe her creativity needed some revamping. Maybe she should reread her previous novels, try to dissect them and see why they had made the bestseller list. How had she written them with minimal hiccups and formed characters that were loved and viscerally hated by so many people that it had made her stories so successful?

With a defeated sigh, she realised reading her old stuff wouldn't help anyway. She was trying to do something new, she was trying to write something real, and she had forgotten what that was like. Maybe she was making it harder for herself to come up with a character for her leading lady because he wasn't meant to be perfect. He was just meant to exist.

Theo's friend opened his apartment door, all dark blond and tall with ruffled hair and a grin that screamed playboy. He greeted her with a wink, followed by a straightforward, "Sorry Taylor was a dick. I could've warned you if I'd had known this dumbass set you up with him. I'm Finn, by the way. Nice to finally meet the girl Theo has been nattering on about forever." He reached a hand forward in greeting, a beer firmly tucked in the other.

"Uh, thank you?" Olivia muttered in response before they were welcomed in.

Georgia, Theo's sister, elbowed Finn in the ribs muttering an unashamed, "Move out of my way, you oaf," before placing two kisses, one on each of Olivia's cheeks, in welcome. "Olivia! About time I met you. My brother has been incredibly hush-hush about you, so you have to tell me your whole life story, please and thank you."

"Of course." Olivia laughed, there was no room for discussion in Georgia's warm but firm tone, and she suddenly knew how she managed to teach a full class of little rascals.

The girls followed behind Theo and Finn, settling down on the plush grey sofa.

A stocky man sat on the single armchair in the far corner, his brown hair ashy and unkempt. He looked tired, his body rigid and unfitting in the cosy penthouse apartment. "Hi, I'm Ross, nice to meet you." He smiled at Olivia. She said hi back respectfully, before Finn passed around booze.

She noticed how Georgia jumped up to help bring beer bottles in from the kitchen, swiping a bag of Doritos from the cupboard on the way, despite the complaints from Finn. "George, not the Doritos. Grab the Walkers. Doritos are mine."

"Doritos are mine," Georgia mocked him in a low voice. "I'm having the Doritos, Finn. Suck it up."

Finn grumbled under his breath, but didn't make any further rebuttals.

The apartment was far fancier than anything Olivia had seen in a while. It was certainly nowhere near being in the same ballpark as her little north London shabby apartment where hot water turned off randomly, and where you had to jiggle the lock four times before it let you enter the property. She should probably get that fixed.

No, this apartment was sleek and grey, with stainless steel appliances, and a large comfy, grey three-seater sofa that sat in the centre of the open space living. The place was spacious and clean, and Olivia could imagine the rugby nights happening here, making note of the bathroom door just down the small hall and to the right of the front door. The same bathroom door Theo had gone through when she had called him after her last godawful date. As they all sat around the small oak coffee table, Olivia felt relaxed.

"Okay, first up: *Trivial Pursuit*." Georgia leapt up from her spot on the couch and opened up the red cardboard box. "Names out of the hat for teams."

Theo sat next to Olivia, his knee knocking the coffee table as he settled into the grey cushions, causing the small, coloured counters she had just set up to fall over and roll onto the floor. "Oops." Theo smirked, leaning back and throwing his arm around Olivia. She tensed at the movement before settling into his side with a small glance at him.

Georgia sent her brother a deadly look. "You better be nice to me; you're not making a very good impression of how you treat family to your new girlfriend."

Olivia felt her stomach pull at the word, butterflies hatching from cocoons and fluttering all around her stomach and chest at the declaration.

It's just pretend, she thought. *I'm just doing him a favour.*

"Good thing I can get away with it then." Finn chuckled, knocking over the pieces once more.

Georgia struck out with lightning speed and slapped Finn on the back of the hand. "Back off, Townsend."

"Never, Constantine." Finn's teasing eyes stayed on Georgia as she read out the instructions before passing a small baseball hat towards Olivia, letting her pick out a name from the hat first.

Reaching in, Olivia pulled out a small piece of paper, glanced at it and looked up with uncertainty as she read out the name "Ross."

The man on the armchair leaned forward and smirked.

113

"Well, I guess we better get to know each other really well in the next five minutes, cause these three have far too many inside jokes."

Olivia shuffled closer to Theo, giving the man a small smile. Despite Ross's words, she felt there was something not quite right about the authoritarian way he sat in the corner, as though playing games were childish.

Georgia let out a loud groan as she glanced at the paper in her hand. Turning to Finn, she sent him a look. "If you make us lose, Townsend, I'll make Mum force you to eat outside in the cold at Christmas."

"Challenge accepted, Georgie pie." Finn shot her a wink.

Georgia rolled her eyes, scooting over and leaning up against the single armchair. She angled her head up and glanced at Ross. "You okay going with Olivia?"

"Are you okay going with Finn?" he rebutted. They glanced at each other for a moment, her eyebrows arching down at his words.

Theo cleared his throat. "Okay, first category. Sports and Leisure."

Finn leaned forward, elbows on knees and glanced directly at Georgia. "Time to be on your A-game, George. If you get the answer wrong, there'll be no more Doritos."

Olivia glanced at Ross. "Are you any good at Sports trivia?"

He shook his head, fiddling with the buttons of his shirt. "No, I'm more of a politics guy, but I'll try my best."

"Shit," Olivia muttered. She felt Theo's chest move as he chuckled beneath her.

"Ready?" Theo asked, and at the reluctant nod of their heads and a few grumbles, the game began. "What team won the FIFA World Cup in 2014?"

"Argentina?" Ross said, his voice uncertain.

Georgia looked up at him with confusion. "Aw, honey. That was 2022, nice try though."

Finn jumped up and screamed, "Germany!"

"Move Finn and Georgia one place, won't you Ross?" Theo asked, picking up his beer and taking a swig while Finn and Georgia were huddled near the armchair, basking in their correct answer with shared grins.

"Next up: Olivia and Ross. Your category is… Geography!"

"I'm sorry in advance," Olivia groaned. Ross looked as though he had accepted defeat in the first five minutes of the game. Given how Finn and Georgia were enthusiastically playing, even her confidence had begun to waver.

Empty beer bottles and a few glasses of wine littered the coffee table.

Olivia had determined that the Constantine siblings were both incredibly stubborn and competitive. When she turned towards Theo and tried to sneak a look at the answer written on the small card in his hand, he snatched it away. "No cheating, Liv. This is a fair game. We play by the rules."

"No one plays by the rules." Olivia rolled her eyes.

"We do," Georgia interrupted. "And stop being so goddamn cute, you're going to make me puke with all your googly eyes at each other."

Olivia glanced up at Theo, noting how close their faces had got during their conversation. Looking into his deep brown eyes, she felt her lips turn up in a cheesy grin, matching his, before leaning further forward until their lips were centimetres apart.

"Since when do you play fair, Theo?" she whispered.

His eyebrow quirked slightly, his eyes gleaming. "What does that mean?"

From the look on his face, and proximity of their bodies, Olivia knew something was about to happen. She could feel the way his hand had snaked around her waist.

If she were to lean forward an inch their lips would touch. Press delicately over each other.

Since she'd known him the scales had been tipped solely in his favour. He never played fair. All hot and dishevelled every time they met up at the coffee shop, brushing his leg against hers, answering her video calls with his breathy baritone that sent her eyes glancing over his plump lips.

She wanted to find out if he tasted like the Americano coffee he ordered, or the spearmint breath mints he always carried around in the pocket of his coat.

"Now you're not playing fair." Theo's voice came out gravelly. As if the words were only for her.

She leaned forward the rest of the way and melded her lips over his in a quick peck, reaching for the card at the same time. Theo moved his hand back as she pressed forward into the brief but firm slant of their lips.

A gagging sound could be heard throughout the room, their kiss ending as Theo turned to throw a sofa cushion in the direction of his sister, causing her to squeal and leap onto Ross's lap.

Ross whispered something into Georgia's ear, making her teasing smile drop as she moved off his lap.

Olivia sulked at her failed attempt at cheating.

"Nice try, sweetheart," Theo said putting the card down

beside him.

Clicking her tongue, she sucked her lower lip into her mouth, smirking as he followed the action, before shifting herself closer to his body and swinging her legs over his lap with a swift movement. She could still taste him, her lips buzzing with the flavour of his beer and a hint of spearmint.

"Our turn!" Georgia suddenly beamed, smile back on her face as she swivelled towards Finn and shook her head slightly at his questioning gaze. Finn raised his eyebrows at her, eyes flicking between her and the man sitting behind her, before muttering something about grabbing another drink.

Seeing Theo's dynamic with his sister made Olivia wish she had a sibling. Their relationship was playful, with sibling banter thrown back and forth around the room at top speed. Despite their bickering, Theo offered Georgia a cushion for her spot on the floor where she was sitting cross-legged, and ensured she had a blanket when the sun dipped behind the clouds and the day turned into night.

Olivia was also jealous of the apartment view. The London skyline looked more beautiful than ever outside the floor-to-ceiling windows. Bright lights from signs, cars and lamp posts dotted a blank canvas of shadowed chimneys and navy night sky.

Half an hour later, and a few drinks in, things had got incredibly heated. Ross and Olivia's team was losing by a landslide, whereas Finn and Georgia were on the very last question. This time anyone could answer. As many guesses until someone said the right one.

Finn bounced on his feet. "Ah, this is a good one. Okay, pay attention, Georgie pie."

Olivia's eyes flicked between the two, who over the past half an hour had got increasingly more cocky and inebriated with each question. Both of them pacing the living room, one minute jumping up and down when they got the answers right and the next yelling profanities and food-related threats at each other when they didn't.

Finn and Georgia were absolutely thrashing them.

Trivial Pursuit used to be Olivia's favourite board game.

Not tonight. Not when she had absolutely no chance of winning when playing against those two.

They seemed to have too many inside jokes just like Ross had said, sharing looks and both answering questions correctly on the first try. They seemed to know nearly every answer. Their antics kept the smile draped over Olivia's face the whole time she watched them. It was as if there was a direct telepathic link from his mind to hers.

Olivia thought it was endearing.

Theo's hand had started drawing lazy circles on the top of her arm. They sat on the sofa, her sock-clad feet now draped over his lap, as she cradled a glass of wine. She swore she had never laughed so much.

"Your sister is quite a character." Olivia giggled, leaning her head against Theo's shoulder.

She heard him exhale a small chuckle. "Yeah, she gets it from my mum."

To the left of them, Georgia leaned down as if she were about to enter a rugby scrum "Pay attention, got it. Hit me."

It was a universal question. First team to answer got the point. Finn and Georgia were one answer away from winning, whereas for the rest of them it meant that, if they got the question right, they'd get one more chance to make the game last five extra minutes.

Theo and Olivia had admitted defeat ten minutes prior, but Ross seemed to hit a second wave of determination, his gaze zoned in on Finn, shooting daggers his way.

Finn paused, rereading the card before glancing at Ross. A look of something malevolent flickered across his face, so quick one might not notice, before his eyes met Georgia's once more. "Think university."

"Oh God, this is going to be interesting," Theo muttered.

Georgia's face paled slightly, her excited jig halting.

"Wait, are we supposed to guess as well?" Olivia asked.

"Try your best, Liv, but these two have a weird sense of shared telepathy." Theo leaned over and kissed her forehead, tucking her further into his side.

Over the course of the night Theo had been really selling the fake relationship thing. So much so that by the time the moon had risen high in the sky and the sound of the London nightlife began to buzz, she had grown accustomed to his light touches. Every now and then she would feel her cheeks heat at the way his thumb caressed the top of her arm as he read out the questions, at the way his eyes met hers as she thought of the answers, at the way he gently nudged his thigh against hers to calm her when Ross clicked his fingers and rushed her to answer.

Georgia's eye twitched, before she muttered the words. "Give me more."

Finn shot another quick look at Ross, who was sitting on the edge of his chair, meeting his eyes with a sharp glare. He looked like a panther ready to pounce on his prey at any moment.

"Karaoke…" Finn continued. "Irish pub."

Ross clapped his hands and leapt up. "Shania Twain!"

"No, dipshit," Finn snapped, standing up straight and titling his head as though he was tired of the man's arrogance.

"Oh! I know!" Georgia jumped up, beaming a winner's smile. "Amy Winehouse!"

By the time they left Finn's apartment, it was very late.

"When you first told me about Finn, I thought he was a playboy, but seeing the way he and Georgia are together I can understand how wrong I was. I'm glad they're getting hitched. Both of them are so in love it's hard to look at."

"What?" Theo laughed; his arm still locked around her shoulders.

"Finn and Georgia. Those two are so compatible, and the chemistry" – Olivia made an explosive motion with her hands – "it's dynamite."

"Ross is her fiancé, not Finn."

Olivia opened and closed her mouth before letting out a small "Oh." Her eyes flashed with unfiltered surprise. "I just figured he was a friend or something. He was really quiet all evening."

Theo frowned. "Why did you think Finn was her fiancé?"

Olivia began to tread carefully with her words. This was Theo's baby sister whom she'd made an assumption about. And his best friend.

"Well, she knew his favourite song, he couldn't keep his

eyes off her, and she was all flirty, and they seemed to have inside jokes that helped them ask questions. Those factors don't scream hate. Quite the opposite. You have to know someone really well to communicate both verbally and non-verbally like that."

Theo laughed. "Sure. Flirty. Those two have been at each other's necks for the past eight years. They're more like siblings than anything else. Plus, she's my sister. He'd never go there."

"Just because she's your sister doesn't mean he can't like her."

Theo shook his head, shoving away the idea of his sister and best friend of nearly a decade shacking up together.

No way.

Finn would've told him.

Plus, Finn found no shame in sharing details about his sexual partners. Of which, he'd had plenty. But commitment wasn't his style, and Theo knew that. There was no doubt that Finn knew one step out of line or attempt at a fling with his sister, and Theo would be there, fist coiled at the ready.

Georgia deserved someone who could commit to her one hundred per cent, not a playboy with a new chick at his side every Saturday night.

"When I was writing my second novel, I took a psychology class all about reading body language. It was really interesting, and I only remember parts of it, but it included a lot of insight on how to tell if someone is attracted to you," Olivia stated. "Finn's feet were pointing towards her all night, and her body was always turned towards his. That's why I thought Ross was just a friend. Although he had his arm around her, she never seemed to notice."

Theo frowned. If what she was saying was true, then neither Finn nor Georgia knew about it either. As far as he was concerned it would be the blind leading the blind when it came to uncovering their true feelings. Especially love.

CHAPTER FIFTEEN

Theo couldn't get the kiss out of his head.

The soft plump feel of Olivia's lips on his was enough to make his blood run hot, all reasonable thought venturing embarrassingly south in the most inconvenient moments. The way her lips had slanted over his, even briefly had him imagining how it would feel to have her tongue poking out and running along the length of his, teasing. Tasting.

He still remembered the hint of summer berries and cream lip balm she had been wearing.

Now that he had felt her in his arms, what it was like to kiss her, Theo knew he was going to struggle to find her more dates to go on. Dates that weren't with him.

It had only been for a moment, and the moment was for show, sure. But he could still feel her, the gentle press of her body against his, the way she smelt of floral perfume, the way she leaned in and whispered those teasing words before pressing her lips to his in the gentlest of brushes.

He was almost grateful Georgia had interrupted the moment, otherwise he might have up and left the games night embarrassed and needy. The only thing that had kept him sane was that he was finding her dates, so maybe now he had a new mission. Maybe now he had to make her see the best man for the job was him.

"So, you're stripes, I'm spots, and basically—" Theo began. The were huddled at the side of one of Robbie's velvet pool tables, the green velvet stark against the dull brown hues of the pub. Dim lamps lined the wallpapered walls, their soft golden glow making the bustling pub feel warm and cosy.

"Yeah, yeah, I know how to play," Olivia cut him off, shoving him out of the way before leaning over the table and lining her aim up. After three Apple Martinis and some shared hot chips, the two had decided to play a game of pool. When he had told her where they were going, and she'd asked why, Theo had simply said that for each bad date she'd had he was going to give her a good one. Plus, he didn't want one bad date to ruin her beloved Apple Martinis for her.

Both were slightly tipsy, but that made for more fun, or at least that's what she'd thought before Theo started ranting at her, telling her all the rules and regulations of the game. "Okay, buttercup, show me what you got," he said, finishing off his beer.

Olivia was about to learn though that understanding the rules and being able to actually *play* were two different things. Leaning down, she placed one hand on the table, pulled her arm back and pushed forward. The pool stick missed, bouncing up and down on the table.

A choked laugh sputtered out of Theo. With a frown, Olivia turned to see him slapping a hand over his firm chest, his head tipping back in laughter. She couldn't help but glance at the thick corded veins which lined his arms, trailing up past his elbows and underneath the double rolled sleeves of his shirt.

He wiped the beer from the corner of his lips as he struggled to compose himself. "I thought you said you knew how to play?"

Poking him with the chalked end of the pool cue, Olivia stuck out her bottom lip with full effect and sulked. "I said I knew how to play, not that I was any good."

His eyes shone in amusement, fingers curling over hers as he pried the stick from her delicate grasp. "Okay. Watch and learn."

Three more drinks later, Olivia was positive that whoever had created the game was stupid. Theo had sunk all of his balls bar two, meanwhile she'd sunk a measly one. By accident.

"Okay, I can't stand to see you suffer any longer. Come here." Theo shook his head as he watched her miss yet another shot.

"I can get it, I swear," Olivia responded stubbornly. She was determined to get this one. She could feel it in her fingertips. This time she would sink it, and it would even swish the net. She would bet money on it.

Ignoring her stubbornness, Theo grabbed her hips, fingers curling around her hipbones and turned them, sandwiching her between the solid table and his body. Olivia felt heat creep up her neck, her body not letting her ignore the press of his fingertips against her lower stomach. The fluttering in her chest increased tenfold, her rationality melting further when the steel hard muscles of his abdomen contracted against her back. Her cheeks were red-hot, and not from the copious amount of alcohol she had consumed that evening.

Taking a deep breath, she closed her eyes before snapping them open once again. This time, they were trained on the striped ball.

Theo leaned down, his breath brushing over the lobe of her ear and filtering down the side of her neck. Cocooned in his arms, she couldn't stop her mind immediately diving head first into the gutter. It practically threw itself in and rolled around in the dirty thoughts the position promised. Her blush grew stronger, her lower stomach contracting in excitement underneath the steady grasp of his wide palms.

Pushing her front closer to the table, Theo leaned them over the table, covering her upper body with his. She breathed in the alluring scent of his aftershave. Musk and pine, with the undercurrent of something fresh. Like the scent of the pavement after it had rained, or the fresh country air. She couldn't describe it other than it was purely him. The broad planes and lean muscles of his chest made her feel as though they were in their own little world within the pub.

He had sheltered them, covered her petite frame with his, the murky bartender and the rowdy stag group at the bar disappearing with the firm reassurance of his chest and the feeling of his breath against the curve of her neck. "Angle your body like this…"

Olivia's breath hitched, forcing herself to focus on anything other than the warmth his chest was emitting. This was embarrassing. She had been single for well over a year now, and it was as if her body was yelling out for Theo to touch her, satisfy the needs her toys at home did nothing but to amplify.

His hand then brushed down her side and grasped her hand clutching the pool stick, manoeuvring her fingers. His next words sent shivers down her spine, and planted a seed of need deeper into her abdomen. "Make a triangle here…"

She liked this position a little too much, and in that moment was thankful he couldn't see the fire that consumed her face. She was mortified. And horny. *Forgive me*, she thought to herself. To *him*. She had sinned. Correction, she was sinning. Every time his hips brushed her backside an accidental gasp would escape her lips, the hand on her hip flexing each time at the sound. It felt sinful. Not wrong, just completely against the religion of celibacy and singleness she had adhered to over the past year. Theo flexed his forearms, the muscles and veins doing nothing to extinguish the throb between her legs.

In that moment, she needed holy water.

"Ready?" he asked, his head almost resting on her shoulder.

"Yes," Olivia breathed softly. She felt him freeze for a moment at her confirmation, a small moan escaping, before he brought their arms forward. Holding her breath, she watched the striped ball roll along the table and fall gracefully into the hole.

Olivia let out an excited yelp and turned, grinning ear to ear. "I DID IT!"

Theo chuckled.

Clocking how close their faces were, the way his hands were now splayed across her belly and back, she looked up into the striking caramel brown of Theo's eyes.

Olivia could count the various shades of gold and brown that made up his irises and found herself slowly and meticulously examining his facial features. The small dimples on either side of his cheeks. His straight nose, stubbled jaw and soft, full lips.

Noticing how the quiet and comfortable pub ambience had invaded their bubble, Olivia went to take a step back, bumping into the table and pressing the pool cue into his chest.

"It's, uh… it's your turn," she said before sliding sideways and grabbing his near-empty drink.

Tilting it back, she sculled the rest of his drink as Theo watched. She knew the action meant her throat was exposed, and the long curve where her shoulder met the delicate flesh of her neck was visible, and as she swallowed the liquid she noted how he gulped, his Adam's apple bobbing in his throat before he turned away.

Olivia pictured taking one step forward, leaning up and licking up the vein that strained along the side of his neck next to that Adam's apple. She imagined him returning the fervour, a bruising reminder of his lips on her neck sounding like a very good idea as she wiped the corner of her mouth with her wrist and slammed the glass back down on the edge of the pool table.

Theo averted his eyes before clearing his throat. Muttering a quick, "Right," he lined up his shot.

CHAPTER SIXTEEN

"Olivia, I've found someone I think might just be the leading man you've been searching for."

It's me, Theo wanted to say. *I'm your leading man.*

Olivia's pause on the other end of the phone line made sweat begin to bead at the edge of his hairline. Did he say that out loud? Why was she taking so long to respond?

Finally, after a few beats of silence, her melodic voice came through the phone and made his shoulders drop. "Really? Who is the next mysterious contender?" The teasing tone sunk deep into his chest and squeezed the air out of his lungs.

Theo was about to hype up another man, something he really did not want to do. Not when he could still feel her soft frame against his chest, the breathy words she had whispered and that goddamn kilowatt smile she had sent his way when she had finally sunk the silly striped ball at Robbie's a few days prior. Through seething teeth, he said, "His name is Edward, he's a lawyer, and I swear he seems better than those previous jerks."

In truth Theo hated the guy, and a small part of him hoped that Olivia would too.

Olivia clicked her tongue. "I dunno, Theo. Your scouting skills are lacking a bit. How do I know this guy won't be a complete disaster date again?"

Theo let out a half-hearted chuckle. "I promise you, he's worth a shot. No more Taylors or Masons."

Theo had to constantly remind himself of the deal which was made. Help her find *Naomi's* leading man, not hers. He had only been assigned the task of finding her fictional character's prince charming. So why was he reluctant to set up these dates? He needed to separate his own wants and needs with what was best for Olivia and her novel. All Olivia wanted was love and fiction. It helped to separate his own wants with this mantra, especially once he realised, lying in bed the night he returned from their date, that the agreement was skewed and completely unfair. It was then, bare chested and under his navy duvet that he no longer wanted to find her a leading man, he wanted to be it. He was capable, reliable, and had been conducting their every meeting in accordance with her leading man list of requirements. He already ticked numerous boxes on said list, and after spending more and more time with Olivia, he'd become transfixed by her. The time they'd shared was better than it had been with his previous partners, their conversations intellectual and interesting. She fascinated him far more than he wanted to admit, so much so that the thought of her going out with other men, real or for research purposes made his stomach squeeze, and his shirt collar feel too tight to breathe.

"What's the plan then?" Olivia sounded just as reluctant to give this guy a chance as Theo did. He had already been unsure of setting her up with him, and now the sound of her uncertainty gave him hope that she wouldn't like him either. That maybe after this third terrible date, she would open her eyes and finally realise that Theodore was the one she was looking for.

"Meet him at the Alice movie theatre tomorrow night at 9:00. I've organised for you to both see a rerun of *Rebel Without a Cause*. Theo knew it was one of her favourite films, he had noticed the small sticker of James Dean on the lid of her laptop, and the way she casually quoted the old Hollywood blockbuster in everyday conversation. Small details that hopefully she would pick up on; how he had set up this date, picked a movie she would like, a movie theatre that served extra butter popcorn just how she liked, and realise it had been all him.

"Wow." Olivia's surprised tone made his chest tighten.

Had he taken it too far? He had planted the idea with Edward the night before, telling him about how she loved old Hollywood cinema.

Edward had eagerly thanked him for the idea and agreed to meet her instantly after seeing the picture that Theo had taken secretly of her on his phone the other day when she had been writing like crazy in one of her many notebooks. Was there such a thing as paying too much attention when it came to Olivia? Theo held the phone up to his face, his feet pounding on the rain-drenched pavement of Oxford Street.

No.

The answer was a solid no. The girl was joyful and far too intriguing in a way that Theo had never felt before. She was beauty and brains and she didn't even know it.

CHAPTER SEVENTEEN

Olivia stood outside the old Alice Cinema, nervously adjusting her dress. She looked around, searching for Edward, whom she had been given a very detailed description of by Theo an hour prior. Long black jacket, tall, pale golden hair and blue eyes. Aka, half the men in London. She did not want a repeat of her previous date, where she had looked like a complete idiot for not knowing who he was. A few moments passed, and a tall man with messy blond locks approaches her with a wide smile, wearing the very outfit described by Theo. Mustering up a smile, Olivia stopped smoothing her hands along her dress as the man stopped a few feet from her.

"Olivia, it's a pleasure to meet you. I'm Edward." He leaned forward, cupping her shoulder in a firm grasp and placed a kiss on her right cheek.

"Nice to meet you too. Theo has told me great things." Why did she just bring up Theo? She'd only just met Edward, and she was already talking about another man. Noting his polite smile, he nodded towards the popcorn counter.

"Should we get some snacks? The movie starts soon."

Olivia smiled her agreement. She had said many times before that she hated first dates, and nothing had changed. They were always awkward and unrelenting. To her pleasant surprise, however, Edward had chosen to see one of her favourite movies for them to watch, and so she would be able to sit in the dark in Edward's company without too much chitchat and not worry about maintaining the same level of conversation and show of interest she had in her previous dates.

"Yeah, that sounds good. Theo told me they had good popcorn here, so to say I'm excited would be a major understatement." Olivia skipped towards the counter, her khaki green coat and skirt flowing around her bare legs.

"Do you like sweet or salty popcorn?" Edward pointed towards the huge case of popcorn, the metal pan popping as corn kernels fell over the edge onto a large pile.

"Salty." Olivia hummed, licking her lips. Cinema popcorn hit different than other popcorn. It was elite. Especially the salty, buttery goodness that was less popular here in England. It was often incredibly difficult to find the savoury snack, and the times she had, her dates had just ordered the sweet popcorn by default. Glancing at the counter, she drew her lips between her teeth. Edward had already overtaken her previous dates by asking what flavour she wanted, and in her head, she mentally checked the box for considerate on her leading man criteria list.

"I thought you would pick sweet," Edward said, his eyes piercing with their bright blue irises.

Olivia quirked her eyebrows. "Why's that?"

"To match your personality." Edward winked, leaving her standing there in the line while he approached the counter. She watched him carefully, looking over his features with interest.

Letting out a gentle laugh, she felt her cheeks blossom with heat as the attendant called them over.

Flirting. He was flirting. A behaviour she was, apparently, not that good at, according to the men she'd speed dated weeks ago.

The old timey cinema was decorated in art deco-inspired architecture. Musty reds and patterned green carpets made the place feel as though you had walked back in time, right back to the golden age of cinema, and sit too close to your neighbours on the small red fold-out chairs. She liked to think Edward might have the same taste in movies as her, and smiled when he leaned over the small marble counter and ordered. Maybe this date wouldn't go as poorly as she originally thought.

"One salty, one sweet popcorn, please." Edward handed over a sleek black bank card before Olivia could blink.

"Oh, are you sure? I can pay for mine." Reaching into her handbag, she rummaged around and began to lift the bright pink purse out.

His hands covered hers, and he looked right at her. "I'm the one taking you out, I'm paying."

Chivalrous. Another box: ticked.

Olivia allowed herself a shameless swoon as she threw the pink purse back in the old leather bag and closed the zip.

They entered the dimly lit theatre of the old cinema. The flickering marquee lights cast a warm glow on their faces as they made their way to their seats. The theatre was nearly empty, besides an elderly couple sitting at the front, the man's arm slung over his partner's, whispering sweet nothings to each other in the dim light, and a rowdy group of five teenagers sitting right up front, their feet propped on the top of the seats in front of them. Popcorn was being thrown high into the air before they tried and failed to capture it in their mouths.

The red velvet seats creaked under their weight as they settled in, the old narrow chairs making their shoulders brush slightly as they sat side by side.

"So, Theo told me this is one of your favourite films. I must admit, I'm not as familiar with it. But I'm excited to watch it with you." Edward spoke while folding his jacket and laying it across his lap.

Olivia was surprised at his admission. She didn't even remember telling Theo such a small, obscure fact about herself. "Oh, really? Well, it's a classic. I haven't met anyone that doesn't like it so far, no pressure or anything," she joked.

Edward turned to her and grinned just as the lights went down.

Over the course of the film, Olivia occasionally stole glances at him, and each time he'd glance back at her, and they'd share smiles like shy teenagers. She noticed his genuine interest in the film, despite his earlier confession of not knowing much about it. She began to relax, and by halfway through the movie she had mustered the confidence to lay her head on his shoulder as they watched.

Despite the first two dating blunders, Theo had found her someone she could finally envision being her leading man.

After the film ended, Olivia and Edward exited the old cinema, warm night air greeting them. Olivia couldn't help but smile as they stepped out of the gold-lined double doors and onto the bustling street. The date had gone well. It had been the best one yet.

She couldn't wait to tell Theo.

"It was just as fantastic as I remember," Olivia said excitedly. Grasping Edward's arm, she turns her gaze towards him. "What did you think? *Rebel Without a Cause,* did it live up to the hype?"

Edward grinned at her gleeful tone. "You know what? It did. I can see why you love it so much."

Her smile widened when he insisted on walking her to her tube line to go home. They continued to talk; the awkwardness of the blind date had completely dissipated, leaving only a warm tug in her stomach, and a bunch of butterflies.

For first dates, this one hasn't been that bad, she thought, glancing up at the blond man with blue eyes who had been respectful, and kind, and so far, everything she wanted. Edward was more than just a contender for her leading man; he had all the makings of a genuine protagonist in her upcoming novel. The way he made her feel, the way he looked at her, it was all too perfect to be discarded.

When she got home, Olivia outlined three chapters, left a voice message for Theo and wrote a new name at the end of her list.

CHAPTER EIGHTEEN

Theo grabbed his beer off the counter, nodding at the bartender in thanks.

"So, let me get this straight," Finn muttered, placing his own beer down and turning to his friend. "You set her up with Edward, the dickhead company lawyer you can't stand and she left you a voice message saying it was the best first date she'd ever had in her life."

Theo gave Finn a pointed look before responding with a curt, "Yeah."

"Sorry for rubbing it in… but you're fucked. Wait, didn't you choose the location, and the movie? Why didn't you just take her out?"

"We made an arrangement, Finn. One that only you, me and her know about. I'm to help her find a leading man, and she's coming to Georgia's wedding with me."

Theo didn't miss the wince Finn let flash across his features at the words, before he picked up his beer and took a long and hard swig.

"I just didn't thing she would actually - Theo's phone rang, cutting off his next sentence. Looking down at his phone, he saw Olivia's name light up.

He immediately answered, lifting to his ear just as Finn

laughed. "Dude, you're whipped."

Theo sent him a harsh glare before speaking. "Hey Olivia."

"Hey, Theo. You'll never guess what happened." Olivia's voice was filled to the brim with excitement, her tone overflowing so much he had to turn the volume down on his phone.

"You woke up and reflected on the date to realise it wasn't as great as you let on?"

I wish, he thought.

He could almost feel Olivia frown. "What? No. It was great. In fact he wants to see me again. Can you believe it?"

Theo winced. "Well, don't fixate too much on Edward. I've got another date for you coming up."

"Another one?"

Finn frowned. "Another one?" he whispered.

Returning the frown Theo spoke into the phone. "Uh, yeah. Another one. His name is Tommy."

He hadn't worked out the logistics of it, and the spontaneous words just spilled out of his mouth like water out of an overflowing glass. He would work something out.

"Tommy?" Finn's eyes widened, shaking his head at Theo.

Theo merely shrugged and gazed away, rattling off the details to Olivia before hanging up the phone.

"I think you've officially gone insane." Finn lifted a hand and gesturing to the bartender.

Insane? Have I gone insane? Theo thought. Sure, Tommy was a unique individual, but maybe he and Olivia could find common ground. Common ground long enough for her to end the date by calling and confiding in Theo about how terrible the date was. That's what he really wanted. He wanted her to come and talk to him.

To need him. To realise that he had been perfectly capable of being her leading man all along. "Why?" Theo said, the corners of his lips tilting up slightly at what had just unfolded.

"Setting her up with Tommy is going to go terrible. The man is insane."

Theo sent another knowing look at his friend.

Finn caught on quickly. "Oh, mate. You want it to go poorly, don't you? You plotting arse. She's going to hate you."

"She's not going to find out. Plus, she's already been on two bad dates, what's the harm of one more?" Theo said, nodding as a burly, overweight bartender made his way towards the two friends. Blame it on the alcohol, blame it on being green, but in that moment, it seemed like it was the only plausible way for her to run back into his arms. *Where she belongs*, he thought as he finished his drink.

Finn's gaze lingered on his friend for a few more moments before he turned to the barman and said, "Give me something strong."

After her terrible date with Tommy, she had messaged Theo asking for a debrief ASAP, with the words:

> I need to eat too much candyfloss and ice cream
> and go on a roller coaster until I feel like throwing up.
>
> Carnival. 7:00 p.m.

He had texted her immediately with a simple:

I'll pick you up.

The county was putting on a springtime carnival, an unusual, but welcome event for when the sun finally began to shine in England.

"The date went downhill though, just as dessert was served." Olivia tore some candyfloss from the cone and placed it in her mouth.

Theo frowned. "What happened with dessert? Did he not let you order the cheesecake?"

Olivia turned and looked at him with amazement. She couldn't believe he remembered the small detail from their coffee meetups. Whenever she ordered a coffee, a fruit muffin or sweet slice of cheesecake always accompanied it. A detail she had scribbled down in her green notebook way back during the night of their first meeting.

Wiping the surprise off of her face, she shook her head. "Worse. Guy tried to woo me. Guess what he did?"

"Humour me."

"Oh, I will," Olivia said, stopping suddenly and sending Theo a knowing glance. "Don't laugh, okay?"

Theo made a cross symbol on his chest. "I would not dare."

"He pulled a bouquet of flowers out of his sleeve. All neon yellow, red and blue." Olivia once again picked at her pink candyfloss.

There were a few beats of silence before Theo's shoulders began to shake. "Hey, you promised you wouldn't laugh!" She began her own round of laughter.

"Did I?" He laughed. "I don't recall any pinky promises

made. I am terribly sorry you had to sit through an impromptu magic show; it must have been torture."

"Are you really, though?" Olivia stopped walking, and turned to see Theo's shoulders shake once again. He had paused in his step, clasping a hand to his muscular pec, and was leaning back slightly.

She had never seen something more magical than the way his dark curls were illuminated by the moonlight behind them, the neon signs flashing around them in a heartbeat of colour and transcendent light. The subtle tip of his head backwards, his lips stretched in a wide smile. One she had never seen before.

It was her new favourite thing about him.

"Nah, not really." His baritone laugh was rich and deep, making her cheeks hurt with the contagious nature of it. Her cheeks had begun aching minutes ago, but she revelled in the pain as her smile matched his.

"You were the one who set me up with him. Didn't you screen him beforehand?"

"For magic extracurricular activities?" Theo teased, smacking his hand to his chest, and turning towards her. "I'll add it to my to-do list."

A group of young teens passed them, swinging stuffed toys in their grasp and laughing with glee. The sounds of pinball machine and food cart fryers were alive and thrummed in the air around them. The smell of deep-fried churros and melted chocolate smothering the smell of British countryside.

Olivia aggressively ripped another sugary cloud of candyfloss off the cone and placed it onto her tongue.

"I'm assuming Naomi's leading man is not going to be a

magician, then?" Theo chuckled. Olivia shoved his shoulder as he let out another round of husky laughter.

She enjoyed this playful side of Theo. "No, definitely not."

"No closet magicians. Got it."

They walked for a bit in silence, both gazing forward into the bustling crowd swarming the Ferris wheel line, and food carts. The breeze flipped her hair across her face. She felt the soft grass under her Converse; the small cardigan draped over her frame doing little to stop goosebumps from flittering over her skin in waves.

"Well, how would you do it, then?" Olivia broke the silence.

"How would I do what?" Theo watched as Olivia pulled a strip of candyfloss from the cone and placed the pink fluff in her mouth, licking her thumb and forefinger.

"Woo me."

They stopped in front of the spinning saucers, the entrance to the clown maze tucked to their left-hand side beyond the purple tent housing a psychic reader.

"Woo you?"

"Yes. If you were madly in love with me, theoretically, how would you make a move?" Olivia bumped his side with hers, before glancing up at him, her face glowing in the neon lights. "What's your game? It's your time to humour me."

He hummed, eyes narrowing as she looked up at him with determination. Fine, if she wanted to know what he would do, he would tell her. In all the over-the-top and conniving ways he'd already used – spoil her, open the door for her, affirm her. He would play the same game he had been all along, since that first night in the bistro when he watched her chat up eight different men in the same night and, despite having made the effort to look gorgeous in a tight black dress and red lipstick, not leave with any.

All those men – no, boys – were idiots. That's why it had been so easy to talk to her and convince her that he was the man to help. A true man who wanted to devour every inch of her body. He would address every love language and pretend he wasn't already halfway to falling madly in love with this spitfire of a woman. Theo could do that. He knew he could.

"Assuming we were already together?" Theo snagged a small cloud of candyfloss, squashing it between his fingers before throwing it in his mouth. He noted the way her eyes followed the action.

"Yes. How would you take care of me?"

Theo liked that question a lot.

How would you take care of me?

He looked over her body, scanning upwards from the scuffed converse on her feet to the floral summer dress that brushed the middle of her thighs teasingly, all the way up over the wrap cardigan, to her golden curls and the brilliant blue of her eyes.

Quirking his eyebrow, he gave her a small suggestive smirk. "How would I take care of you?"

In all the dirty, sexual and romantic ways I know how, he wanted to say, and with her blue eyes shining under the multicoloured string lights of a carnival stall, it was if she saw right through him.

His eyes had said it all.

"Oh, keep your head out of the gutter, Mr Constantine." Olivia gave him one hard shove on the arm, the beginning of a smile lingering on the corner of her mouth.

Theo let out another booming laugh, before turning to her accusingly, lifting his hands is surrender. "Hey, I didn't say anything…"

She gave him that knowing look, the one that lifted the corners of his lips in return. Jabbing him in the ribs with a pointed finger, her own smile slipped out.

"You… it was implied…" she stuttered. "Don't look at me like that."

"Like what? How did I look at you?"

But Theo knew he was gazing at her like she was the whole world, and like that floral summer dress she had been teasing him with all evening would look better hiked up over her hips while his wide palms squeezed the soft curves of her sides..

Or, even more honestly: on the floor.

Her words came out breathy and stilted, as though his thoughts had permeated her and sent her the visuals of what exactly he had on his mind. "Like you want to rip this dress off of me and get down and dirty in the clown maze."

A rush of warm filled his cheeks at her words. They had stopped to the right of the rotating cup and saucers, and a small ball throwing game. Theo glanced at her and blinked. He hadn't expected her to be so blunt in her answer. She was right, that was exactly what he wanted to do to her. And more.

He would take care of her in many ways. Kiss her. Comfort her. Worship her.

Glancing at the clown maze across from them, he gave

her another devilish look, the image of having her pressed up against a mirrored wall, the thrill of getting caught with her smooth legs around his hips, and her hands tangled in his hair, their lips locked in a mess of lipstick made his breath falter halfway to his lungs.

Candyfloss and her light rose perfume. The mere thought of just tasting her. Licking the pink sugar off her plump lips.

It all ran through his mind like a movie, the front of his jeans growing tight in anticipation. "I mean, you're not wrong..."

"Oh shush, you." She looked away from him bashfully.

How he was fascinated by that brush of red spreading up her neck and across her freckled cheeks. When he had first met her in the bistro, he hadn't noticed the small dots that painted a constellation over the bridge of her nose and across her high cheekbones. Now, in the dim light of the evening and with little make-up on, she still looked undoubtedly beautiful. He found himself constantly playing connect the dots, noting how the golden-brown freckles made her blue eyes shine brighter on her face.

After all, he thought, *if I were to fall in love with her, surely it wouldn't be that hard, he was already completely infatuated with her.* He was supposed to help her. What if he could be that guy? He knew he could, now all it would take was for him to try to convince her.

After all, what could possibly go wrong??

Chapter Nineteen

"I raise you five." Finn peeked at his cards once more before tucking them neatly in front of him with a smug grin.

It was poker night, and Theo had gladly accepted the invitation, stopping at the local Metro and knocking on his best friend's flat door with a six-pack of Corona under his arm.

The group of five – Theo, Finn and two other mates from their university days, Danny and Jono, met up every now and then, when their schedules would allow, knuckle down at one of their small dining tables and gamble their spare change. Some would say that they gossiped, but to be honest, nothing extraordinary had happened in any of their lives other than Danny getting hitched and divorced and remarried all in the same year. Long story.

Danny sighed, slapping his bad hand of cards on the wooden table. "I fold."

Theo glanced down at his cards, before meeting Finn's eyes. The bugger was grinning his face off, something that Theo knew he did when he had a good hand. His best friend had a pitiful poker face. He could read the lad better than his own family sometimes. One glance from Finn and he knew there was no point playing on with the shameful cards in his hand.

"I fold."

"Fold." Jono echoed before slamming his cards down in defeat. "Finn, I swear to God, you better have a good hand. If not I'm gunna have no trouble taking back my twenty from the pile."

Letting a wicked grin fall over his face, Finn retorted, "That's against the rules, mate."

Jono shrugged, spinning his beer bottle between his forefinger and thumb. "We're playing for fifty bucks and some footy tickets. Not even good ones at that. Fuck the rules."

Finn groaned. "Oh fine. Come on, guys. You make this so easy." With one swoop, he laid his cards down.

Groans resounded around the table as they glanced at his royal flush. If there was one thing about Finn, it was that he was a damn lucky poker player with a shit poker face. Unfortunately, that meant you had no idea what kind of hand he had been dealt. It irritated Theo and the others to no measure.

"I'm not drunk enough for this," Jono stated, before pushing back from the table to retrieve another beer.

"Do you still want your twenty back, mate?"

Jono glowered. "I don't want your dirty money, Townsend."

Danny glanced at Finn with annoyance. "You've got to be shitting me."

Finn grinned, his eyebrows raising in contempt. "What can I say? I was taught by the best."

The best being Theo's father. He'd have to have a word with his dad about teaching Finn poker tricks. It seemed unjust. Theo was his son, he should be the one thrashing them at the game rather than staring as Finn scooped the loose change, five-pound notes and tickets to the next England match at Wembley into his hands.

"I'm going to use these tickets wisely. Hey, I might even take a chick to the game." Finn lifted the football tickets and slapped them into his palm.

"Yeah, maybe you could take Theo's new girl," Jono joked.

"Theo's got a girl?" Danny asked, just as Theo frowned and said, "What girl?"

"You know, the one you've been ditching me for, for the past three weeks." Finn wiggled his eyebrows. "Olivia."

"She's not my girl." Theo took a swig of his beer as all of his friends scoffed. "Plus, you can't speak Jono, you've got that journalist you're seeing…"

"Yeah, sure. Keep telling yourself that mate." Jono laughed. "And Freya is away in the US reporting on that hurricane, so at the moment I'm not doing anything."

"Or anyone." Danny laughed.

Theo set his bottle back on the table, before placing a drink coaster underneath as he watched Finn's gaze focus on the ring of condensation that now adorned his tabletop. "She's… Olivia is a writer, I'm just helping her find a little inspiration, that's all."

Finn grinned, finishing off his own drink. "Yeah, helping her find inspiration in the bedroom more like it."

"It's not like that. Olivia is… she's different." Theo cracked open another beer as Finn started shuffling the cards once more.

The men had been playing poker for well over two hours, the sky completely dark outside, the sounds of London filtering in through the window. Sirens, drunken laughter and cars could be heard, dim lights littering the skyline view outside of Finn's open-plan living space.

"I'm helping her find a man. She's dating guys to come up with ideas for one of her characters."

"So you're setting her up on blind dates?" Jono said.

Theo sighed. "Well, yeah, kind of. But she's not looking for anything romantic, to her it's just research for her new novel."

"Who have you set her up with so far?" Finn asked, dealing out the next round of cards.

"You know that guy you told me about, the one in the HR department at your firm, with the blond hair and weird obsession with filing systems?"

Finn choked on his beer. "You set her up with Taylor?"

"Yeah. She said it was a total disaster. Hate-wrote a whole chapter and scolded me about it afterwards.."

"Oh, that's who you ran off to talk to," Danny teased.

"I didn't run off," Theo said, shuffling the cards between his fingers.

"Nah mate, you totally ran off. One minute you were cheering on the team with the rest of us, the next minute you were hiding in the bathroom, clutching your phone like it was the most precious thing ever."

"Shut up, man." Shaking his head, Theo grabbed his drink and took another gulp. If he was busy drinking, he would be less inclined to tell his friends how he really felt about Olivia, and they wouldn't be able to make fun of him anymore than they already were.

Not giving them any more ammo, he turned back to the table and asked, "Are we playing another round or what?"

CHAPTER TWENTY

Olivia felt the cool breeze brush against her skin as Edward held the glass door open for her. Stepping out onto the restaurant balcony, she glanced at him before turning to see the sparkling night sky before them. It was their second date, and she had agreed to go out with Edward again in the hopes she could write a further few chapters.

Olivia had to admit she felt a bit like a bitch using men to write her novel, noting down all the things she did not like about each man and highlighting what she did, just to write a few good chapters and come up with descriptions for her now-forming leading man. Her male protagonist was coming to life, and although Edward had blond hair, she had begun writing her male character with black wispy hair that curled around his ears. After all, in real life (a concept she found absurd since here she was, in real life, on a date with a man but acting on behalf of her leading lady), Olivia was more attracted to dark-haired men.

Across the tiled balcony, a small two-person table was dressed in a crisp white tablecloth, a bottle of expensive-looking bubbly perched on the edge, along with a board of small but elegant appetisers.

Edward had done this for *her*.

For Olivia. Not Naomi. At the realisation she felt her stomach squeeze, a wash of guilt as Edward stepped aside to let her take in the balcony.

He had come up with the idea of dining at one of London's must-visit rooftop bars and restaurants, and he'd had dinner set up under strings of fairy lights and the city's bustling early summer night sky. Her mouth agape, she pushed the guilt to the back of her mind. "This is amazing. How did you even do this? It's absolutely beautiful."

Edward grinned, taking a few steps towards her, hands deep in his suit pant pockets. "I knew you'd love it."

"Well, I sure do." Olivia glanced around and saw no tables on the balcony other than theirs. By the door, a man wearing a black tuxedo stood quietly, a small white napkin thrown over his forearm. "Are we really the only ones up here?" A romantic date with dim lighting and candlelit table was something Olivia had never experienced before. "She had thought that the movie theatre was a grand gesture, but boy, this made it look small compared to the delicious appetisers and bubbly wine sitting in front of her.

Where did Theo find this guy?

Edward gave a short laugh, as she gazed out into the London skyline with awe. The soft blur of city lights from business buildings and downtown streetlamps made the view sparkle as the twilight slipped into a blanket of dark blues. "I rented the whole place out for the evening. The balcony is ours for the night."

It must have taken him a while to plan this, she thought. It must have taken a lot of *money*.

Olivia was too busy staring into the night sky in disbelief

to notice Edward move until she felt his firm hand across her lower back, turning and leading her towards the small table. Pulling out her chair, he waited for her to settle before pushing her in like a gentleman and making his way around the table and settling into the dining chair across from her.

He offered her a glass of bubbly, before lifting it high in the air. "Cheers to our second date: one hope is as magical as the company I am keeping."

The line was cheesy, like something written in a Hallmark movie, but Olivia still felt her heart begin to hammer slightly in her chest, a flush creeping up into her cheeks at the compliment. "To our second date." Olivia cheersed her drink before taking a timid sip. The fresh burst of summer berries hit her tongue and she hummed in approval.

As the night progressed, the smooth jazz continued to hum in the background. They had eaten a creamy broccoli soup for starters, before having grilled salmon and vegetables cooked in a sauce so delicious it made Olivia wanted to bottle it up and take it home with her. By the time they shared a small chocolate souffle, Olivia was stuffed. Despite the grandeur of it all, the delicious food and private location, she still felt a small seed of guilt in her stomach. She was enjoying this date far too much.

Scooping another mouthful of the souffle into her mouth, she let out a small moan of approval. "Where did you find this restaurant? I swear this dessert is heaven." She sighed, licking the back of her spoon. It was incredibly unladylike, but she wasn't used to glamorous nightlife, or balcony restaurants on the top floor of one of London's most prestigious locations. She could see Big Ben in the distance, the night-lit glow of Tower Bridge reflecting a collage of colour and light onto the glassy surface of the River Thames.

Edward took his own mouthful and nodded as he placed the silver spoon on the small napkin. "A client told me about it, said it one of the finest places in London to dine, and immediately I knew I wanted to bring you here."

Olivia felt warmth blossom in her cheeks. But this time, for all the wrong reasons. *Immediately I knew I wanted to bring you here.* His words were meant to feel like butterflies in her stomach, but instead they felt like acid running down her throat. Edward knew he wanted to bring her here. He had no idea that this was a job for her, that she refused to allow herself to get tangled up in a real love affair. This was purely for research and the seemingly perfect man sitting across the table from her had no idea about her writing. Edward was in the dark when it came to the fact that he was just a piece in a much larger, fictional puzzle. A piece that she would add to the picture but would ultimately forget about once the others all clicked into place.

"Are you trying to impress me?" Her flirtatious tone matched her actions as she reached across the table and ran her hands against the back of his. If she were to finish writing her leading man, she had to play the part of her leading lady, and with Edward ticking all the boxes, it wasn't that difficult. "Because if you are, it's working."

Edward leaned forward; their heads huddled close together. His eyes flicked to her lips, before focusing on her gaze. "That," he spoke in a hushed tone, as though it were a secret to be shared just between the two of them, "is exactly what I am doing."

Before she had a chance to blink, he had grasped her hand in his and leaned back with determination. "Dance with me."

She let out an unsure giggle as he pulled on her hand gently. "Pardon?"

"Dance with me." Edward grinned wickedly at her. "We have the whole balcony to ourselves and have been listening to some of the best jazz ever composed. It would be a shame to let the music play without at least one dance."

Olivia smiled up at him as he rose from the table, hand still grasped in her own. Drawing her close, he wound his long arms around her waist. His arms were softer than others she had danced with, and she couldn't help but imagine the strong, defined lines of Theo's arms and chest, and how they felt against her during the carnival, how he had felt holding her at the games night. How warm he had been. Edward was tall, yes. But he was lanky, his elbows too sharp, his shoulders narrow and undefined. Where Olivia fit into Theo's arms as though they were made for her, with Edward there was all of this... space.

Olivia let out a shaky breath, her body rattling with a slight chill.

"Are you cold?" Edward asked as they rocked side to side.

Goosebumps raised on her arms as the cool night air drifted between them. She could understand him wanting to be gentlemanly, but would it kill him to hold her closer? Tonight had been amazing, definitely one of the better second dates she had been on, but it felt colder than when she was spending time with Theo.

"A little," she responded.

Edward ran his palm up and down the tops of her arms, "It's okay, I'll keep you warm." Before she knew it, he was leaning in, body still too far from hers, all long limbs and rigid. His face came close to hers, his eyelids fluttering closed as he began to close the distance between their mouths. Pulling back at the last second, Olivia turned her head sideways. The night really had been amazing, but that didn't mean she was ready to kiss him. Maybe after another date she would, when they were more comfortable with each other. As much as she wanted to get to know Edward, as much as he ticked all of her boxes, she felt scared. She was beginning to like this man, who had now plastered a polite kiss on her cheek and brushed off the near kiss with gentlemanly sophistication, sending a smile her way. The desire to see him for a third date was definitely in the forefront of her mind. If she could imagine going on a third date, and hell, even entertaining seeing him long after she had finished writing the book, then why couldn't she stop thinking about a certain dark-haired man?

Chapter Twenty-One

"Why is my mother calling me and asking to meet my girlfriend?" Theo adjusted the phone on his shoulder as he leaned on his sofa, television humming in the background with the World Cup on.

The boys had all been supposed to meet up to watch the game, but Finn was out of town on business and was having to watch it on an ancient box television set in a run-down bed and breakfast near Bristol, Jono was visiting his long-distance girlfriend, and Danny had to work.

England was winning, and Theo's spirits had been high and mighty until his mother had called him thirty minutes into the second half demanding to know how and who he had spent his past few weekends with.

"Mate, I don't know what you are on about." Finn demurred, the sound of the game also echoing from his side of the receiver.

"Nice try, man."

"She name-dropped me, didn't she?"

"Yep."

"I swear Gladice can't keep a secret to save her life." Finn huffed. "Okay, you caught me, man. But what was I supposed to say? She was asking about who you were hanging out with.

When it was just me, Georgia and Robert going to weekend family dinner she caught on pretty quick."

"His name is Ross, and he's Georgia's fiancé."

"Yeah, yeah. Robin. That's what I said," Finn nonchalantly muttered under his breath.

Theo huffed. He couldn't help but notice now how Finn had a strong vendetta for his little sister's fiancé, one that caused every weekend family dinner to be incredibly strained and not at all like the calm, humorous and obnoxiously positive dinners they used to have.

"I thought I did enough to get my mother off my back about my love life, or lack thereof, but clearly not." Theo opened another bottle of beer with a shiny silver bottle opener, a present he had received from his father after their family trip to Canada a few years back. It was tacky, incredibly different to Theo's minimalistic taste, but it did the job: opening cold bottles of beer and helping him forget about his nagging mother for half the duration of a football game. She couldn't even wait the full ninety minutes before pouncing.

"Your excuses to miss family dinner have not been great. You can only have the flu once, Theo. Any more and your mum would probably call an ambulance and demand you see a doctor."

Theo took a long thoughtful swig of the brew before leaning his head against the back of his sofa. "Yeah, I guess you're right. But that doesn't stop the fact that she's invited me and Olivia to dinner with her and Dad on Friday."

"Would that be such a bad thing, though? After all, aren't you supposed to be dating? Georgia has been very adamant about what she wants for her wedding. Random hook-ups immortalised in photos are not one of them."

Theo frowned, eyes narrowing. "How do you know what Georgia wants for her wedding?"

"She was over at Mum's looking through their wedding box," Finn stumbled, a curt laugh weaving around all of his words. "Something about borrowing stuff and then they just rambled about wedding nonsense. I didn't understand half of it, and to be honest, my ears are still bleeding a little bit."

"You're just jealous cause you're not invited," Theo said pointedly to his friend.

"Don't even start on that, T." Finn huffed on the other end of the line. "Plus, you have other things to worry about."

"You're right, instead of rubbing salt in your wound, I guess I better brief Olivia." Theo glanced at the screen just as the opposing team stole the ball, and cursed.

"Uh, yeah. You probably should. God, sometimes I feel as though you should pay me. I give out enough advice. It would be nice to get something in return." A loud crash sounded on the line, just as the crowd went wild on the TV, England shooting another goal. Theo shook his head at the volume of Finn's cheers before tipping his bottle back, this time taking a celebratory swig.

Maybe England winning the game would give him good luck, and maybe, just maybe, he'd survive the family dinner with Olivia.

Small stones of white and caramel crunched under Olivia's feet as they approached Theo's family home. For a girl who grew up in a small, terraced house in the middle of nowhere, the grandeur of the building was overwhelming. It loomed, filling her mind with a sense of inadequacy and making her feel like the lower-class peasant girl she supposed she'd always been. Before her words had unlocked wealth – monetary and otherwise – she had never understood what it meant. She wasn't rich by any means. Her bank account now reflected a comfortable number, and for that, she was grateful. Having financial security was something that had made such a difference for her and the more time she spent around those who'd always had money, something her success forced her into, the more she felt alienated from such circles, as she couldn't relate to people who took it for granted. Even more so, that people actually purchased them.

"Do you think they'll like me?" she asked, turning to Theo as they came to halt outside a wide, prune-purple front door. Olivia glanced up at the obnoxious gold-plated lion door knocker. Everything about this place screamed wealth.

"I like you. So yes, they'll like you," Theo assured her.

Taking in a rattling breath, she smoothed her hands over her dress, partially to get rid of the creases that had appeared from their car journey, but also in attempt to dry her clammy palms. "Am I dressed alright? I feel underdressed. Is that even possible? I haven't even seen them, but you're dressed in cashmere, and I'm just in a cheap black dress—"

"Olivia," Theo butted in, halting her ramble. He grinned. "You look beautiful. What you're wearing is perfect."

He always had the right thing to say to calm her, and she didn't quite know what to do with that information. Theo Constantine had a way of stopping her pinball thoughts, instead pulling her down to reality with an invisible string and tying her feet to the here and now. Reaching up, he took the mouth of the lion in his hand and rapped it three times against the solid wooden door.

A screech of excitement sounded from beyond, before it swung open revealing a woman with wavy grey hair and warm honey eyes. She was dressed in a navy blue and white striped top and red cotton dress pants, her neck adorned with a string of statement red blown-glass pendants.

"Ah! Teddy, you're here." The woman reached forward and squeezed Theo into a suffocating hug. "I missed you, my Teddy Bear."

"It's nice to see you too, Mum," Theo replied, sending Olivia a look that said *don't you dare comment on the Teddy Bear thing.*

Lifting her hand, Olivia pretended to lock her lips closed, and threw away the key with a smug grin. She would definitely be using that nickname in the near future. She found it incredibly endearing. Her father had never called her anything other than her full name, and this type of informality reflected the warmth and love of a stable household. Something Olivia was not familiar with.

Gladice turned her thin frame towards Olivia and held out her arms. "And you must be the mystery woman who keeps stealing my baby away on the weekends." Her smile was warm, the corner of her eyes crinkling with age and a lifetime of laughter.

Olivia felt herself blush, as she stepped into Theo's mother's arms and gave her a soft squeeze. "Uh, yes. I guess that's me."

"Mum, this is Olivia." Theo placed a gentle hand on her

lower back.

"Oh Teddy, she's just gorgeous, where have you been hiding her?"

"It's all kind of new, really. Can you blame me for wanting to keep her all to myself?" Theo grinned.

His mother was squeezing the life out of Olivia. She was quickly learning Gladice Constantine's hugs were just as deadly as her stare. They were often all consuming, the kind of hug that crushed you with love until you had to tap her on the shoulder like a pro wrestler just to break the hold.

"Theo has told me such wonderful things about you, it's lovely to meet you, Gladice." Olivia's voice was muffled into his mother's shoulder, as her hand began slow tapping on his mother's upper back.

"Okay, Mum. That's enough. I don't want you to squeeze her to death. I'd like to keep her around for a while," Theo joked.

His mother pulled out of the hold and gave him a glare. "Are you saying I would scare her off with a hug? Don't be ridiculous, there's no such thing as too much when it comes to hugs, don't you agree, Olivia?"

Olivia glanced between the duo and gave a small grin at the way their features mirrored each other's so well. Both their eyebrows furrowed in a way that made the bridge of their noses scrunch up slightly in the middle. Sending a smirk Theo's way, she looped her arm in Gladice's. "Yeah, *Teddy*. There's no such thing as too much when it comes to hugs."

Theo glared playfully at her, stepping forward to reach for her, but she turned quickly as his mother guided her through the front door.

"Come on, deary, let's get you a nice cup of tea. My husband's just finishing up dinner and he's so excited to meet you…" Gladice led Olivia through a tiled foyer, the dark red walls littered with framed pictures of Theo and Georgia as kids, as well as hand-painted landscapes probably worth a fortune. As they walked past the kitchen, a tall man with whispery black and silver hair stood by the stove, turning something in a saucepan.

"Denis, come and say hello to our guest. This is Olivia, Teddy's girlfriend." The elderly man looked up from the pan and gave Olivia a once-over before nodding his head and letting out an awkward, "Hello."

A man of few words, Olivia concluded as Theo's mum ushered them around a large oak table for dinner.

"I hope you're not allergic to anything, Theo didn't tell us much about you, but if there's anything you don't like then you don't have to eat it. I wasn't sure what you ate so I went a bit overboard with everything." Gladice gave Olivia a motherly smile, before untying her husband's apron and ushering them into the dining room next door.

"This looks sublime, darling," the old man said, before settling into a red-cushioned dining chair. Once they were all seated, he turned to the younger couple and told them to dig in, or it would get cold.

Theo's parents were unusual, quirky. Their outfits matched in a way that made Olivia look twice. From his mother's red pants and navy and white striped top to his father's navy pants, white shirt and red pocket hanky. It was all very formal, and despite Theo's reassurance that her outfit was alright, she couldn't help but feel a little bit underdressed.

"So, tell us a bit about yourself, lovey." Gladice smiled. She looked like an older version of Georgia, the same honey brown eyes shining back at Olivia as the ones she had seen during the games night.

"Well, I'm an author." She gulped, waiting for their reaction. Waiting for the hesitance that often came after she said this, the way their smiles turned tight and unsure. Waiting for the 'why are you doing that when you could be doing something else' comments that her own mother voiced.

Instead, Gladice responded with a surprising, "That's lovely. We are a family of booklovers." She gestured to her husband, who was busy tucking into a gravy-covered slice of turkey. "Denis here even published his own short story collection back in the day. I've got so many copies hidden away. I'm sure I could find one for you to flick through…"

Olivia turned to Denis with a surprised look. "Theo never told me…"

"They're just some silly short stories," Denis cut in, forking a parsnip and plopping it in his mouth.

Theo leaned close to her, nudging her shoulder with his as he spoke. "Dad likes to keep his writing more private these days. He does small clips for the local county magazine every now and then, but for the most part, it's just personal writings."

"Published or not, it's great to meet a fellow writer." Olivia smiled at the old man, who gave a curt nod in response before asking Theo to pass the gravy.

Dinner came and went with pleasant conversation. Olivia learned a lot about Theo's family, about how alike his father he was, but with the warmth and kindness of his mother. She heard how the seemingly gruff old man spoke of his daughter, how his eyes lit up when talking about Georgia's teaching. By the time they got to the end of the main course, Olivia was smiling ear to ear, watching as Theo laughed at his mother's bad jokes, and how his father kept getting up to fill her drink, lift the heavy pots and ask everyone if they wanted seconds.

They were lovely.

"Now, time for dessert!" Gladice sprang up faster than anyone could blink and began taking everyone's plates and bowls. "Teddy, give an old girl some help would you and take Olivia's plate into the kitchen for me?"

"Sure, Mum." Theo gathered her plate in his arms before turning to Olivia with a small grin, "Will you be okay if I leave you here with my father?"

Olivia blinked up at him, their faces a hair's breadth away from one another as he gathered the cutlery. "He's not that scary, I'm sure I'll survive," she murmured.

Theo grinned at her before leaning down and planting a firm kiss on her forehead. "I'll be back in a second," he whispered into her ear before disappearing into the next room.

CHAPTER TWENTY-TWO

Theo followed his mother into the crystal white kitchen, the dirty bowls and plates stacked in his hands. Taking them from his fingers and transferring them to hers, Gladice looked him dead in the eye. "You better be careful with that one, Teddy."

Both mother's and son's eyes wandered towards the door where the sound of Olivia's laughter, matched with his father's rare bellowing laugh echoed through the hall and sank into every crevice of the home. He was going to lie to his mum, but as he stood there, looking into the same honey eyes that had loved him and preached about honesty his whole childhood, he just couldn't bring himself to say anything but the truth. "It's nothing serious, Mum."

Gladice Constantine placed a pair of yellow rubber gloves in her son's hands and gestured to the pile of dirty dishes before them. "I gave birth to you; you can't fool me. A magnitude of romantic flings, and you have not once brought any of them back home to meet us. Not even that nasty woman you were *living with* for god's sake. But this girl? She's wonderful and light, and Lord knows how but she makes your father laugh."

The two of them shared a small smile and, as if on cue, his father's boisterous laughter once again followed Olivia's, the two sounds somehow melodic despite the brutishness of his father's and the light bells of Olivia's.

Theo grabbed a pot and placed it in the sink and got to work, washing until suds appeared and it was sparkling clean. "I can't get into anything serious right now, you know that."

"She's not just any girlfriend, Teddy. Even a blind person could see that she's already so much more."

Theo's jaw tensed as he looked back towards the sink and resumed scrubbing the dirty saucepan. He didn't know what to say. He certainly wasn't going to deny it. His mum was almost always right, and he would be silly to argue with her. Gladice Constantine was a wild woman with a quirky nature and a sharp sense of honesty and compassion that he wished he had inherited.

"Most importantly" – his mother passed him another pot – "you're happy."

Theo looked over at her with questioning eyes. It was no lie that he had been miserable since his break-up, he just hadn't realised how much his mother had taken notice. "How is it you know everything?"

"Oh please. I am your mother." Gladice hit him gently against his side with the end of the tea towel. "Annika was a rotten apple and good riddance to her, I say. This one is different, this one is special."

Olivia's laughter rang out once again, before a small "aw" was sounded. *Oh God*, Theo thought, *Dad's showing her the baby album.* Both of them stood in silence, listening as Olivia and Denis laughed together in the next room. Before he even knew it, Theo could feel the corners of his lips curl up at the sound.

"I haven't seen you smile like that in a long time, boy.

She makes you happy, and for that you get my approval a thousand times over. All your father and I want is for you and Georgia to be happy. You're our children. We don't care who you're with, as long as they make you smile like you are now and laugh like you did at that silly 'leek in a boat' joke your father made earlier."

Theo's grin widened. "He really needs to get some new material, doesn't he?"

"Well" – Gladice patted her son on the shoulder – "I encourage you all to dream, but his days as a stand-up comedian? Never going to happen." Winking at Theo,, his mother gathered a cup of tea in each hand and gestured to him to get the dessert behind them.

"Trust your gut, kid. If you have feelings for her, then go for it, go all in. And if you insist that it's nothing serious, well just don't be surprised when she starts to feel differently."

And with that, she was gone. "Denis, get your cup off my oak table; where is your coaster?"

"Sorry, my treasure…" Theo's father's voice droned out.

Shaking his head, Theo grabbed the dessert and headed back out towards the dining room, and back out towards the woman he was madly in love with.

CHAPTER TWENTY-THREE

"I think I'm in love with your mum."

Theo turned to see Olivia nodding as if she was confirming the statement to herself. They were walking side by side down the dimly lit street after a post-dinner cup of tea and a generous dessert. Theo had had to park a little way down the street as parking was always a nightmare out front of his parent's town house.

Sending him a kilowatt smile, she wound her arm through his, swinging slightly as the bounce in her step resumed its normal bob.

"I'm serious. Did you see those cabinets? The anchor brooch on her jumper?"

Theo was more than aware of his parent's tendency to match their outfits. His mother had decided today was sailor day and had somehow also convinced his usually stern father to wear a matching handkerchief and shirt combo. They were a joyful couple, and he had grown up feeling incredibly loved and slightly embarrassed of their complementary dressing habits.

"And did you hear what he called her? His treasure," Olivia gushed, curling her painted nails around his forearm and squeezing firmly.

To Theo, who was so used to his parents' antics, it was strange hearing someone enthusiastically give opinions about them. All their small nicknames, laughter, terrible jokes and complaining about everything under the sun before uttering 'I shouldn't be complaining' and listing everything they were grateful for in life, had been the soundtrack of his childhood.

"If a man ever called me his treasure, I think my ovaries would explode."

Theo laughed at her blunt comment, slinging an arm around her shoulders and pulling her into his side. The soft cashmere of his jumper brushed against her cheek, her face blossoming red in the twilight.

Theo opened the car door for her before moving around the front and sliding into the driver's seat. Turning the heat on, he directed the car fans towards Olivia, the warm air blasting over her. He noted how her body visibly slumped into the leather seat with a shiver of satisfaction as her body defrosted. "My parents loved you. I swear my mum is expecting me to bring you to every family meal."

"Oh, well, if they make that lemon tart again, how could I refuse?"

Theo flicked the indicator on before glancing at her out of the corner of his eyes. God, she was so fucking beautiful. She had fully reclined back into his car seat, eyes closed, hair splayed wildly across the headrest and curling slightly around her shoulders due to the misty rain that had begun to fall on the walk back to the car. She was a sight to see. And a wonderful one at that.

Gulping, Theo knew he was doomed. His mother was right. Olivia wasn't just a friend. He didn't want to be her friend. Not when every time she breathed the same air, shared the same space and existed on earth at the same time, he couldn't seem to think coherent thoughts. His chest began to ache again, and he reached up, splaying a hand over his hammering heart as the headlights beamed through the windscreen, illuminating her in threads of gold as they passed car after car on the suburban road.

No, he most definitely did not want her as just a friend.

"You offered to do the dishes; that makes you officially welcome anytime." He chuckled finally, squeezing down the fog of lust covering his eyes and forcing himself to remain calm.

"I think I'm dessert drunk." She spoke softly, placing a hand on her stomach and looking at him with a grin.

Theo felt the corners of his lips tilt upwards as he gazed out into the dark street ahead. He loved her strange sayings and weird facts. She researched a lot for work, and you could tell. By now, he had her Netflix recommendations memorised, and the 'continue watching' section, he had taken note, had been filled with nature documentaries and low-budget romance films.

Her date with Tommy had been mediocre, and Theo was happy about it. He was slowly filtering out the dates until it was just him who was left. He had already planned their next non-date. Except now they felt less like pretending and more like non-fiction.

Olivia hummed, turning her body towards him, her stocking-clad knee bumping the top of his thigh. "Do you wanna know what I think?"

"All the time."

"I think they are like me. They love love." Olivia grinned at him, the small purse of her lips making that thud return, and the feel of her knee resting against him increased it tenfold. The caress of her body, connecting to his in the seemingly most innocent ways, made his stomach tighten and pants zip feel more confining than before. He coughed, reaching down and skimming her leg with the curve of this thumb before changing gears. He was a poor sucker and was not ashamed to take every opportunity to accidentally touch her. Be near her. Listen to her.

"When I write," she continued, eyes focused on where his fingers had brushed the side of her knee, "I try to think of people, meetings and love stories like theirs. Matching outfits, teasing each other about the smallest things like coffee coasters, and silently swapping newspaper sections. The kind of love that's vibrant and noticeable but not yelled. Love that can be seen through the small things. The unconscious way their bodies move together in synchronicity. When she moves, he moves. They adjust. Your parents… they just fit. I love that. I love that kind of love. As sickening as it may be for you – which I'm sure seeing them kiss so openly would've been mortifying when you were younger – it's real. What I can't seem to believe is that they're real. And tangible examples of love. Even more so, you grew up with that example. It's all rather beautiful." Olivia glanced out the window at the moving cityscape.

Theo had never thought of his parents' relationship that way before. Sure, they used to dance in the kitchen, arms wrapped around each other, so freely he would feel nauseous as a teen whenever he saw it. He now was grateful, though.

Grateful that his father, no matter how stern, had been an example of chivalry, respect and honour. His mother was affectionate and loyal. Almost to a fault.

Hearing how Olivia viewed his parents' thirty-year marriage was eye-opening; it was always a delight to see through Olivia's lens. He found her mind fascinating. And that view, the view he had been given access to through her ocean eyes, he couldn't help but agree with. It was beautiful. Their dynamic was certainly something to marvel at. It was something he aspired to have eventually.

He changed gears again before his hand settled above her knee. When she didn't pull away, he curled his fingers around the inside of her leg and stroked the soft flesh gently. "I'm definitely aware of how fortunate I was to grow up with such loving parents. That's something I'd never take for granted."

"Good. If you did, I might just have to steal them. What do I have to do to have parents like yours?" she joked, glancing up and staring directly into his eyes.

Marry me.

The thought crashed into Theo's head like a freight train. Sudden and dizzying enough to rattle his bones down to his core. With a gulp, he straightened up, removing his hand from her leg, noticing her small frown at the movement. But he didn't replace his hand. Instead, he tightened his grip on the steering wheel. The thought of Olivia walking down an aisle in a white dress made his stomach with something other than nausea. Something that spread warmth through his veins and relaxed his mind into a state of calm, while tugging hard for attention at the muscle in his chest. It left him just as breathless as when she had bitten her lip and teased him about putting cranberry sauce on his Yorkshire pudding and eating it like a fruit pie, smirking at him, eyes sparkling across his parents' dinner table mere hours ago.

How beautiful she had been, all smart-lipped and blushing. He'd had to remind himself where he was. If he hadn't, they would have been in a very different situation right then – one where he tasted cranberry sauce straight from her lips instead of from a fine china dining set. The fluttering came back full throttle, and he once again squashed the thought of getting used to having her at family dinners... before he got caught up thinking about what forever would look like with her.

Looking over at her comfortably cruising beside him in his car, he let himself indulge in the fantasy of forever with her for a moment. For them to have what his parents have – in her words, a dynamic love that *just fits*. He let himself imagine what it would be like to wake up every morning with her beside him, tucked against his chest and curled in his arms. If he ever got the privilege of holding her there, one thing was for certain: he didn't think he'd ever have the strength to let her go.

"You okay?" she asked, snapping him out of his pressing thoughts. He had been staring for far too long. Thank God they were at a red light.

"Yeah." Theo cleared the lump that had settled in his throat. The idea of forever with her made more sense than he should admit. "I'm good." He shook himself out of the dream.

Thinking of forever with her was silly, wasn't it? Certainly not something that was possible after only knowing her for four short weeks.

He needed to reel himself in and get back in line.

He was doing her a favour. She was trying to write a bestseller, and he would be damned if he wasn't going to give her the best leading man she had ever written.

That's all.

That was the agreement.

Not occupying his mind with thoughts of her linking her arm with his and drinking fancy champagne from flutes or drowning out the sounds of their families cheering as their lips covered one another's after responding to the priest with, "I do."

Theo pulled up on her street and put the car in park. Forever definitely was not part of the agreement.

"Thanks for today. It was fun," Olivia said, too casually for his liking.

The night, which to Theo, had begun feeling all too real, had ended far too quickly. If he had it his way, he wouldn't just say a simple 'goodbye' and drive back to his apartment. The very one that now felt cold and empty in contrast to what he could imagine to be her eclectic and warm abode.

Maybe I should get a rug, Theo thought. *Or a lamp. Maybe even a picture. A piece of art.* Something to liven up the dull interior of his home and heart. If he had it his way, Theo would not hesitate to reach across the centre console, tug her closer by her cardigan, slip a hand below the freckle stamped on the bottom left of her jaw, drag her onto his awaiting lap and kiss her senseless. Until both their lungs burned and fingers trembled with desperation for more. Until she let out that sensual sigh he had heard when she took her first bite of dessert that evening. The same bloody sigh he had been replaying in his head ever since.

"Are we still on for Sunday?" Olivia asked shyly, one hand opening the shiny black door.

With a nod, Theo got out of the car. They silently walked across the small pavement to her apartment building.

Olivia leaned over, plastered a surprising but soft kiss along the scruff of his cheek, and said goodnight before disappearing into the small building.

Back at his car, the leather seats suddenly feeling colder than before, he turned the key and listened to the engine roar to life. He waited until the front door of her apartment was firmly closed, and his phone had dinged with the text.

Go home, you weirdo :)

Theo shook his head, letting a smile flicker across his face before returning to the street and heading west.

Sunday.

Oh, he couldn't wait until then.

CHAPTER TWENTY-FOUR

Sunday was flower market day, and for the first time since the accident, Olivia found herself standing in front of her friend's florist market stall dressed in a camel apron with Danielle's business emblem on it. The Columbia Road Flower Market was among the most renowned destinations for fresh flowers in the capital, and tourists loved the unique and magical feel of walking through its stalls. In season blossoms lined the streets and transformed the area into a collage of colour and scent. Olivia had occasionally helped out in the past, wrapping the stems up and placing them in the black flower holders, exchanging money and giving change. And when she'd texted her friend Danielle and said that she would be up at the crack of dawn to help haul the flowers into the back of the van and set up ready for the eight am market opening, her friend was delighted to have extra help.

"You're different today," Danielle said as her friend opened up the back of her pink florist truck.

"I told you on the phone; I just want to help out." Olivia reached in to lift the first crate of flowers delicately from the back of the vehicle.

Narrowing her eyes, Danielle tilted her head to one side in thought. "You coloured your hair."

"No."

"Got a facial?"

"No."

"Got laid?"

Olivia bit her lip as she went under the tent and disposed of the box on the fold-up table. Danielle gasped at her silence just as her husband came around the side of the van, lifting one of the heavier boxes and tucking it under his arm almost too easily.

"You bitch," Danielle exclaimed, looking at her friend with wide eyes.

"Who's a bitch?" John muttered.

"Olivia." Clipping the black flower buckets to her display, she began shoving them in their spots in frustration. "She got laid and didn't tell me."

"I did not get laid," Olivia said.

The early summer morning was bright, the sun rising steadily and making the slight fog that had covered London overnight melt away like it had never been there. The bustle of other florists setting up their stalls made the road buzz with excitement. Pigeons were scattered, hobbling in all directions across the concrete path, and eager tourists hovered awkwardly near the market entrance.

"Took you a while to answer," Danielle sang teasingly. Grabbing a bouquet of flowers from Olivia, she wiggled her eyebrows suggestively. John stood behind his wife, a smirk on his face as he lifted another box of flowers down.

Olivia looked between them before letting out a small huff. "I did not get laid!"

"Promise?" Danielle stuck out her pinky finger like they

were in primary school. Rolling her eyes, Olivia linked her pinky with Danielle's and looked her friend dead in the eye.

"Promise."

Danielle pulled back with a small pout. "Well, that's no fun. I was excited for you for a second. Stop giving me false hope."

"When have I given you false hope that I might get laid?"

"Uh, every time you mention your little dates with Theo. That's when." Danielle stated. "Which, by the way, is more often than you call me nowadays."

"Hey, I call you." Olivia frowned at her friend. The market was growing busier, the sun shining down through the tent and in their eyes as they rolled out parchment paper onto the table in preparation for bouquet making. "I've just been busy. I'm almost finished with my writing, and between Edward and Theo—"

"Wait, hold up." Danielle paused with a bunch of baby's breath in her hand. She stared at her friend in confusion. "You're dating *both of them*?"

"Well, yeah. Kind of."

"What do you mean 'kind of'? Are you dating them at the same time?"

"Wow, I didn't know you had it in you, Livvy," John joked.

Olivia shoved a bunch of roses into another slot. "Like I said, kind of. Theo is helping me with research and Edward… well he's Naomi's perfect man. I have to keep seeing him."

"How long have you been seeing both of them?"

"Well, you know how long I've been seeing Theo. It's almost the end of summer. Edward was date number three or four so I've been seeing him for a couple weeks now."

178

"Livvy, have you been on more than one date with Edward?" Danielle gasped.

"We've been on two. The first was what Theo set up and the second was this dinner in a place that overlooked the Thames. It was private, and the food was amazing. John, you really should take Danielle 'cause she would just love the chocolate souffle—"

"I can't believe it," Danielle cut her off. "You slayer. You're dating two guys at once." Her laughter rang out in the early summer air.

John stepped up next to his wife, his hand caressing the top of her arm, halting her booming laughter with a simple question. "Wait, do they both know you're seeing someone else?"

"About that..." Olivia shuffled her feet, her fingers brushing over the stems of another bunch of flowers. She was doing everything she could to distract herself from the fact she hadn't told Edward she was seeing Theo, in a professional capacity or not. She had also neglected to tell Theo about her second and upcoming third date with Edward. Perhaps she felt a bit guilty continuing to see Edward after the conversation she'd had with Theo about him replacing her every bad date (which, at the present, was a fair few) with good dates. Dates with Theo. As if he was going to step into the shoes of her character Naomi's leading man. A task which Olivia wasn't sure she wanted him to do. Was it unethical and, perhaps, mean to neglect to inform her dates about each other? Yes, there was no doubt about it, but she was determined to get her leading man down on paper before the June deadline whether they liked it or not.

Feelings aside, this was what she had to do… and, shamelessly, she was having fun doing it. At her words, John's eyebrows raised before he coughed, face turning a beetroot red, as his wife's jaw slackened so much, Olivia was sure it was in danger of unhinging and landing land on the floor like one of those funny cartoons they used to watch as kids.

"You're… you… Olivia." Her friend gathered her thoughts, scooping them off the floor like the marbles she seemed to think Olivia had just lost. "You can't be serious."

The sun glared in Olivia's eyes as she turned and took in the shocked faces of her friends. "Okay, but just listen for a moment."

John's gruff laugh sprang out. "Oh my God, this is gold." At the comment, his five-foot-nothing wife elbowed him sharply in the side with the clipped edges of a handful of poor, now crushed roses.

"Theo promised to help me find my leading man, that was what we stated in the agreement we made months ago. He would organise dates, and I would go on them. Edward was one of those dates. Now, is it wrong for me to not tell Edward? Yes. But I'm not planning to officially date, and after *Micah…* I have no interest in falling in love."

At first she thought that her friends were just mulling over what she'd said, taking in her justifications and coming to the same understanding she had the previous evening. Instead, she looked over to see them frozen in their spot, even more perplexed than five minutes earlier when she had told them she was scandalously dating two men at the same time with little to no intentions of romance.

"What?" Olivia's eyes flicked between the married pair at

rapid speed, her heart racing. They were looking at her as though they thought she was completely bonkers. Maybe she should have just kept it to herself. After all, it wouldn't be the first time Danielle had accused her of doing something completely mental.

"Darling, did you just hear that?" Danielle whispered to her husband. His laughter was long gone as he stared at Olivia.

"Yes, I did."

"She said *his* name."

"She did."

"For the first time since…" Danielle's hands came up and cradled her mouth as a small tear fell from her eyes. Before Olivia had time to blink, she was engulfed in the all-encompassing squeeze of her best friend's pale arms. Danielle smothered her, head tucked firmly over her shoulder as she held her.

"You said his name. Micah's name." John spoke carefully.

Olivia awkwardly patted her friend's back. "What's the big—"

"I am so proud of you," Danielle mumbled in her ear. Leaning back, she took Olivia's face between her hands and looked into her eyes. "You. Said. His. *Name*."

Realisation sank deep into Olivia's bones, and she felt it bubble up her spine and settle behind her eyes with a heavy sting. "Oh, my God. I said his name."

"You said his name."

"I said his name." Olivia took a step back from her friend and rested a hand on the edge of the table, settling herself down on a small wooden stool John had unpacked from the van as part of their display. "I said his name. I... I didn't even realise."

"How did it feel?" Danielle asked.

"Natural." Natural. That's how it felt. It hadn't even registered. *Micah*. She hadn't spoken his name since his funeral over a year ago. When she was settling the will and passing his belongings back to his family who, after the accident, had cut her off like she hadn't been engaged to be married to their son. As if she hadn't attended three Christmases at their house in north London. After the accident, which had left her heartbroken and fiancé-less, she had pushed aside her belief in love. Adamant there would be no other for her, she'd guarded his name as though it were the last scrap of him in her reality. God knew it was the only thing his parents let her have of him. His name, his memory, and his Yale University T-shirt, which she had shoved so far deep in the back of her chest of drawers it had stopped smelling of him far too quickly and instead smelt of moth balls and her.

A year ago, she'd have thought uttering his name once more would kill her, the pain being too much. Acknowledging that love that had far too quickly been ripped away from her seemed like the complete opposite to natural. It had once felt impossible. But between the dates, and her finally writing, the gaping wound his death had left in her chest had somehow begun to scab over, the ache dulling and being replaced with something peaceful, reassuring.

As she'd been writing this fourth novel, she had felt him, sitting in his spot on the sofa, whispering encouragement in her ear, giving her suggestions about her main protagonist. She had felt his encouraging motions whenever she spoke into the abyss of her living room, typing away on her laptop about Theo, and the dates she had been on. Olivia had spent far too long talking out loud to *Micah* as though he were right there beside her, at first feeling guilty for going on the dates, but later explaining it was all in the name of research.

Just like she had said to Theo about their arrangement. It was all just for research.

So when she said it felt natural to say his name, she meant it. Closure had crept up on her quicker than she had expected, hitting her like a freight train, pushing her off its tracks and onto her own. She had never breathed cleaner air than this, standing there under that bloody tent, organising roses with her friends and talking about him. It felt like her lungs could finally take in a big gulp of newness, and promise. Promise that she was going the right direction, and that she had him leading her the whole way. *Micah.* The man who had been her leading man in reality. The man that was now giving her the green light to enjoy dating again. The man who was whispering in her ear with every word she wrote: *"Just because my story is over, doesn't mean yours hasn't only just begun."*

At the thought, Olivia felt a ghost smile drifting over her lips as her friend pulled her close for a second time. "Come on, you." Danielle gave her a quick but just as smothering hug before dragging her over another box of flowers that had yet to be dealt with. "Let's finish getting set up, and then, after we sell my whole shipment of peonies, we're going for a drink."

CHAPTER TWENTY-FIVE

Edward had picked her up for their third date at approximately two in the afternoon. Sliding into the passenger side of his Audi, she'd gaped at the smooth, black-lined interior and leather seats. They were driving out to Surrey, where he had something planned, giving nothing away other than saying to 'dress comfortably'. On the way, they'd driven down motorways and were now passing through quaint villages, the crisp smell of British country air filtering through the cracked window and filling her lungs with the earthy scent of home. Olivia looked over to Edward, who clasped the steering wheel at a perfect ten and two position, his eyes never straying from the winding road ahead of them.

"So, where are we going?" Olivia broke the silence.

Edward grinned as he rounded another sharp country bend, thick bushes on either side of the one-way road. "It's a surprise. Just enjoy the ride."

When he'd picked her up from her apartment, he'd offered her a single rose, and asked, "Do you trust me?"

A bit apprehensive, and despite the thought *I don't trust you, but I trust Theo*, she had accepted the rose and smiled into the red petals all the way down to his car. Now they had been driving for a solid forty minutes, out of the city and into the grass-laden Surrey countryside.

"Are you driving us out to the country to murder me? If so, I've told multiple people I'm with you." Olivia had told a total of three people: Danielle, John and Hannah. All of whom told her to keep her location settings on, and phone fully charged. Only one of which she had done, her phone being at a mere thirty per cent charged by the time he had rung the doorbell of her building.

Letting out a booming laugh, Edward's eyes turned to her before focusing back on the winding roads ahead. "Don't worry, I'm not going to murder you. My only aim is to impress you, hopefully."

"Ah, so you're trying to impress me?" Olivia bit her lip to stop the smile from taking over her whole face.

"Of course. It's our third date, the third of what I hope will be many more." His eyes flicked to hers again for a fleeting moment before reluctantly drifting back to the road.

Heat bloomed in her sun-warmed cheeks, and she turned to glance out of the window once more. Another thirty-five minutes later, Edward signalled right and pulled into a gravel drive. Hopping out of the car, he ran a short twenty feet to undo the latch on a large metal gate before pushing it open and running back to the car. They continued down the drive before pulling into a tall, grassed paddock. The afternoon sun was beginning to set, golden hour taking over in full force as they parked up in the middle of a vast field surrounded by lush greenery. Olivia stepped out of the car, her eyes widening with amazement as she took in the sight before her.

A hundred yards in front of her, an old pickup truck was parked; dozens of roses in various pots circled the truck. Along with multiple fluffy pillows and thick duvets. The truck bed was filled to the brim with thousands of vibrant roses. The sweet scent of flowers filled the air, and the colourful petals created a stunning contrast to the green backdrop. Edward had created a rose garden oasis in the back of a truck, in the middle of the lush green fields and rolling hills of the British countryside. It all felt too romantic.

Edward took her hand and led her towards the truck through long blades of grass. Beside the truck was a big pile of blankets and plastic candles, glowing softly in the daylight. Olivia gazed at the display with a hint of confusion. "Edward, this is… I mean, it's beautiful."

"Do you like it? I wanted to do something special for you, and I remember you saying that roses were your favourite flower." His smile was too bright for Olivia to admit he was implicitly wrong. Roses were her *least* favourite flower. Despite this small detail he had attempted and failed to take note of, Olivia was still touched by the gesture and took comfort in knowing that he'd gone out of his way to set up such an elaborate and thoughtful third date. One she felt was not warranted at all.

Jumping up onto the truck bed, Edward reached down and offered a hand to Olivia. "Milady?" he said, grinning at her as she placed her hand in his. Olivia let out a small and embarrassed giggle as he pulled her up, before she settled on the blankets and pillows.

"So, tell me about your writing," Edward asked, leaning over and pulling a bottle of wine from a cooler tucked behind the decor.

Olivia watched as he retrieved the wine, as well as some

cheese and crackers from behind a plush fluffy pillow. "Where did you…?"

"I had one of the villagers drop it off while we stopped at the petrol station." He popped the cork off the bottle.

Olivia's spirits lifted at the promise of wine. He was interested in her writing, and that was one of the things she found most attractive in men. "Well," she huffed slightly, accepting a small plastic cup of wine from his awaiting hand. "I've been working on a novel recently…"

Edward's prolonged gaze made her feel unsettled, unlike the comfort of Theo's warm brown orbs. Instead, the sun reflected in Edward's blue eyes so piercingly that she felt herself falter in speech. He was listening so intently, his eyes transfixed on hers, as if he were sucking up every word she said like a vampire feasting on blood. Talking about her novel seemed almost holy, and for some reason she felt reluctant to share the same details she had with Theo months ago.

Looking away from his heavy eyes, she instead scanned the sea of red roses surrounding them. "It's a romance novel about an independent woman who learns how to let love in after a previous—" Olivia paused, noting how he'd gulped his wine and shuffled further into the blankets. "What are you doing?"

"I'm getting comfortable," Edward said, lying back with his hands behind his head, eyes closing underneath the setting sun. "Wanna lie down too?"

Olivia glanced at him before saying, "Uh, sure," then lying on the duvet beside him. Their shoulders brushed, hips joined, and thighs touched. The truck was small, and suddenly, with the summer evening heat and the warmth emitting from Edward's large frame, she felt hot. Too hot.

"Please, continue." Edward swung an arm around her and looked up at the orange and pink clouds littering the sky. "You were telling me about your book." Although he listened intently, his voice wasn't enthusiastic as he asked her short and generic questions about her planning and writing.

Olivia decided to change the subject. Turning onto her side with a small smile, she glanced up at his face and at how the sun hit his gold hair making a halo of light around his profile. "What about you, Edward? Is there a particular area of law that made you want to practise it?"

Olivia noticed his hesitancy as he cleared his throat loudly before answering her question. "Well, to be honest, it's a demanding job. Being a divorce lawyer... well, it's not all sunshine and rainbows."

"But don't you feel good helping people?"

"Unfortunately you're not always fighting for the good guys, Olivia. But it's fulfilling in its own way, I suppose."

Olivia hummed. Leaning over to a pile of roses, she ran her hands through the flowers. "So how did you come up with the idea to— Ow!" Looking down, she saw a tiny drop of blood form on the tip of her thumb.

Edward leaned up onto his forearm. "Are you alright?"

"Yeah, I just pricked my finger." She shook her head, waving his concern away.

"Let me have a look." Edward quickly took her hand, noting the small injury on her thumb. Bringing her hand up to his lips, he kissed the wound gently, the act making her heart race faster. "There we go, all better?"

"Y-yes. Thank you," Olivia stuttered, trying to hide the

breathlessness that came as a result of her racing heart. The gesture momentarily distracted her from her previous doubts about the over-the-top gesture of the truck full of roses. It distracted her enough to almost not feel the first few drops of summer rain that pattered against the truck roof behind them.

Gazing up at the evening sky, she felt another drop on her face, causing her eyes to squeeze shut.

She started to laugh as the rain began to fall harder. The sudden shower caused Edward to jump up and gather the blankets with a low mumble of "shit."

She let herself enjoy the moment, laughing at how he worried and floundered around gathering the electronic candles he had set up around the field and the blankets that they had lain on. He filled his arms and shoved them into the boot of his car with frantic movements.

"Don't just sit there and laugh. Help!" he snapped from across the field, hands full of decorative items.

"Okay, okay, I'm coming!" Olivia laughed, her dress now damp, hair sticking to the back of her neck in thick wet strands. Forget summer rain; this was more like a thunderstorm rolling in at the same speed as a Formula One racer.

"For fuck's sake, hurry up! It's getting heavier," he snarled.

Her giggles halted as she realised that he was genuinely annoyed. Sobering up, she picked up as much as she could and walked quickly to his car, shoving the damp cloth into the back seat.

After running around and gathering as many things as they could, Edward snapped the fabric roof of the convertible onto the windscreen before they slumped onto Edward's leather car seats in silence. The cool rain soaked into her bones, and following his snappy demands, she turned her knees away from him as they began to pull out of the paddock and back down the gravel road.

"It's too rainy to drive back," Edward stated, nodding towards the constant patter of rain against the windscreen.

"Oh, I'm supposed to be back in the city for—"

"We'll have to drive to the closest village and stay the night," Edward said.

"Um, okay. How far is the nearest village?" she asked, with a glance out the window at the heavy rain splattering against the window and deduced that Edward was probably right. It wouldn't be safe to drive back now, the rain came down so hard that he could barely see out of the windscreen, the wipers working overtime to make the road visible.

"We passed one about nine miles west, on the way here; I think I remember there being a pub, they might have rooms."

They pulled up to a small pub advertising rooms about twenty minutes later, staggering into the reception where an elderly woman sat, pink-marbled glasses perched low on her nose as she frowned down at a word search on the bench in front of her. At the sound of the bell above the thick black wooden door, she glanced up, gasping at their drenched frames.

"Good gracious, you two look like drowned rats," she nattered, placing her pen down in the centre of the page to not lose her puzzle place.

"Do you have a twin room available?" Edward asked. "We

got caught in the rain and it's too heavy to drive in."

"Well, I'll have a look, young man, but we are quite busy this time of year with all the tourists flocking here." Turning to a small, black leather book, she flipped the pages, humming while she looked down at the paper. Olivia's body was racked with a round of shivers, goosebumps raising on her arms. She really should have dressed more appropriately. The forecast hadn't said anything about rain last time she had checked, but that's England for you, the weather perfect sunshine one moment and torrential rain the next. Her eyes drifted to a small pamphlet stand, displaying the pub's roast dinner offer and a brochure for a small tour of the folk museum.

"You lucky ducks, I have one room spare. Not a twin though, and one night only as I have a reservation for tomorrow. Room 12, second floor on the right-hand side." The lady's voice snapped her out of her thoughts as she saw Edward take a key off the counter.

Together, Edward and Olivia made their way up the narrow staircase and down the dimly lit hallway to the right before stopping at an old wooden door, the black brass lock looking original to the Tudor building. After a few wiggles and a reluctant click, they swung the door open and made their way inside.

Olivia stood in the doorway, glancing around the small, low-beamed room, noting the bed cover's old, musky fabric and the velvet armchair cushion. "Well, this is certainly not how I imagined our date ending up." She laughed and pulled at her wet sundress, the floral fabric stuck to her curved frame like a second skin, and although she had felt confident in the flowy skirt and light cardigan, she suddenly found herself anxiously trying to cover her shivering body.

Edward laughed back, the sound lacking genuine mirth and his smile not quite reaching his eyes.

He brushed a damp lock of hair out of his face. "Yeah, who would've thought a rainstorm would ruin everything?"

"Our date isn't ruined. Plus, running through a field in the rain holds its own kind of romantic flare, don't you think?"

Edward hummed, ignoring her question and scanned his eyes across the room. He picked up a small decorative cushion before flinging it onto the armchair.

"There's only one bed." Olivia frowned. "I thought we asked for a twin room?"

"Oh, yeah." Edward coughed. "She said there wasn't one available, I hope that's alright?" He glanced over her sodden form, his eyes lingering on where her dress clung to her chest, the beads of rain sliding beneath her neckline. "I must say, being stuck here with you isn't so bad," he teased.

Olivia blushed, taking note of his flirtatious manner. "Oh really?"

Reaching for her hand, he grasped hers in his calloused grip. "Absolutely. Plus, I get to know you more, and I couldn't be happier about that."

Olivia forced herself to lift her lips into a smile and nodded once at his forwardness. "Sure." Grabbing one of the towels from the edge of the bed, along with her small clutch purse, she said, "I'm gonna jump into the shower, okay?"

Edward grunted. "While you do that, I'll go ask the front desk for the kitchen menu." He strolled out of the room.

Taking a deep breath, she assessed the situation. She was alone in the Surrey countryside with a man she had only known for a few days, drenched head to toe in rain and in a room with one double bed. Edward had definitely been more touchy during this date, and a flicker of uncertainty hit her.

Rather than jump into the old claw tub and get warm, she decided it was most important to get out of her wet clothes and call Theo. Stat.

She crossed the old cream rug in a few steps to reach the bedroom door, locked the door and made her way to the bathroom. After cringing at her appearance in the mirror, she clicked on her phone to see five text messages from Theo, one from Hannah, and a stream of missed calls. With a short glance in the direction of the main bedroom, she closed the bathroom door, sat on the edge of the bathtub and clicked onto her contacts. Taking a deep breath, she pressed call and waited for the sound of Theo's voice to settle her racing heart.

Chapter Twenty-Six

"Olivia. You okay?"

"Yeah, I'm okay, there was just a small hiccup."

"Are you heading back to the city now? I can meet you at your place in twenty minutes." Theo's voice filtered through the phone and settled into her bones like warmth from a fire. "Oh, wait. Make it an hour, my train just got cancelled."

"About that… I'm not gonna make it back tonight," Olivia said, her fingers picking at the hem of her sodden dress. She pressed them into the flesh of her thigh, watching the impression turn a stark white before blood rushed back into the spot.

"Oh, are you staying at Danielle's?"

"Um, no. I'm still in Surrey actually. The rain came out of nowhere, and Edward said it was too dangerous to drive so we've got a room at this pub—"

"Wait, you're still with Edward?" His tone was laced with surprise. A train announcement sounded in the background and he let out a small profanity before muttering, almost to himself, "I guess I'm getting a taxi."

"You don't have to worry, he's been nothing but a gentleman. We've got a room and he's gone to get some food…"

"Nothing but a gentleman…" Theo repeated on the other end of the line.

"Pardon?"

"You're in Surrey, staying with a stranger on a third date." Theo spoke each word carefully, as if he was saying it to himself. If Olivia didn't know better, she'd think he was *worried*. About her.

"Yes. But I'm safe. We'll drive back first thing in the morning, you have absolutely no need to worry," she confirmed carefully. Placing her phone on the basin, she clicked the speaker button and went back to lift her dress and wiggle herself out of it. The thin fabric was not budging as she pulled. On the other side of the bathroom door, she heard the main door click closed and Edward's voice notified her that he was back.

Irritated that the dress was barely budging off her damp frame, she huffed in annoyance just as Theo's voice came through the speaker again.

"Okay…alright. So how's it going?"

"I think I found him."

Theo paused for a moment, before carefully asking, "Your leading man?"

"Of course, silly. Who else?" The small bathroom was decked out with old, gold wall lights and pristine white towels that hung in a zigzag on the rack. Olivia took a deep breath before grabbing the straps of her dress and pulling them down, forcing her arms out of the holes.

"So. Do tell."

Olivia hummed. "Well, he's tall…"

"And?"

"Theo?"

"Kind."

"And…?"

"Handsome. Very Handsome." Olivia huffed, perching herself on the edge of the old claw foot bath with resounding defeat.

Theo chuckled. "Let me guess. He has dark hair, eyes the colour of chocolate and his name rhymes with Leo."

Olivia let out a laugh. "Theo…" He was making it impossible for her to wipe the grin off of her face.

"I knew it." His teasing tone came through the receiver just as a loud thump sounded followed by Theo muttering a small "sorry," to someone.

"And…"

Theo paused once again. "There's more?"

Grabbing a crisp white towel from the heated rack, she unfolded it, before beginning to cocoon herself in the fluffy material. If she couldn't take her dress off, then this would have to suffice. "His name is Edward."

"Oh." Theo went silent on the phone; all she could hear was a choked inhale that caught mid-way.

Olivia paused, towel half thrown around her shoulders at Theo's abrupt change in tone. "What do you mean, oh?"

"Nothing." Theo brushed it off. "Why are you talking to me when you've got handsome Edward waiting for you? Hang up."

"But…" Olivia didn't understand. One minute they were joking around and then all of a sudden she's brought back to ground; gravity working its hardest to remind her that only a few steps away she had her personified leading man waiting for her on the other side of the thin wooden door.

"Have fun, Olivia."

Olivia closed the bathroom door with a swift click. With a jolt she realised Edward was back in the room. How much of her conversation had he heard?

"Did you fin-" she began.

"You didn't tell me you had a boyfriend." Edward's words were low, menacing.

He jumped up and started gathering his things. He was still soaking wet; the thin linen shirt he had been wearing was beginning to crinkle and harden with the remnants of the rain.

Olivia looked at him dumbfounded. "What?"

"Someone called Theo?"

"I don't have a—"

"Why would you sneak off to call a man when you're supposed to be here with me? What kind of person does that?" He shook himself irritably, like he was shrugging her off, ridding himself of her even as she stood there in front of him. "You should have told me. Why did you even agree to date me if you were already with someone else?"

"I'm not with someone else…" Olivia took a step forward, the old wooden floors creaking under her step. As she did, Edward began to step back towards the door.

"Don't lie to me, Olivia. I may have been naïve enough to believe a gorgeous woman like you was single, but I'm not stupid enough to believe you're not lying to me right now."

The thin windows rattled under the weight and velocity of the summer downpour outside.

"I… just let me explain," Olivia muttered, her eyes pricking with tears. She was embarrassed. And ashamed.

"I really don't want to hear it."

"I'm an author," Olivia rushed. "I've been dating men because I can't write a character…"

His laughter spat out like acid. "So it's all just been a game to you. I'm just some pawn for you, a man to help you write?" Edward's voice felt like knives against her skin. His tone was accusatory, his question exactly right.

Olivia hesitated for a moment, realising how horrid the situation made her sound. She'd never meant to hurt people's feelings, that wasn't part of her research. "Edward…"

"I don't know what's worse. You having a boyfriend, or you using me for nothing but a quick research session. Did you even take any of our dates seriously?" Edward huffed and walked across the small room, grabbed his damp coat off the back of the armchair and opened the door. "Don't answer that question. I'm going to leave now. Enjoy the room."

"But it's really coming down out there…" she gasped, taking another step forward.

"I'll take my chances." Edward slammed the door shut leaving her in the soft glow of the fireplace, feeling more alone than ever.

Shrugging off the towel from around her shoulders, she hung it on the back of the armchair and pulled the quilted throw off the end of the bed. Wrapping the itchy fabric around her shoulders, she slumped to the floor in front of the warm fireplace and let the tears begin to fall.

CHAPTER TWENTY-SEVEN

Theo pulled into the side street faster than he should have. After an hour of driving in the pelting rain, he was brimming with adrenaline and angst, not knowing what he was going to walk into once he entered the small bed and breakfast across the small village road.

The rain had continued to fall, and the wind had picked up about a half hour ago, making trees fall in some areas of the county and decreasing driving limits to a snail's pace.

He didn't care though. The only thing that kept him going forward was her. Olivia had called him only a short while after he had hung up the phone. He could tell there was something wrong before she had even spoken. The only words she had uttered were: "Theo," before her sobs pierced his heart.

After sharing her location with him, and a swift "I'll be there soon." He had rushed home, grabbed his car keys and had begun the agonising drive to her on the motorway, the bad weather making the traffic move at a snail's pace out of London. None of that mattered though. Not the traffic, nor the rain pelting his windscreen.

He had to make sure she was safe, and she wouldn't be safe until she was firmly planted in his arms.

He had spent the whole drive thinking about what he

would see when he got there. Perched on top of Edward, the two tangled in bedsheets. He pictured her waiting at the bar like he had asked her to, with wet hair dripping down the back of her dress, and mascara running all over her soft cheeks. When he arrived the bar was empty, except for a single, elderly lady wiping the bench top. He spent ten minutes trying to get Olivia's room number out of her, thinking of the worst possible scenarios he might find Olivia in. The woman finally gave him her room number after he slid her a twenty-pound note, before telling him how a blond lad had stormed out of the inn half an hour ago, angry and muttering about her.

Edward.

Running up the old staircase, Theo made the trip to the second floor with his heart thudding in his chest and found her room at the end of the hall. He pressed down on the black door handle and swung it open to see the small double bedroom she was in.

He had imagined everything but how he actually found her. Curled up at the end of the bed in front of the fireplace, she sat there shivering, the bed covers thrown haphazardly across her shoulders.

He had barely made it into the room three steps before her words hit him.

"Am I a horrible person?" she asked, her voice shaking.

She had been crying. Although her face was turned away the telltale signs were obvious, and as soon as he saw them, all the anger, angst and hatred he had mustered up on the drive fall away as if it were snow melting off his shoulders in front of the warm fire.

"No, of course not." He made his way to her, feet not

going as fast as he wanted. With a thump, he slid down the edge of the bed and landed beside her on the matted rug.

"I feel like a horrible person." Olivia sniffled.

Theo let out a breath before pulling her into his chest and rubbing up and down her arms in hopes of warming her up a bit. She was freezing.

"Edward thought you were my boyfriend." She let out a sad laugh, leaning her head against his shoulder and wiping her nose on the corner of the throw blanket. "When I told him the truth about my novel he said he didn't know what was worse: me having a boyfriend or using him for my research." She sniffled again, lifting her head up and glancing at Theo for the first time since he had entered the room. "That makes me horrible right?"

"I don't think you're horrible," Theo said, his voice low and crackling like the fire beside them. He glanced over her features, noting her bloodshot eyes, the warm flush of pink across her cheeks from sitting too close to the open flames, and the way her hair had begun to dry in a mass of curly ringlets.

"You don't?"

"I think you're perfect," he whispered.

Olivia shivered once more as the window rattled in the wind. After a quick glance to the cold outdoors, and back to her shaking form, Theo stood up and offered her his hand. "Come on, let's get you dry."

CHAPTER TWENTY-EIGHT

After a hot shower and some tea, Olivia felt worlds better.

The rain had shown no sign of stopping, and with the wind picking up even further, they had been told to hunker down for the night as the roads had closed back to the city. One of the big oak trees a mile down the road had fallen, leaving the village cut off until morning when the council could move the tree safely.

Theo had gone back downstairs and spoken to the owner, gathering a spare pair of sweats and a jumper from the lost property bin.

After taking some time to consider everything that had happened that evening, Olivia found her fingers beginning to itch with the need to write.

Rifling around the side table, she found an old leather-bound bible, and a small notebook and pencil. Grabbing the notebook, she sat on top of the floral bedding and began scratching the pencil across the paper in cursive twirls.

It was as if her hands couldn't move as fast as her brain, and before she knew it, she had filled pages, ripping each piece of paper off the notebook and laying them all before her like a puzzle, to then continue writing on the next page, adding her dots and triangles and markers.

She wrote until her hand cramped, until her fingers seized and until Theo came back through the door for the second time, now with some cheese and crackers, two packets of unopened crisps and a single pack of peanuts.

"The lady said that this was all they had until breakfast tomorrow morning." Theo wandered towards the bed, putting the snacks on the bedside table before leaning over her shoulder and glancing down at the numerous scribbles she had made.

"You're writing?" he said, giving her shoulder a squeeze.

"I just found myself wanting to let it all out, you know?"

Theo said nothing, just squeezed her shoulders once more and gave her a kiss on the forehead. "Can I convince you to take a break for a golden, unopened packet of unsalted peanuts?"

Olivia felt the corners of her lips pull up into a smile. She hated how much she loved that he could make her smile when she felt down. It was as if she couldn't help but feel happier whenever he was around.

While she had been in the shower he had restocked the fire, found her clean and dry clothes, found her food. In the meantime she had been bawling her eyes out behind the thin, wooden bathroom wall, coming to terms with everything.

Theo was here, and despite not wanting him here initially, she was grateful he had been so pushy about finding out her location. Edward had been nice, but she had to admit she felt a lot safer with Theo.

Halting her pen Olivia looked at where Theo was fixing the fire. "Why did you come here?"

"I wanted to know you were all right." Theo prodded the

fire with a poker, before placing another log on the pile.

Olivia glanced at the man before her, eyes draping over his strong frame. His forearms bare, olive-toned skin gleaming golden under the firelight. The strong corded muscle moved and shifted with every step he made towards her, and when he leaned his closed fists on the bed beside her, before sitting his body down a foot from her on the plush duvet, she couldn't help but stare at the way his veins wound around the back of his arms and disappeared underneath the sleeve of his jumper. She wanted to discover where they led.

"When you called..." Theo whispered, his deep brown eyes moving to hers. It was only now that she noticed how there was a golden streak in the right one, or how his gaze kept glancing down towards her dry lips.

Flicking her tongue out, she licked her lips and let out a sigh. "I'm glad you came," she whispered.

Theo hummed, shooting her a warm grin and looking down at all the small papers around them.

"Theo," Olivia whispered, pushing herself up onto her knees and moving closer towards him.

"Yes?"

"I..." she began, before leaning forward and brushing her lips against his. She had been dreaming of tasting him again since the first time at the games night. The taste of him had plagued her mind for weeks, the brief kiss playing over and over in her head.

Spearmint was now her favourite flavour.

After a moment of hesitation, she felt his lips press firmly back against hers, his hand reaching up to grasp the side of her face.

The papers crumpled under Olivia's knees as she moved forward, her chest meeting his, his other hand coming around to rest on the back of her thigh, pulling her further into him until her knees fell either side of his abdomen on the bed.

"Olivia," Theo moaned into her mouth, the baritone of his voice against her lip making her shiver more than she had when she was cold.

"Wait," Olivia gasped as his lips began their sweet torture along the length of her neck, leaving quick bites and kisses on her delicate skin.

"What?" Theo growled against her collarbone, gently sucking more of her skin into his mouth.

"I— we need to keep this professional, okay?" Olivia parted her lips, which were still tingling with the remnants of their kiss.

Theo's kisses stopped, his head coming up to brush his nose against hers. His hands remained on her face, cradling her cheeks in his palms and brushing his thumb back and forth along those swollen, plump lips he had just tasted. Wiping his thumb across her bottom lip, his eyes followed the action as her cherry chap-sticked lip puckered at the movement.

"Uh huh," he rasped, biting his bottom lip. "Professional."

Without a second thought, he slammed his lips back down onto hers, their mouths colliding like a tsunami onto flat plains, slanting, licking, biting greedily at each other's lips. They both dragged in heavy breaths of air with each reluctant parting, as though they were drowning and the only thing that could save them was the taste of each other's lips.

Theo struggled to contain his composure as Olivia's hands began tracing the tough, corded muscles of his back, pulling him closer with fevered need.

Keep it professional.

Yeah right, Theo thought. He had known he wanted her from the first night at the bar. She compelled him. She was the hunter, and he was the prey, and God how he loved to be hunted by her. They shouldn't be doing this. He knew that they were walking across dangerous landmines that could explode at any given moment.

They were putting everything on the line. Her book, their date to his sister's wedding, their friendship. Theo's feelings for Olivia had been slowly increasing every time she looked his way, every time she texted him, every time he goddamn thought of her. Simmering, then bubbling to a high temperature of need and unmatched desire.

Theo had known exactly how this was going to go from the very beginning, only Olivia had no idea. Trying to find her leading man when he was right here. Maybe not the leading man for her novel, but her leading man in real life.

God, she's beautiful, Theo thought as their lips broke once more, her head tipping back, a small smile melting onto her face as he began kissing the two dimples on her cheeks, the freckle on the left of her jaw line.

He wanted to kiss each and every inch of her.

The shower had plastered her long blonde hair against her neck, the water made her skin taste refreshing, like lavender and honey. His hot lips against her cool skin caused goosebumps to erupt across it, the good kind, as he leaned back up and captured her lips once more.

Olivia could feel the burning heat between them as he pressed her firmly against his tall frame. With a gentle push, they were both falling backwards, the crunching of paper underneath their needy bodies not an obstacle to what she imagined Theo wanted to do to her.

She wanted to be as close as possible to him, the urge to wrap her leg around his waist flickered in her brain and with that she knew they had to slow down.

"Theo," she breathed, her chest falling rapidly as he hummed in response against her neck. "We have to stop."

He groaned, placing a firmer kiss against the curve of her neck, making her laugh turn into a low sound of protest as he continued his path downwards.

"Theo," she moaned as his hand made its way underneath the lost property jumper, its dark green fabric bunching in his fist, his cool knuckles brushing the naked skin of her abdomen.

"Do you want to stop?" he said, his voice raspy and low. She felt a pull in her lower stomach, and she knew she couldn't wait any longer.

She wanted this man. Of that she was certain.

She leaned up, wrapping her arm around his shoulder and kissing below his ear. "God no, don't stop."

Theo's inhale spoke a thousand words as he lifted her upper thighs and laid himself between her legs, their bodies meeting in a delicious roll of friction. "As you wish, my treasure."

Theo's fingertips buzzed with anticipation, and he could feel Olivia's heartbeat thudding with excitement. With her consent, hands began to pull clothing off, trying desperately to peel one another out of the scratchy material of her jumper and his rain-sodden clothes. Both of them laughed as the fabrics fell to the floor with heavy thuds.

At the sight of her creamy white skin, Theo groaned, skirting a hand across the curve of her shoulder, his mouth following the movement as he pulled the strap of her bra down slowly. "You have no idea how long I've waited for you, Livvy."

Olivia sighed, her eyes never leaving his as she lay back on the bed, her hands pulling at the hem of his white T-shirt. As much as she loved the way it clung deliciously to his muscles, outlining every curve of his strong chest, she would rather see the real thing, no fabric coming between them.

At that moment she wished she had worn one of her fancier bras, one with lace and detailing, instead of her basic white cotton bra, the cup decorated with simple panelling and a thick underwire band.

How could she have known, though, that less than twenty-four hours after going on a date with another man she would be crossing so many lines and about to have sex with Theodore Constantine. The one who was supposed to find her a leading man, not be him. She laughed at the idea, watching his determined actions with delight, as his lips tried to meet every freckle on her body, and she had a lot of them.

"I want to kiss every inch of you, over and over," Theo whispered.

Lifting her torso up, she took his hand and guided it to where her bra clasp was. "Take it off," she said, her eyes half-lidded with impending pleasure. They were really doing this.

After the end of her last relationship, Olivia had thought there was something wrong with her. That she would never enjoy sex again if it wasn't with Micah, because she was afraid she would never connect to someone again on that level of intimacy. But with Theo, in this small double bed full of floral frills and squashed cushions, he had proven her wrong.. It was like their bodies buzzed with need.

His hands snapped the back of her bra, the fabric curling into his fist before being flung across the room.

"Fuck," Theo said, his eyes taking in every inch of her heavy chest.

"What?" she asked, her body tensing.

"You're even more beautiful than I imagined." With that comment, he leaned down and pulled one of her erect nipples into his mouth, swirling his tongue against the flesh and tugging it further between his lips. He groaned into her chest, his tongue moving back and forth, flicking the nipple, biting the skin around it while he palmed the other in his hand, squeezing the delicate skin.

Olivia gasped, her toes curling at the sensation, her chest arching further into his mouth, as though she couldn't get enough, the pit of warmth curling in her womb, growing hotter and hotter as he continued his thorough attack on her body.

Pressing her body eagerly against his, she rolled her hips, taking solace in his low groan, and the gentle undulation of his stiffness against her core.

He felt big, the bulge in his pants growing heavier and larger with every thrust. The seam of his jeans rubbed against her clit, causing a loud moan to bubble out of her throat.

"I want…" She gasped, her hands threading into his dark locks and pulling his lips back up to hers. "More. I want more."

Theo's lips tilted up into a devilish smirk, his hands

running down the plane of her stomach, grasping the sides of her tummy and hips and squeezing gently. "I love these."

"My love handles?" Olivia breathed, following his wandering hands with lustful eyes.

"Yes." Theo rubbed the full flesh and kissed each side of her belly, pulling the fatter flesh between his teeth and biting it. "They're perfect for me to hold as I fuck you."

"Is that what you're going to do?" Olivia bit her lip, heartbeat increasing with every bite. Lick. Kiss.

He paused in his attack, eyes lifting to hers from above the junction of her thighs. "If that's what you want."

Her gasp turned into a choked moan as he placed a firm kiss upon her clit, his tongue running up the seam at her centre, over her panties, his mouth leaving a wet trail where she needed him the most. "Yes, please," she whined, as he pulled her underwear to the side and drew her clit into his mouth, sucking on the sensitive bud with intent.

Her eyes rolled back into her head, and she let out a gasp. She should update her list.

Add 'must know where the clitoris is'.

Because damn, Theo had just opened a whole other realm of expectations for her as far as men were concerned.

Hot, needy and ready, Olivia weaved one of her hands through his tousled black hair, curling the locks around her fingers and pressing his head right where she wanted him. Right where she needed him. Right where she had him.

The heavenly torture of his tongue against her made her want to roll her eyes back again, but she kept them open, watching him attack her body in the most sensual way.

This wasn't fucking, this was more.

His tongue slowed down, causing a surge of warmth to rush into her stomach, an impending orgasm on the horizon..

With one hand curled into his hair, the other grasping onto the cool duvet covers beneath them, she didn't dare take her eyes off him. The dim light of the bedside table lamp washed the room in gold, making his soft olive skin shine a deeper tone and the warm chocolate swirls of his eyes sparkle as he placed a firm hand against her lower stomach and pressed down.

Olivia squirmed beneath him, her lips bitten and bruised from the way she was trying to contain her moans.

"Theo." She gasped, her body arching upwards.

"Yes, darling?" He hummed against her centre, stroking one of his fingers over to her core before thrusting it upwards, his tongue continuing its assault on her clit. With a few strokes, she could feel the coil in her stomach tighten, the need for release becoming torturous with his attack.

His wonderful, delicious, earth-shattering attack.

"I need you," Olivia moaned, dragging him back up and connecting his lips to hers.

His fingers slowed down, stroking her just where she needed, his tempo teasing. With each thrust, he kissed her face, from her eyebrows to her cheekbone, across her nose, until finally his tongue flicked out and licked into her open mouth slowly, matching the pace of his fingers inside of her.

The anticipation thrummed beneath her skin, every nerve ending set ablaze.

Their mouths impacted, tongues stroking, teeth biting, lips sucking. Olivia moaned, her fingers raking down his back, leaving angry red lines across the muscle planes. Her fingers brushed across his waistline, her finger dipping into his jeans and pulling his front against her.

Theo broke free of her lips and leaned forward, grinning as her eyebrows raised with the increase of his fingers' tempo, her mouth falling open in a heady plea.

"Come for me," he commanded, his voice deep and velvety. With the three words, she fell apart on his hand, her chest heaving, muscles tightening around his fingers as he continued to pump them in and out of her liquid core. She let out a loud moan, biting her lip to try and conceal the sound.

Leaning down, Theo captured her bottom lip between his teeth and let out his own groan of pleasure as he watched her continue to fall apart beneath his eyes.

She was the most beautiful creature he had ever seen, and from that moment on he knew he wanted to be the only one to see her like this ever.

Untamed. Completely ruined and undone.

Chapter Twenty-Nine

The airport was a nightmare, busybodies everywhere all at once, lounging on the black plastic chairs, and wandering aimlessly up and down the north terminal, playing chicken with luggage trolleys and children pulling wheeled carry-on packs who were too stubborn to move out of their way.

Slumping down on the dark leather seats of the small Starbucks, Olivia watched as Theo went up to order their drinks, her heart pulling taut when he refused to let her pay.

"You're doing me a favour. So, I'm paying," he said.

"But…" Olivia started. But it was hopeless. Theo gave her a stern look, silencing her feeble protest before telling her to go find them a seat. Over the course of their… friendship? Relationship? Business agreement? If she had learned one thing it was that Theo never let her pay. It was silly to keep arguing about it, but it was only fair that she pay sometimes so she continued to reach for her purse every time a bill came their way. It had nothing to do with gender or him repaying her favour of attending his sister's wedding, he simply always reached for his wallet first, and refused to let her split anything. Instead, he would just brush off her offer and swipe his bank card.

The coffee shop was busy, a sea of MacBook Pros adorned

the seating area: university goers and video callers all using them simultaneously as a rowdy French family conversed further along the leather booth. They were passionate in their discussion, passing each other gingerbread men biscuits and half empty coloured drinks while making wild gestures and laughing loudly when one of them said something that sounded incredibly rushed but poetic in their romantic drawl.

Since April Theo had become a staple in Olivia's life. When she was not parading around on his arm, or on one of the dates he had set up for her, she was writing. Since meeting Edward and, in recent weeks, spending more time with Theo than ever before, she no longer felt extreme pressure over her impending deadline. Even when she had received another email from Hannah this morning that simply said: *'Don't have too much fun in Dublin, deadlines wait for no one. Meeting time for the end of June to be sent in a follow up email soon.'*

Staring at Theo as he waited at the beverage pick up station, taller than the other travellers beside him, and with his hands deep in the front pockets of his dark-wash jeans, Olivia had to admit that she enjoyed her research. If it meant watching a handsome man rock back and forth unconsciously on the heels of his feet as he waited for the barista to say his name, then, yeah. The research was no trouble. Especially when that man felt her gaze and met it, giving her a wink and lifting the side of his mouth into a grin. A grin that was so effortless it made her own lips lift in return. The kind of grin that said, *I caught you staring at me, but it's okay; I like you looking at me.*

Taking in a deep breath, she broke eye contact and instead busied herself with her phone, sinking further into the questionable brown leather.

"One latte for the lady," Theo said, placing a takeaway cup on the small, round black table between them. Pulling his chair out, he took a seat, his long legs stretching under the table and brushing up against hers in the tight space.

"Why, thank you, kind sir," she teased, moving the cardboard closer to her, fiddling with the heat-protective sleeve he had placed around the cup and cradling it in her hands. People must think her mad, ordering a hot beverage in the height of summer. But she felt better after noticing that Theo was just as crazy, steam rising from his small takeaway cup.

"What did you get?" she asked, nodding her head towards the cup in his large hand. It was almost comedic how small the takeaway cup looked. Olivia bet he could drink the beverage in one gulp.

"Double Espresso." Theo took a small sip.

"So… straight bean juice then."

His lips curled up around the cup. "Ah, but hot, delicious bean juice."

"Can I try it?" she asked, immediately regretting it. Casually sharing drinks seemed almost too intimate. They were friends, but were they really that friendly? Especially after the night they had shared together last weekend, which had left her in a week-long recovery. *Did it really happen? Did I dream it?* She had written a good chunk of her novel after that night, and now only had one final chapter to write and a quick edit sweep to do before she contacted Hannah with the news that she had done it. Created a leading man she was proud of and finished the book. She expected Theo to say no, but she had never tried an Espresso before, and the rich coffee aroma wafting across the table towards her seemed heavenly. Rich and full-bodied arabica.

"Knock yourself out," he said, sliding it along the table. "Be careful though, it's hot."

Olivia picked up the small cup, her eyes never straying from his as she took a tentative sip. For a moment their eyes locked, a flash of something dark and brooding flickered in his brown orbs before his gaze flickered down to her lips, wrapped tentatively around where his own lips had just been.

The scalding liquid hit Olivia's tongue much faster than she anticipated, making her pull back with a harsh gasp and quickly chase it with a mouthful of her own frothy beverage. "I think I just burned all my taste buds off of my tongue."

Theo let out a laugh, taking his small cup back with a shake of his head. "I told you to be careful."

"I thought I was but then you—" *You looked at me like you want my lips on yours instead of on this recyclable paper cup...* Olivia blushed at her thought, looking around the café a failed attempt at smothering the heat rushing into her cheeks.

"I, what?" Theo glanced at her, his eyes gleaming with the same glint that had shone brightly like a spotlight when she had taken the sip of his drink. The glint that highlighted mischievous intentions and reflected every dirty fantasy she'd imagined doing with him across his face in a determined flicker.

She was immediately disappointed by the flavour. After travelling in her early twenties she had learned the glory of Australian coffee and had been on the hunt for a British equivalent ever since. She was yet to find it.

"Do you want some of mine?" she said. Her latte was

nothing like his beverage of choice, but it was only polite.

"I'm alright, darling," Theo muttered before gazing down at the sea of travellers below.

The café was on the second level, numerous restaurants and coffee shops littering the narrow airport wing. They had passed a Mexican place on their short walk there, and her mouth had watered at the smell of warm quesadillas and fresh guacamole.

At least Ireland was a short plane journey. From speaking to Georgia, Theo had the inside scoop on the reception menu, and Olivia had to admit, the grilled steak was sounding more and more delicious as time went by.

The flight had been delayed a half hour, and they were cutting it fine. With Olivia needing to write and Theo wrapping a few things up at his work, they had booked a later flight. The wedding was starting promptly at two in the afternoon, and they needed to be on it once the wheels touched down. With that thought, she polished off her latte and sighed. Ten minutes later, their boarding call was announced.

The venue Georgia had picked to get married in was stunning.

Gorgeous grey bricks were built up to five stories tall, thick pillars lining the double entrance doors. Vines of wisteria crawled up the walls, kissing the old building with flashes of green and violet purple. White rose bushes bloomed in a row against the front walls of the estate, with small gravel stones not too dissimilar to the ones at Georgia and Theo's parents' house creating a circular driveway around a lavish stone fountain.

It was over the top but traditional, and completely Georgia.

After arriving in Ireland, Theo and Olivia had raced to the taxi and made the short drive out into the countryside where this grandiose manor house stood proudly amongst the relics of a small village. It was close enough to Dublin to be accessible, yet far enough to feel as though you were in a completely different world.

"Wow," Olivia muttered to herself as they exited the taxi. "This is beautiful."

"I'll go check us in," Theo said, heaving both bags, one in each hand up the stone steps and through the grand door.

"Yeah… sure." Olivia turned and faced the garden, which curved around the right side of the house. In the distance, about thirty feet away from the patio, she could see white fold-out chairs stationed on the grass, fairy lights hanging down from a huge oak at the end of what she assumed was an aisle of Persian carpet rugs. It was beautiful.

People were already heading to their chairs, wafting their faces with the order of service in a desperate attempt to find relief from the unusually hot summer heat.

Hurrying up the stone steps, Olivia was on a mission. With the ceremony a short thirty minutes away, she had a lot to do. Hair. Make-up. Dress. She had better get inside and get ready.

Her face was bare, her hair losing the curls she had hastily put in them earlier that morning, and the bridesmaid dress she was to wear waiting for her in the bridal suite. Georgia had been incredibly specific about what time the bridesmaids were meeting in the bridal suite, and with the clock ticking, Olivia's time was running out faster than it had during her university exams.

Catching up to Theo, she refused to take in the decor of the reception area. She could do that later. Right now, she had to go get changed, slather on some foundation, blush and mascara and head down to play her part as doting bridesmaid and wedding guest. The last thing she wanted to do was let Theo's sister down. It had been a complete surprise when Georgia had insisted, she be one of her bridesmaids, and quickly welcomed her to group chats and wedding day preparation details that she didn't really need to know but was happy to acknowledge.

Olivia headed down a long, carpeted corridor, eyes bulging at the rose detailing on the ceiling and the gold-painted skirtings. Making her way across the plush carpet, she looked around noting the two sets of white double doors on either side of an old-framed portrait.

The bride on one side, the groom on the other.

Olivia had given little thought to if she wanted to get married in the future. After Micah, she couldn't picture herself standing, as Georgia was, white dress billowing around her, crystals littered in her hair, but with time, and the ability to heal, maybe, if she found the right person, maybe, she could think about again. Someone for her, and not for her leading lady. Someone who met Olivia's criteria, someone who would make her believe in love again. Someone who was understanding about the smutty romance she wrote and did not judge her for writing it. A leading man who would make her realise that she was ready to love again.

Her eyes met Theo's as he stepped towards the groom's door, the slow smirk that settled on his lips sending heat down her body. With a deep breath, and her bag tucked to her side, she sent Theo a wink and brief salute of good luck, before swinging the white double doors open and entering the chaos of bridal squeals, silk fabrics and floral bouquets.

Chapter Thirty

Theo adjusted the black tie that looped around his neck. He had been nervous for this weekend. Nervous for Olivia to meet his extended family and friends, all of whom would give him that knowing glance he hated.

Smoothing his hand down his chest and checking the button was fastened on the tuxedo, he began walking towards the door. The wedding was due to start any minute now, and Theo had to get downstairs and in his place alongside Olivia in the fold-out white chairs before people made comments about the bride's brother being late to his very own sister's wedding. Knowing half the bodies in attendance would do just that anyway, he wanted to minimise the side effects of gossip and drama by being there at least before the flower girl.

Theo knocked sharply on the double white doors that lead to the bridal suite. Georgia's friend opened the door, holding a mimosa in one hand, and a bouquet of flowers in the other. "Oh hey, Theo."

"Jessie." He nodded in greeting, glancing over her shoulder at the sea of pink silk dresses and champagne glasses.

"Are you here to wish the bride good luck?" she asked, clicking her tongue and leaning her body closer to his.

Trying to ignore the woman's not-so-subtle attempt to

invade his personal space and flash far too much cleavage his way, Theo looked beyond her.

It was safe to say he didn't like her.

She was a flirt and had absolutely no shame taking her shot at any man who would glance her way, on purpose or by accident.

"I'm here for my date, actually. I spoke to Georgia this morning."

"Date?" Jessie asked.

"Theo." Olivia's voice sounded out through the doorway, her petite figure waltzing up to them with purpose.

"Yes, my date," Theo remarked, flicking his eyes back to Jessie in time to see the hope drain out of her face and her shoulders droop in defeat.

The dress Olivia was wearing made him take in a deep breath. It was a light pink silk; the fabric draped over every curve and angle of her body. The cowl neckline was torture, giving him a glimpse of the creamy flesh of her chest and the dark beauty spot that was situated perfectly over her beating heart.

He had to calm himself down before he went absolutely feral. Before he tore it to shreds and took her right then and there like a wild animal, against the gold-lined French doors. That was the moment he knew he was in trouble.

Big trouble.

The dress made him think of things. Things far too indecent for his little sister's wedding.

It made him remember the kiss. The night in the hotel.

The way her lips had slanted perfectly over his, the way he had bitten her cupid's bow gently, how she had swiped her tongue across his bottom lip as if she wanted to savour the very taste of him, of his lips, and burn it into the depths of her memory.

And in those moments, he had memorised the way she tasted. Like sweet honey and fresh, juicy strawberries.

Shit. He remembered how the beautiful woman in front of him had curled her body around his in her sleep, the smell of her floral shampoo and the way she had skimmed those plush lips against his. It made him want to taste her again.

She still had a few feet of ground to cover before joining him and Jessie. He still had a few seconds to not think about how her soft flesh had felt as it was pressed up against his. Her hand skirting down his chest and—

"Theo, you ready?" Olivia shot him a smile, which went straight to his chest, where he felt his heart tighten at the light sparkle of her eyes and the melodic nature of her voice.

"Olivia." It was like his brain had short-circuited, the only thing he remembered was her name, her lips, her smile.

Just her.

All of her.

Mine, he thought, his gaze drinking in her curvaceous form in that bloody silk dress once more, because looking once didn't seem like enough to drink in how gorgeous she was standing in the doorway, the bright summer sun shining behind her, making her hair look like strings of pure gold. "Yes," he replied, "I'm ready."

CHAPTER THIRTY-ONE

Theo's sister was not much of a traditionalist, but as they sat in the front row of white wooden chairs, the wedding march played out into the summer breeze.

"Georgia looks gorgeous, just wait until you see her dress, Teddy. It's something out of a dream. She just glows," his mother said, sitting to his left. Gladice Constantine had spent the morning hunkered down in the bridal suite, helping her daughter get ready, running back and forth across the venue snagging bottles of bubbly and asking anyone if they had blotting powder. Now, she sat next to her son, her pale pink mesh hat protecting her face from the harsh sun, waiting for her only daughter to walk down the aisle and marry the man of her dreams. She squeezed Theo's hand, shot Olivia an excited smile, her shoulders raising up as though her excitement was an atom deep.

One minute passed, the big smiles of the guests remained on their faces, despite the head turns and unsure looks. The groom had told the wedding planner to begin with the flower girl and bridesmaid's walk, reassuring them that he would be there soon. Before the bride.

Olivia shifted in her spot, glancing forward at the pastor who was waiting patiently, bible in hand. Two minutes.

Olivia shifted in her seat, readjusting the small clutch

she held in her hands and crossing her ankles. The heels she had on were high, much higher than she normally wore, but with her five-foot nothing height, Georgia had ordered her a pair of six-inch heels with the simple explanation that the bridesmaids needed to be the same height as each other in photos.

Theo turned to his date, stunned once more by the way the fabric of her dress draped so perfectly over her frame, and curled an eyebrow at the front of the aisle. Pastor. Check. Groomsmen. Check.

Three minutes.

"I know your sister isn't that traditional, and correct me if I'm wrong, but doesn't the groom typically wait at the end of the aisle?"

Theo glanced over the crowd quickly. "He said he would be here." Olivia knew better than to take his words at face value, her eyes drifting down to where his thigh had begun bobbing up and down, his inability to remain still echoing the nerves Olivia felt in her stomach.

After a few moments, the wedding planner came to a halt in front of all the guests, giving everyone a curt smile.

"Ladies and gentlemen, please remain seated, the ceremony is about to start any moment now, we have just run into a small hiccup. The bride and groom will be here shortly."

Gladice glanced around, tilting her head in question at her husband who stood at the end of the aisle waiting to walk his daughter down it.

"What does that mean?" a guest sitting in the row behind them whispered to their plus-one.

"I'm not sure."

"When will the groom get here? The wedding was supposed to start ten minutes ago," another said.

"We'll just have to be patient and wait, I'm sure they'll be here any moment now," Gladice turned and responded, trying to reassure the guests with the same motherly smile she had given to her son and Olivia earlier.

As if anything could justify the groom not waiting for his bride. Four minutes.

Theo narrowed his eyes.

A small hand grabbed his thigh and squeezed. "A hiccup?" Olivia's face looked confused.

The wedding planner shifted from one foot to the other before letting out a short cough. "No, ma'am. Nothing is wrong, I promise the wait won't be much longer."

Another squeeze of his thigh.

"I'm going to check on the bride," Gladice said under her breath as she stood, fixing her hat before hurrying down the aisle with determined steps.

"Something is wrong," Olivia whispered.

Theo tried not to let the nervous feeling in his stomach make him run back up to the manor and drag Ross down the aisle to make his sister happy.

He covered Olivia's small hand, his long fingers giving hers a squeeze as if to say, *I'm alright*. Even though his worry was filling every vein in his body. He wanted this day to be perfect for his sister, and as he sat there with Olivia, he got a nauseous feeling in the pit of his stomach, as if something was inherently wrong.

"Something is definitely wrong." Olivia echoed his thoughts once again, this time more insistent.

Theo felt the same way. He turned to where his mother had got up from her chair and had scurried back up the aisle and into the manor house faster than Usain Bolt.

"This is like a Julia Roberts romcom," a bridesmaid sneered in annoyance from the front. "My feet are hurting from standing up here so long. Where is Georgia?"

Theo pulled his phone out from his breast pocket.

Where the hell are you?

He sent the message to the groom, before waiting as he saw three little dots load onto the screen.

Be there soon, bro.

"Something must be holding them up. Ross said he'd be here soon," Theo muttered, putting his phone back in his jacket pocket and giving a reassuring smile to Olivia, who looked about five seconds away from biting her nails off.

Five minutes.

Six minutes.

Seven minutes.

Gladice wandered down the aisle and took her seat once more, giving Theo a small, less assured smile. "Not long now."

"Mum," Theo started, a worried frown gracing his handsome face, "is everything okay?"

"Bride will be here soon," she affirmed before someone

patted her on the shoulder and she welcomed another guest with the same kilowatt smile as half an hour ago.

Ten minutes later the wedding march began playing for the second time.

"Finally," the sore-footed bridesmaid whined.

"This is it," Gladice whispered as they all stood and turned to the doors where Georgia stepped through, her arm wound around her father's. The smile that brightened her face fell in the span of half a second, and Denis Constantine's eyes narrowed into a deathly glare.

The bride was here, looking as beautiful and elegant as ever. The only problem?

The space where Ross should have been waiting to get the first glimpse of his future wife, the space where vows should be exchanged and promising kisses given, was empty.

The groom was nowhere to be seen

The flight back to London was bumpy. Harsh rain and heavy winds whacked against the side of the small plane, and Olivia had to imagine she was in jelly, bobbing up and down in the whirlwind of turbulence, and that it was a scientific fact – or at least she convinced herself it was – the plane wouldn't suddenly just drop from the sky.

The seatbelt sign had been on the whole time, and somewhere during the flight Olivia found herself gripping Theo's hand like her life depended on it. It was almost as if the big man upstairs was having a laugh. As if the non-existent wedding hadn't been turbulent enough, and he had to shake things up even more to make everyone pray for the safe return to London. Olivia had never been to Ireland before, and she hadn't heard about the turbulent crossing of the Irish Sea.

Instead of complaining, Theo sat there, grasping her hand back, letting her squeeze the living daylights out of his firm grasp.

"It's okay," he reassured her, wincing in pain as her fingers dug into his in fear. "We'll be back home in no time."

After collecting their bags from the bag drop and hopping in a taxi, Olivia saw the crescent marks she had left in his arm and hand and instantly felt guilty. She apologised the whole way back to her apartment.

"I told you, it's okay," Theo said, lifting her bag up the stairs.

"But I feel terrible. Honestly, please let me get you some cream or a cup of tea. I feel so silly."

He sent her a small smile, pulling her into his frame after settling the bags down by her front door. She curled into him, and they stood there embracing for a few moments. "You can hold my hand anytime, Livvy. Flight of death or not."

Releasing a pent-up breath, she pulled back and unlocked her flat. The curtains had been left open during their short time away, the sky dark and luminous due to the unexpected dark rain clouds overhead.

"Can we talk about the elephant in the room? That was terrible. I almost feel physically sick," Olivia groaned, flopping down on the sofa with a heavy, exaggerated thud.

The wedding had not happened, and everything essentially went to shit. The groom was still nowhere to be found. What was supposed to be Theo's sister's lucky day, had turned into the worst.

He dragged a hand down his face and huffed. "I feel the exact same way. In some ways you know, I feel responsible. She's my baby sister. I should protect her."

"You can't protect her from heartbreak."

"I wish I could go back. Grab that bastard by the scruff of his collar and drag him in, not just send that stupid text."

Olivia was quiet for a moment. As awful as it was, maybe *not* marrying him was the best thing for Georgia. "Don't do that to yourself. You did everything you could have."

"I just wish I could have done more. This whole situation is messed up."

Olivia glanced at the man before her. His crinkled shirt and dark circles under his eyes were a telltale sign of his rough weekend. She couldn't remember a time when he had been this dishevelled.

Patting the spot beside her, she watched as his shoulders slumped, his body falling onto the sofa with the same defeated air as she had. Their shoulders brushed, his broad frame taking up most of the space on the sofa. But she didn't mind. As far as they were both concerned this quiet apartment in east London was the most relaxing place to be.

The heavy rain did not look as though it was going to break anytime soon, and with a slight nudge, Olivia found herself doing the unexpected.

"You should stay here tonight. The weather's crap and, to be honest, you look like you might fall asleep at any moment."

"I really should get back—"

"Theo." She sent him a pointed look. She was a woman who wouldn't take no for an answer, not when someone needed help. If she knew there was an opportunity to help someone, she took the ball and ran with it all the way to the goal.

"Okay, fine. I'll stay, but we should at least be productive." Theo turned his body towards Olivia's until their thighs brushed against one another. The grey daylight hit his face in a way that made him look like a 1940s film noir star. All angular and mysterious. Even more handsome than she'd thought him to be.

"Deal." Licking her lips, she listened to him begin a monologue about her novel heroine and her leading man, all the while trying to stop herself from memorising the gold flecks and various shades of brown in his eyes.

CHAPTER THIRTY-TWO

"So let me get this straight: you went to Ireland for 0.2 seconds, only not to attend his sister's wedding, take what sounds like a terrible flight back to London and spend the whole weekend talking to Theo about your novel for hours and hours in your living room?"

Olivia nodded, stepping forward into triangle pose. "Yes."

Danielle followed suit. "Damn."

Upon returning to London, Danielle had bought a coupon for a new Hot Yoga place in Fulham, and promptly invited Olivia, saying it would be a prime opportunity to destress from her less-than-ideal weekend.

"What?" The instructor sent Olivia a dirty look as she passed, the directions for the next pose coming out far more pointedly than the others.

Together, Olivia and Danielle lowered themselves – less gracefully than the other women in the class – down to their mat.

"You let that poor man listen to you natter on about your novel the whole night and you didn't even give him a blow job?" Danielle's arms shook as she pressed up into cobra pose.

"Correction: Theo asked about my novel. He listened of his own volition."

"You didn't deny anything about the blow job."

"Ssh," the instructor snapped, hand cupping over the microphone.

"I did not give him a blow job. We just talked," Olivia whispered as she felt a drip of sweat make its way down her back. At the thought of her evening with Theo, their heads huddled together as they sat side by side on her sofa talking about everything to do with her book, the main character's motivations and the leading man's attributes, a grin began to take hold over her face. "It was actually really… nice."

"Nice." Danielle coughed. "Nice is a word you use to describe the butt ugly wallpaper your mum has put up when she asks you what you think, not an intimate evening with a potential boyfriend."

The instructor told them to take three deep breaths, giving Olivia time to mull over her friend's words. Was Theo a potential boyfriend? Sure, they'd had a few kisses and that one night at the hotel, but could Olivia see her starting a relationship with him? She was unsure.

Olivia drew in a third and final deep breath before placing her hands together.

"… and with your final breath, bring your hands together in a prayer pose. Our class has now ended, take your time to clean your mats, and I hope to see you all next time for another Hot Yoga session. Have a lovely week. Namaste." The instructor nodded her head, hands in prayer pose as she let the music play in the background.

"Namaste," a chorus of voices echoed back, before the familiar shuffling of people getting up sounded throughout the small room.

Danielle sat up, her body slick with sweat as she leaned forward and grabbed her drink bottle and took a large gulp of water. "I mean, do you see the two of you going any further, perhaps going on some *real* dates?"

Olivia stood, pushing herself up, and began to roll up her mat with careful hands. "I'm not sure. My first draft is almost finished, and I've technically already completed my side of the agreement going to Georgia's wedding. I'm not even sure if I need him any more to write. I've planned it all out, I just have to write."

"But do you *want* him?" Danielle asked, rolling up her mat and slinging it over her shoulder.

Olivia wiped her forehead and bit her lip. There had been a moment, somewhere in the collage of time, when the dates she had been on with Theo transformed from fake to feeling real. The subtle touches, the whispered sweet nothings that became sweet somethings. The way he reassured her, encouraged her, supported her. The only other time she had felt this way was with Micah, and although that scared the living daylights out of her, it made her feel exhilarated, as though her nerves had been struck by electric lightning, shocking her with the possibility that one day, yes, she would want him.

The library Olivia had chosen to write at today was bigger than the usual community one, with over seven floors and independent research areas you could book out to study, write or read. Inviting Theo had been spontaneous, but with her manuscript almost finished, she wanted one last meeting with him to make sure she had gotten everything right. That her notes and scribbles made sense, and as silly as it sounded, Theo helped her think clearer.

They hadn't spoken much since the wedding. He had been busy at work and had cancelled their weekend meet-up to go to family dinner again for the first time since the wedding trip. He said it had been awkward as hell, Georgia nowhere to be found, and Finn not in attendance. His father had tried to make conversation, and his mother had pulled out all the stops, making his sister's favourite food in the hope it would lift her spirits, but alas, she had not shown and the three of them had sat there in stagnant conversation, all still a bit shocked over the events of the previous fortnight.

"I've spoken to Georgia a few times, but I just don't know what else I can do for her." Theo let out a sigh. His response to Olivia asking him how his sister was, nothing but truthful, and the hurt in his tone making her clutch her notebook tighter as they made their way to the space she had booked out.

"You're a good brother, Theo. She's lucky to have you." Olivia sent him a reassuring smile.

"Let's not talk about this anymore. Give me updates on Naomi and her leading man." Theo followed her into the small section, a table and chairs resting against the wall of windows. Behind them, dark rows of books and journals were crammed together, blue lettered cardboard signs dividing the books into sections. They were the only ones there, the library thrumming on the level across from them, with the faint sound of people walking down the hallways on the other side of the large wooden staircase.

"We're the only ones here." Theo frowned, looking around the space in amazement.

"Isn't it great? I found it when I was writing my third book. Who would have thought in the middle of a library in London you could practically have a whole section to yourself?" Olivia placed her notebooks down on the wooden table with a smile and slid into the green chair, snapping back the plastic and clicking her pen.

An hour, and some sneaky biscuits later, Theo scanned the notes of her final chapter, eyes skimming over the outline as Olivia typed away on her laptop.

"Your writer's block is gone."

Olivia looked up from her laptop and nodded. "Yes, it is."

"When did you realise it had disappeared?" he asked, closing the notebook and leaning on his elbow. Sometime during her typing he had stood to pace, making his way closer and closer until he sat sideways on the chair next to her, legs crossed, locking her into her chair at the table. She couldn't move even if she wanted to, the warmth of his skin burning into her side, making her blush more than the love scene she had written fifteen minutes ago during his trip up and down the aisles.

When did you realise it had disappeared? Olivia knew the exact moment, she had been sitting at her dining table, typing with the same enthusiasm as just now. She had been typing when *he* had appeared, sitting at his space on the right-hand side of her old shabby loveseat, eyes searing into her back as she typed.

"Stop that," she had said out loud, as if *he* were really there, a tangible being rather than just a figment of her imagination. There or not, he had once been real. *Micah.*

"Stop what, my love?" she had heard him whisper back. She could picture him leaning forward on his arms and exhaling a breathy sigh.

"Stop judging me. It's already hard enough to write without you."

"I'm not judging, I'm observing." His gaze moved from the white screen of her laptop, where a blinking cursor could be seen, to the small wispy hairs that had fallen out of her messy bun framing her high cheekbones. Sitting there in the small plush seat, her knit cardigan falling off her shoulder revealing her smooth skin.

"You're writing again."

Olivia had paused her writing and pulled her lip firmly between her teeth. Was she really imagining her dead fiancé talking to her as she wrote? Yes, yes she was, and as silly as it sounded, she was going to allow herself this brief moment of insanity, because she got to speak to him again. Even if it was just her imagination.

Micah stood from the armchair and walked towards her with long strides, his brown curly hair let down and wild, his hazel eyes shining as he continued to look at her in complete and utter wonder. *"I always thought you were the most beautiful when you wrote."*

She could feel his figure drawing closer to her as she pressed down on more keys, the cold waft of air brushing the back of her neck and sending a shiver down her spine.

"Your mind, Livvy, is exquisite. I'm so glad you're allowing yourself the freedom to write again."

"You're not angry?" Olivia had asked, eyes brimming with unshed tears.

Micah frowned, looking at her with questioning eyes. *"Why would I ever be mad at you, my love?"*

"Because I forgot your birthday, because I grieved you for so long, because… when I'm with *him*, I'm not thinking of *you*."

"When you're with him, I see my Livvy again. That doesn't make me angry in the slightest. If I was there, I would shake his hand and tell him how thankful I am for him. For Theo.*"*

Olivia had frowned at her late fiancé's words, letting them settle in her mind as she pressed enter and began another sentence. "How can you feel that way, when all I feel is heavy with guilt."

Micah placed a hand on her shoulder, watching as she continued to type words about her leading man down on the document. *"I feel that way because he has made you smile again. How can I be angry with you for moving on?"*

"But you were mine."

"And now you've found another."

"I don't want to forget about you."

"You won't. I'll always be with you, Olivia." Micah bent his head down, brushing his lips against her cheek in a whispered kiss. *"In here."*

Olivia remembered reaching up, placing her hand on her chest, covering the cool touch of his. Closing her eyes, she let out a strangled breath, feeling the steady thrum of her heart beneath her touch. By the time she had opened her eyes, Micah was gone, and so too, was her writer's block.

CHAPTER THIRTY-THREE

Olivia wiped a tear from her eye as she gazed at Theo still sitting next to her.

"Do you remember when we met at the coffee shop, you asked me why I had writer's block in the first place?"

Theo nodded. He remembered that day as well as she did. The smell of burned coffee, the blueberry muffin he had ordered, the gold necklace that tormented him for days afterwards, how it complemented the soft pale skin of her collarbone in that cream cardigan... It was the day he realised he liked her, and the day he had promised to do everything he could to help her find her leading man.

Nodding his head, he watched as Olivia reached up and began to fiddle with her necklace, a thin silver ring looped through a thin chain. "Well, I said I was struggling to find a genre, that I wanted to write something real. That was true, but not the only reason for my writer's block. About a year ago, there was an accident." Olivia halted, taking a deep breath before continuing. She had not dared speak these words out loud for a long time, and even then not to anyone except for a therapist. She had gone, reluctantly, and despite their recommendation never went again. "My fiancé, Micah, was on his motorbike coming home from work one night when a truck came out of nowhere."

Theo's eyes scanned her face as he registered her words.

"The ambulance got there, but he... he haemorrhaged internally on the way to the hospital and, well, he didn't make it."

Theo lifted his hand and brought it to Olivia's shoulder, his thumb drifting over her skin softly as if to say, *I'm here, I'm listening, you're okay. I've got you.* He couldn't possibly imagine what she had gone through, but he could listen, and from the small drop of her shoulders and shaky exhale, he could tell, in that moment, that was all she needed. Someone to listen.

"He had proposed a few months beforehand, during our Christmas holiday to his family's house. We were both so excited to start our lives together. To love each other for the rest of our lives."

Theo now understood her writer's block. She couldn't write her character's leading man because she had just lost hers. It must have been hard writing about love and happy endings when she never got the happy ending she thought she would. His heart dropped at the thought. She had worked so vigilantly over this past summer to write someone she'd thought was impossible to bring back to life. Dating strangers seemed like such an insensitive idea to him now. He should have just done the job himself, entirely; taken her on dates, supported her more, as she did what must have been the hardest job she'd ever do. *Heal.*

"I didn't find out until the next morning. His mother called me. She just said that *her* Micah was dead, and that the funeral was being arranged. That she would email me an invite." Olivia shook her head as if she still couldn't believe it.

"As if I needed an invite to grieve for my fiancé.

"Micah was always so supportive of my writing. Sometimes I think that he thought everything I touched was magic." She let out a broken laugh, completely unaware that Theo thought the same thing.

"A silly compliment when I think back on it, but it was enough to give me confidence and pursue my writing career. My mother wanted me to be a teacher, or a counsellor, something that held certainty, but writing was my passion and Micah saw that. He was my leading man, and after he died, I found it difficult to write male characters, not just love interests. Every time I tried to picture someone, I'd picture him. His brown curly hair, his hazel eyes and the silly dance moves he used to do whenever the radio was on and I just... couldn't do it. Hannah was courteous enough to push the deadline back a few months to just give me... time, but it wasn't until we made our arrangement that I realised I had to get it done. I had a responsibility, both to myself and him. Even if it emotionally drained me, I was going to write another leading man.

"Then, after some of our meetings, and some of the terrible dates too, I said his name out loud. I hadn't said his name since the funeral, and for some reason it felt like I had his blessing. As if he was helping me write the character, whispering in my ear and giving me strength to continue on without him. At first I felt so horrible, like I was betraying him in the worst way; that, in some capacity, I was cheating on him and his memory. But then things started happening during our dates, like you ordering that stupid blueberry muffin that was his favourite, or swapping my tomatoes for your gherkins, or just the gut feeling that I had to speak to you before or after dates, which you were terrible at organising, by the way." Theo let out small smile at the comment. "Those small things made me think that maybe this is what he would want: for me to be vulnerable enough to entertain the thought of liking someone again."

"He sounds like a very sensible man," Theo said, his thumb reaching up and brushing aside a golden wave that had broken free of her braid as she had been talking.

"When he wanted to be, he was. Other times he was quirky, the funniest person I've ever known. *Knew.*" She corrected herself quickly. "Danielle and John were both in shock when I said his name, but after it settled, they said it showed how much I had healed since his passing, that they were so proud of me. Micah had helped me then, and you are helping me now. It was only then I realised that it was because of him, and because of our agreement, that my writer's block had disappeared."

Her admission scorched his skin. The pads of his fingers drifted down her neck, hot to the touch as her body sent sparks up his arms and into the muscle in his chest. He was glad she had known a love with Micah like that, she deserved someone who thought the world of her, and by the sounds of it, his had revolved around her.

Theo grasped her jaw and turned her head so his eyes could meet hers for the first time since she'd begun speaking. He wanted to know what it meant to him that she'd told him, that she'd explained and answered the one question he had been asking himself over and over for the past three months. Why did she need his help, when she was so articulate, so precise in the way she planned out chapters, the ways she created arcs and actually wrote? It wasn't her talent that had ever been in question, it was her. She was hurting, and now she needed to know that Theo was grateful for the opportunity to help her, that by writing this book, she had demonstrated what a goddamn amazing, strong woman she was.

"Thank you for telling me, Livvy," Theo whispered, as if the quiet library rule still applied to them despite being what seemed like miles away from any other person in the building.

Her blue eyes shone back at him, reflecting the dull lights of the literary review section. "You're welcome. I thought it was about time I gave you a proper answer."

Theo's eyes took in every aspect of her face, from the small freckles littering her nose, to the soft wisps of hair falling against her jawline perfectly. She looked like an angel. "I hope you realise that Micah was right?"

"Right about what?" Olivia asked, her eyes becoming dark and heavy as she leaned towards him, their heads huddled together like they always ended up whenever they were sitting next to one another. Theo moved his legs, his thigh knocking in between hers and slotting in between her chair and the edge of the table, their knees knocking together under the dark wood surface.

"Everything you touch is magic."

Olivia's eyes darkened as she leaned forward, plastering a firm and deep kiss upon his lips. Theo's lips curled up into a smile against hers, and she broke the kiss.

"You really think so?"

His forehead came to rest against hers. "Oh yeah," he whispered before their lips met once more. With one kiss, all of Theo's self-control went out the window. All he could do was think of her. The way her hip bones dug into his, the subtle thrust of his jeans against the short black shirt she was wearing, their cores rubbing together as he devoured her lips.

Strawberry flavoured, plump and perfect.

Theo grasped her jaw, curling his fingers around the delicate flesh below her earlobe, trailing kisses ferociously across her pale jugular. Brushing aside the golden curls that he adored so much, he bit down.

Hard.

Olivia's moan was the sweetest music he had ever heard. And it was his.

She was his.

Her pleasure transferred to him, and he loved it. He would make sure she felt everything, everywhere. Simultaneously giving her pain and pleasure and love.

Olivia's nails dragged down the planes of his chest, her index finger teasing the waistline of his boxers.

"Darling," he growled. "You better stop that right now or I'll have to throw you over my shoulder and find the closest bedroom."

Olivia's laugh boomed out down the rows of bookshelves around them, her head resting against the dusty novels and magazines behind her.

Grinning, she leaned up and left desperate, open-mouthed, assaulting kisses on his neck and Adam's apple. He felt her lift up onto her tiptoes, a second finger looping under the fabric of his boxers and brushing the skin of his pelvis. Bringing her mouth up to his ears, she thrust their hips together once more.

"Bedroom?" she teased. "I'd rather you take me right here in the literary review section."

"Liv," Theo moaned in warning, hoisting her leg up and hooking it around his waist.

With another thrust the pair moaned in synchronicity, their lips millimetres apart, chests heaving, eyelids heavy.

A buzz radiated around them, sexual static making every touch, every whimper feel like an electric shock of need and lust. Theo had never been so desperate to have someone in his whole life. Olivia just did something to him. It was like there was a chemical reaction to her, every part of his body craved her touch.

She did something no one else did to him. Things no other woman had before.

He looked down the aisle, then glanced back at Olivia who had a smirk on her face.

"Are you sure no one will find us?"

"I've booked this section for the next twenty minutes." She grinned.

Grunting, he hooked both her legs around his waist and palmed her backside, pressing their centres together in a slow roll before walking her down the aisle and towards the back wall of books.

If she wanted him to take her right up against these flimsy library bookshelves then so be it.

Slamming her back against the wall of books, he felt her body arch into his as she gasped at the contrast of his warm body with the cool metal bookshelves.

Olivia's hands shook in anticipation as her hand reached down and unclipped his belt, pulling the strip of leather through the belt loops slowly as he continued to watch her undress him. Making haste with the zipper, she pushed his Levis away from his hips and squeezed his backside between her fingers, drawing his solid core towards hers.

His hands were everywhere. Trailing her neck, squeezing the soft mounds of her breasts, flicking her nipples harshly before moving further down over the thin fabric of her shirt and hiking it up around her waist.

"You want it off?" she asked, her breath harsh and uneven from the attack of his lips.

"I want it off," he growled. "Now."

Shimmying the garment over her head, Olivia was left in a black lace bra and her black skirt. She'd never thought a man would ever look at her the way Theo did right then, pressed up against the F section of the library's literary magazines, as his eyes flickered with something.

Dark with lust, she watched as he took in her gasping chest, the firm hold of her hands against his chest, the way she was entwined around him like ivy around an old house.

He looked at her like she was the most beautiful thing he had ever seen, and for the first time in her adult life, she believed it.

"You're beautiful." He cut off her thoughts, capturing her blush with his lips and continuing his torture down her neck and across the hem of her bra.

As much as he wanted to fuck her against the bookcase, he would make sure she was properly prepared first. He wanted to make her legs shake. Kneeling onto the wooden floors, he grasped the tops of her thighs and slung one over his shoulder, kissing down her stomach.

"What are you doing?" Olivia asked, glancing around to double check no one was coming their way.

"Stay still." Theo hummed.

"But…"

"Open your legs for me, princess." Theo ran a finger along the lace of her underwear with a promising caress before pulling them down around her thighs

Her eyes flickered shut for a moment. Theo had been dreaming of this moment since the bed and breakfast. He couldn't wait to taste her again. Without hesitation he dived in, lapping her centre with determined licks. He had one mission. Make her come at least once before he had her against the flimsy bookcase of the public library.

Her fingers wound around his wavy dark locks, pulling his head closer to where she needed him the most. Grasping her thighs, he hummed against her centre, letting out a deep chuckle when he felt her muscles contract at the vibration, her mews and moans coming out faster and louder with each thrust of his tongue against her centre.

Without warning, she crumpled in his arms, her core clenching almost painfully as he devoured all of her release, tasting the sweet honey on his tongue.

Standing up, he grasped her face between his hands and thrust his tongue into her mouth, allowing her to taste herself on his tongue, before reaching down and aligning their cores. Thrusting into her slowly, he felt her muscles contract around him, squeezing his cock further into her heat. Entering her slowly was the sweetest torture, but the guttural moan Olivia released as their hips lined up was like music to his ears. Her hands reached up and grasped onto his shoulders, and she rolled her hips, pulling him deeper and deeper until she held him captive to the hilt.

They groaned loudly in pleasure, and despite being so turned on, Theo looked round, worried that someone would walk past the far end of the section, glance in between the wood and glass openings and see them joined in passion.

Olivia kissed down his throat, rolling her hips once again in determined need. "Faster."

Theo grunted, his body obeying her command, and with the fast rolls of his hips all they could hear was the sound of their panting breaths, their skin meeting with each heavy thrust and the small rustle of books shifting as the bookcase gave slightly with every move of their bodies.

It was dangerous.

It was thrilling.

It was addictive.

Her.

Having her like this made Theo's brain short circuit, the only thought he had going through his mind was to try and delay his release. The hot molten core of her was enough to make his eyes roll back into his head, and for his lips to devour her mouth once again with passionate, punishing kisses.

He wanted all of her.

All the time.

He knew that this was far more than a simple arrangement now. He wanted to be her leading man in real life.

"You feel so fucking good, Liv," he moaned.

She responded with a breathy laugh before it cut off and turned into a whine as he thrust once again, hitting just the right spot inside of her to send fireworks throughout her body. "Right there. Right there, Theo…"

"You'll only come when I tell you to come, understand?" he breathed into her ear, watching as her body shook with untamed pleasure, the need growing unbearable for her.

"Yes, please. Right there. Don't stop." Olivia's breath hitched as he thrust even faster, sweat falling down the side of his temple, jaw muscle tensed as he tried to contain his own pleasure.

When it all became too much, he grasped her throat with one hand, and brought the other under her knee, pulling her leg up even further to hit that magic spot inside of her deeper. With a single word from Theo's mouth, they both fell apart.

"*Come.*"

Thirty minutes later, with their clothes haphazardly fitted back on their flushed frames, Olivia and Theo walked through the front entrance of the library, childish grins on their faces, hair slightly astray. She looked up at him, as they swung out onto the street, their footsteps hurried as though someone was after them. They ran down the pavement, both slightly out of breath, bodies still thrumming with exhilaration.

"Oh my God, I can't believe we just did that." Olivia laughed. Lifting her hand up she brushed a lock of hair that had gone rogue on the top of Theo's head. His hand came to her waist, giving her stability as she balanced on her tiptoes to reach his height.

"I can," Theo said with another grin, kissing the side of her face quickly. "Trust me, I want to do much more than that."

"I'll have to find another writing spot."

"Why?"

"Because after we did that… I'm not sure I'll be able to come up with any coherent ideas, let alone think of anything other than you, me and the spine of an analysis of *Pride and Prejudice* digging into my back."

"Let me take you out."

"What do you mean? We are out right now." Olivia hummed.

Theo shook his head, hands still clutching her waist. "No, not like this. Can I take you out?"

"Like on a date?" She let out another laugh, almost as if his question was silly.

"Yes, like on a date."

"Theo, we go on dates all the time."

"No, I want to take *you* on a date. One for you, not your research. A date for my own selfish want to have you spend more time with me. As Olivia and Theo. A proper date."

Olivia flicked her gaze between his eyes, noting the sharp, serious glint that brightened his face. He really was someone that she wanted, and as much as that scared her, she decided to push the fear so far down that it dissolved into nothing. "Okay."

"Okay?" he asked.

"Okay. You can take me out, Theodore Constantine."

"Saturday? Seven o'clock. I'll pick you up." He spoke as if he had already planned it all out, and Olivia knew that he probably had. He was that kind of person. Prepared, romantic, attentive. "It's a date."

Olivia's lips, still tingling from their passion in the library curled up with excitement. "It's a date."

CHAPTER THIRTY-FOUR

Theo took Olivia back to where they had very first met. The smooth songs playing in the background were the same, the steady piano rendition of Dean Martin's *On an Evening in Roma* filling the room with warmth and richness. They sat in the same chairs, navy blue suede, the pillows soft and sinkable. The table was adorned with the same familiar carved candlesticks and wicker breadstick basket, a little pot of olive oil stationed on the ironed white tablecloth next to the salt, pepper and parmesan pots.

Bringing her back to where they first shook hands, to where he'd written his name in her silly green notebook seemed almost nostalgic.

"I figured this was an appropriate place for our first official date," Theo said, pulling her chair out for her.

Olivia couldn't conceal the cheesy grin spreading across her blush-laden cheeks. This was perfect. All night she had been pacing her apartment, imagining where he would take her. She'd never expected this: sitting in the same small bistro they'd first met in, where he'd pulled the seat out across from her and said those words that had changed everything, *"I believe you've been waiting for me."* It felt like they had come full circle.

Oh, Theo had no idea how right he was. How she had dated numerous terrible, questionable and some decent but not-right-for-her men, before he had sat down and given her that stupidly handsome smirk.

"It's perfect," she replied.

Two hours later, after many teasing jokes, banter and the same charming grin that made her want to kiss his face until all of her breath escaped her lungs and her chest burned for air, dessert arrived. Their date was going well, far better than any other date she had been on, and for the first time, she knew her date didn't care if she cut up her pasta or not, no matter how childish it was, or illegal it seemed to be in an Italian restaurant. Theo knew her. Inside and out. Mind and body. The fact sent shivers down her spine at the thought of what would inevitably happen after they finished their desserts. *Back to his place, or mine?* she thought. It didn't matter. She was sure he could tell how much she was aching for him to—

"Theo! My man, it's so great to see you!" A voice rang out across the small bistro, the thick south London accent making Theo's face go stark white as he took in the lanky figure approaching them.

"Hey, Rick."

Rick, a man with a short blond buzzed haircut and buggy hazel eyes, glanced between the two of them before flicking his gaze up and down Olivia's dress-clad form. Rick whistled. "Oh damn, are you on a date?"

"Yes, we are, so if you wouldn't mind—"

"Oh, hey, did that guy do that job you wanted?" Rick cut Theo off and grabbed a breadstick off their table and began scoffing it down with no sense of etiquette or manners. "Got

253

any more gigs coming up? I could really use some quick cash, ya know?"

Theo shook his head, looking at Olivia with an apologetic smile. Olivia wondered who this man was who had just sauntered over to their table and was talking to Theo about stuff that sounded more like a drug deal than a normal business conversation. "Uh, no. No, I don't, and I don't think this is app—"

"Tommy said the date went well," Rick continued. "Bragged to the whole office that the woman's face was so funny when he pulled the flowers out from his sleeve. Classic move, by the way. He even told me he'd teach me a few tricks if you ever needed to help sabotage a woman's date ever again. You know, more options and such."

"What?"

Who knew a one syllable word could shatter a person's whole sense of reality?

The sound of Olivia's utterance rang out in the space between them, small and laced with the devastating realisation of betrayal. Confusion washed over Olivia and she glanced at Theo in hopes he'd say it wasn't true.

"Oh yeah, get this. He offered me fifty quid to date this chick, for some research thing. Told me to make it the worst date ever. I offered to do it, 'cause, you know… quick cash."

Some chick.

That chick had been Olivia. Suddenly all of it seemed to fall into place like an immoral game of Tetris.

"Of course." Olivia hummed as though she would do the same for a quick payment. Drawing her lips between her teeth, she continued to listen to the stranger, her eyes not daring to look up at Theo again. His silence was confirmation enough.

"Cheeky bastard, isn't he? Anyway, I heard through the grapevine that he ended up giving the fifty to my mate, Tommy, instead. Something about magic tricks..."

The black wooden legs of her chair screeched against the hardwood floor with a piercing whine. Olivia gave a curt smile to the stranger, her blood running cold at the confirmation. Magic tricks. Tommy. "If you would please excuse me."

Olivia avoided the eyes of the man she had been on a date with. Had. As in no longer and never again would she be going on another date with Theo Constantine.

"Olivia—" Theo leapt up from his own chair. "It's not what you th—"

She barely got the words out, turning and storming away with a quipped "I need some air."

Passing the questioning gazes of perfect strangers, she stormed out of the Italian bistro, only stopping to grab her coat before swinging the glass door open and stepping out onto the rain-soaked pavement. Olivia breathed in deeply. Shrugging on her coat, she lifted her palms and covered her eyes, as if pressing them tightly would stop the sting brewing in the corners. Without even registering it, she let out a broken whimper before her hands fell in defeat.

Behind her, the restaurant doors slammed open, Theo's tall once-protective frame now looming in the doorway. She had to give it to him, he was smooth. Yes, the dates she had been on were terrible, comical even. It was only now that she knew it had all been by design. He had paid those men to make the dates purposely bad. Dates he knew she needed for her research. To help find her leading man, her character's love.

"Olivia, please it's not—" Theo said, his voice, smooth and deep; the voice that had one told her how perfect she was as he held her sounded *wrong*.

Filled with hatred, and with the slimy remnants of the truth making her top cling to her back in uncomfortable twists, she felt her lip tremble before pulling it back into a firm line. Theo was a snake. He had been sneaky. He had planned it all out, and the realisation made it pierce deeper than the sharpest dagger. Olivia had dated snakes in the past, she had rivalled, she had fallen for their cunning ways, and now karma had come back to bite her with a poison.

"I trusted you." She halted his words, her hair swinging around as she turned to face him. With her coat unclasped, she let the summer night air permeate her skin, cooling the heating anger bubbling beneath her skin. "I trusted you with *him*. I trusted you with *me*. How could you?"

She watched as Theo's face fell, his mouth opening, before he had the chance to utter a single word she shook her head, not able to stop the now evident tremble of her lips, the water gathering in the corners of her eyes.

"No." Olivia shook her head, turning away into the busy London street. "I can't even look at you. Let alone allow you the decency to make up some excuse that you think will persuade me to ignore the fact that you tried to sabotage me. My book. My dates. My life."

"Please, Olivia…"

Another step. She could almost smell his cologne. She took one last greedy gulp of his delicious scent, the one she used to find comforting, before stepping back with the realisation that it had all just been a lie. He was a liar.

"I know it's probably futile to say, but it's really not what it looks like."

God he was so handsome it hurt to even look at him, think of him. She had to leave.

"I'm going home. I suggest you do the same."

Theo stepped forward, his eyes pleading with her. "Let me at least drive you home."

Lifting a hand, she closed her coat with a sharp tug. "No, thank you. I'd rather walk."

"In the rain? In the middle of the night, in central London?" Theo took another step forward, his hand reaching out to her. "Please…"

"Is this man bothering you?" A young woman in a smart business suit stopped on the pavement next to Olivia, looking over at Theo with a suspicious glare.

"No." Olivia's gaze met Theo's, seeing the hurt in his own glassy eyes. "No, he's not bothering me."

"Are you sure?" the woman asked, beginning to take out her phone. "I can call someone for you if you need a ride somewhere…"

"Really." Olivia said to the woman. "I'm okay. Thank you though."

The woman sent Theo one last look before nodding. "Okay, if, you're sure." Then, she turned and left the broken pair standing there, drops falling over them in soft wisps of late summer rain.

"You'd really walk home by yourself rather than letting me get you home safely?" Theo said, a lock of his black hair curling around his forehead, heavy with water. She understood his logic, and, of course, in the moment that she hated him he still had to be courteous and act like a perfect gentleman.

The answer was yes, though. She knew it was silly of her to walk home alone, take the tube alone, but she was feeling brave, and completely reckless.

If it meant getting away from him to think, she would take it. Looking straight into his eyes, she let herself spit the words she knew would hurt him. "Yes, at the moment I would like to be anywhere but near you."

"Olivia—"

"Go home, Theo. This date is over."

CHAPTER THIRTY-FIVE

Theo's footsteps landed heavily against the gum-ridden pavement, his trainers slapping the ground with a fast succession of steps as he turned the corner, breath rushing in and out of his lungs in controlled pants. He had spent the past few days running back over his dinner with Olivia, and each time he let his mind entertain the idea that it wasn't that bad, his conscience gave him a quick and firm kick in the backside.

Yes, it really wasn't that bad, it said, *it was much, much worse.*

Music blared through his earphones, but Theo wasn't listening. Instead, he kept his eyes forward, weaving through the wandering businessmen and tourists who crowded the street leading up to Tower Bridge. Morning runs were something sacred to Theo. He always chose to go out first thing, especially in the summer when it was coolest, the light chill settling in the air belying the heat he knew the day would bring.

He'd never planned for it to go this way, but he was sure no one would ever expect it go any other way. It had been clear from the beginning. He was an idiot. But Theo couldn't help it. Thinking of Olivia, of the golden waves that cascaded around her heart-shaped face, framing those enticing, sparkling blue eyes, made his mind muddled. Just thinking of her made him make stupid decisions, her presence was even worse. Whenever he was with her his heart was never steady, nothing like his controlled breaths as he jogged onto the bridge, eyes and feet weaving through the early morning tourists taking their photos along the railing.

He had been so selfish. He had been so... in love. It all made him feel sick. Sick with shame, and bitterness. This was not how his mother had raised him, and when he'd phoned her to say he and Olivia had broken up, she called him exactly what he now accepted he was.

"You're an idiot."

"Thanks, Mum."

"Well, I'm not going to sugar-coat it, Teddy. You remind me a lot of your father at your age. Both of you are too blind to see what's right in front of you. Olivia is a nice girl, selfless and loves to help others. She's successful and just a pure delight, and you, my boy, have screwed up. Big time. Idiot with a capital I."

He paused on the bridge, hands resting on his waist as he looked out at the sun rising against the water of the River Thames. Despite the heavy clouds scattered in the sky, a thin strip of gold had broken free from behind them, lighting up the murky water and making the morning warm. He had no qualms about Olivia's character, no, she was perfect.

It had been him who had hired the damn guy, it had been him who lied and withheld the truth. It was no excuse at all, but in a city of nine million people, he hadn't even thought about bumping into that one other guy he'd offered the job to.

Just thinking about the idea made him realise how goddamn stupid it was, how hurtful. He hadn't considered her feelings, and now he was paying the price. Theo had left numerous voicemails and texts for Olivia, her number constantly on the 'Recents' page of his phone, both tormenting him and giving him hope that maybe, just maybe, she'd reply or call back.

And if she didn't, he would understand.

Huffing a breath out into the morning air, Theo pulled his sweat-laden top away from his frame and checked his watch. It was barely 7:30 and the city was bustling with activity. Turning back, he retraced his steps, running into the oncoming foot traffic and hoping that the five miles he had to go to his flat would be enough to shake his mistake off his mind, and knock some common sense into him.

"One IPA for the sad-looking fella, and a whiskey on the rocks for me," Finn muttered, placing their drinks down on the small round table between them.

"Sad-looking fella?" Theo grumbled.

"If you pout any more, people are going to think your puppy died or something." Taking a swig of his drink, Finn clicked his tongue and whistled at the smooth whiskey, before turning to his friend. "So, what's going on then? Get fired? Someone stole your phone? Forgot to record the Premier League game?"

"I fucked up, man. Big time." Theo watched as the froth of his beer bubbled.

"Olivia?"

"Olivia." Theo sighed. "You know a few months back when I was a complete idiot and decided to hire that magician?"

"Oh, shit. Yeah, you fucked up," Finn said.

"I knew I shouldn't have done it. I didn't even bloody pay him. I couldn't go through with it, but he still went. The date still happened and now I feel like a complete twat." Running his hand through his hair, he pulled at the edges, causing a few strands to stand up in messy disorder. "Olivia deserved better. She's made it pretty clear that she didn't want to hear from me again."

"Did she say that?" Finn asked.

Theo shook his head. "She didn't need to. The look on her face said it all."

"You really like her, don't you?"

Theo frowned. Like didn't seem a strong enough word for how he felt about Olivia. It was more than *like*. Love seemed a bit rash to say, but it was stronger than a typical crush. That's what hurt even more. The fact that the feeling didn't diminish after she'd shouted at him. Told him to go home. No, the feeling seemed to grow, and bend, morph into something more, something that made her silence pierce his heart even more than a sharpened dagger.

Theo shook his head. "Nah, it's more than that. She's…"

"Oh," Finn spoke. Theo was a mess, he could only imagine what Finn thought of him sitting there with darkened circles underneath his eyes, the dishevelled hair, the crinkled shirt. The man sitting before him was lovesick, it was painfully obvious and knowing how that felt, Finn winced, before downing the rest of his drink in one. "Fuck, man."

Theo nodded.

"Have you tried to contact her? Apologise?" Finn asked.

"Yeah, I've tried calling her, but it's always gone straight to voicemail. I've left way too many messages. She needs space now. Away from me. Without me blowing up her phone with silly voicemails and text messages that make me feel eighteen again."

"You love her."

Theo let out a sad chuckle, his words coming out dry. "Is it really that fucking obvious?"

"Try again," Finn said. Theo looked up at his friend, eyes sceptical. He had tried and tried and tried. Each time he was ignored, each time the stone in his stomach feel heavier and heavier with regret. "You love her. Then she's worth fighting for. Don't give up. You can't just give up on a girl like that. She's special. You said so yourself. And if she's the kind of girl that will make you willingly drink piss like the IPA in front of you, then you need to try again."

CHAPTER THIRTY-SIX

Hannah scanned the pages slowly. Much too slowly for Olivia's liking. Sitting across from her literary agent she anxiously jigged her leg up and down, feeling her palms become numb where they lay under her thighs.

It was a rainy day in London, and it brought her back to a few months ago, when she was sitting in the very same chair, being told to figure it out and hope for the best.

Well, she had.

She had figured it out, and she was hoping for the best.

"It's really rough," Olivia stated. Olivia had felt her fingers pause above the keyboard, protesting to write another word.

Not because of writer's block, but because, for the first time in her whole writing career, the story felt unfinished.

"Hmm." Hannah's eyes continued to scan the last few pages, looking down through her black-rimmed glasses.

"I'd have to work with the editor and revise a few aspects."

Hannah didn't bother looking up, instead she seemed to flick back to the beginning of the story.

"It's rubbish... I know—" Olivia began.

"It's not rubbish." Hannah held the pages in her hand, gnawing on the side of her mouth as if she was considering something.

Olivia's mouth remained poised in objection. "But…"

"It's not rubbish," Hannah repeated. "It's actually really, really good."

Olivia closed her mouth, releasing her hands from under her legs and flexing her fingers.

"It's actually pretty fucking great. He's great," Hannah continued, before flicking through the manuscript once more. "How he always walks her back to her door after a date, how he lets her order her favourite food at the restaurant, unlike that guy you told me about a while back when you went on that date. The way he always makes her coffee the right way without having to ask. It's fucking fantastic." Hannah opened the manuscript up once again as if she couldn't get enough of it, eyes skimming over Olivia's words.

All morning Olivia had written and rewritten the ending, her perfectionism having a dangerous hold on her words. Often she would anxiously think, what if her words weren't good enough? What if people didn't like these characters she had slowly fallen in love with as they had fallen in love with each other on the pages? But by the end, Olivia had sat there at her dining table in silent disbelief.

The characters had said everything she had wanted them to say, and since finishing the bulk of her novel,, she had gone back, edited, changed, adapted and rewritten parts. None of which she'd used. Her previous edit, she had decided, was her best. It was as though the last sentence was the final piece in a one-hundred-thousand-word fill-in-the-blank puzzle.

Hannah seemed consumed once again by her words. Her story telling. The scenarios and characters that she had thought up, planned, written and rewritten until the perfectionist in her screamed at her to stop.

It hadn't taken long to overcome her writer's block. Thinking back to those few non-dates with Theo, as per their agreement, she had written a chapter, the leading man still nameless, but now he had bones. To Olivia, her character was perfect.

Why continue to work when it's perfect?

The meet-cute, the slow burn romance, the first kiss, the admission of love. Why try to fix something in her leading man's character that wasn't broken?

Even Olivia had had to admit, as she sat on her fluffy living room rug the night before, after finishing the final words of her novel, that her leading man was everything a modern woman wanted. Or at least everything that she wanted.

Her character was the embodiment of what it meant for a man to be respectful and honourable to a woman, and worship her, both in everyday life and in the bedroom.

This was by far her favourite leading male character she had written.

"There's just one thing," Hannah stated.

Olivia glanced up at her, noting the way she gazed out at the London skyline with a slight grin. "What?"

Hannah's grin widened as she turned back to face her, as if she knew something Olivia didn't.

"What is it?" Olivia panicked. The book was perfect. He was perfect. Leading man search complete. There was nothing more but to cross the t's and dot the i's. The doubt Olivia had had for the last two months began to appear again.

Had she changed her mind? Was the meet-cute not good enough? Was it all too cliché?

"What was the name of the guy again?"

Olivia frowned, taken aback by the question. "What guy, you mean the character…?"

"The one who helped you. Your muse." Hannah closed the manuscript and handed it back to her.

Your muse.

Olivia had never thought of Theo as her muse before. Their three-month agreement had gone quickly. After only a short time into the summer she had found herself typing words, letter by letter, forming scenarios and scenes. Scandalous sex and sweet kisses. After a month of meeting, Olivia had written over fifty thousand words, some more risqué than others, and had begun to fall in love with the man she was creating on the page.

"Theo?" Olivia asked, confused. She grasped the sides of the manuscript between her fingers, toying with the golden clasp that held the printed pages together. She hadn't given him much thought since their date. In fact, she had done everything she could do to make herself forget about him. He had lied to her.

Hannah reached down and tapped the batch of paper in Olivia's hands. "Yes. Theo."

"What about him?" Olivia acted disinterested, as if his name didn't have any effect on her. Liar.

Snatching the manuscript out of her hands, Hannah smacked the cover with the back of her hand. "Olivia, I swear to God. I will not hesitate to whack you with your own manuscript if you don't realise who you've written."

Realisation drained into Olivia's mind.

No.

It wasn't possible.

There was absolutely no way.

"No." Olivia snatched the pages back just as aggressively, smoothing out the creases that had appeared from their to and fro. Biting her lip, she flicked through the pages, feeling the need to reassure herself that it was all just in her head.

That what Hannah was indicating was wrong.

A mistake.

Reading chapter five, she skimmed her writing. The leading man walked the main character to her front door after each date.

Every. Single. Date.

"Let me at least drive you home…"

"You'd really walk home by yourself rather than letting me get you home safely?"

Every single date, every time they'd met up, he would wait for her 'I'm home safe' text before walking or driving off each time. He had driven all the way to Surrey for her. She realised her male character, whom she had named Micah after her lost love, stole glances at her female character, just as she had noticed Theo do. During car rides, during dinner with his parents, at his sister's almost wedding.

She turned to the page where the two characters finally kissed and noted the similarities to how Theo had kissed her, palm curled around her jaw, other hand wrapped right around her waist. The way he had brushed his nose against hers as he pulled away.

All of it was the same.

Oh God.

"Oh God," Olivia repeated aloud.

"Finally," Hannah stated, crossing her arms and looking at Olivia with a knowing look. "You wrote him."

"I wrote him."

All his stupidly perfect imperfections, right down to the small birthmark he had on the side of his neck. Olivia had given her character the very same birthmark, the size of a ten pence coin, which she had kissed so fervently in real life only weeks prior. The memory of the soft skin beneath her lips making her stomach pull and lips tingle.

The realisation washed over her with a heavy impact.

"At the moment I would like to be anywhere but near you."

Those were the words she had uttered to him with such hatred.

"I never let him explain," Olivia whispered to herself. "I was just so angry."

As much as she hated to admit it, without Theo her life seemed so much duller. Her apartment was colder, her writing harder. He gave her inspiration, encouraged her to keep going. Supported her through edits, whispered sweet musings to her. He had delivered his end of the agreement, despite setting up horrible dates for her. It was only now, as she read her manuscript back with brand new eyes, that she could see him woven between every line. His restaurant orders, the way he taps the side of his coffee mug three times after stirring in te sugar. Things she wouldn't have noticed unless she had gone on those silly update meetings after said horrible dates. Things that made her laugh and forget about those dates altogether. Things that made her realise that maybe she preferred their dates over the ones he had set up for her. That maybe that had been his plan from the very start.

"No, I want to take you *on a date. One for you, not your research. A date for my own selfish want to have you spend more time with me."*

"You need to go and find him," Hannah stated at the same time that Olivia spoke the delicate but determined words, "I need to go."

Picking up her bag, and slinging the worn leather bag over her shoulder, Olivia clutched the manuscript harder between the fingers of her left hand. She no longer cared about the creases and lines she was creating in the draft, no, she had more important things to do. More important places to be.

She needed to find him.

"I'll be back. Promise." She rushed to turn and exit the office, leaving Hannah sitting at her desk.

"Take your time, sweetheart! You found your leading man, now go get him!"

CHAPTER THIRTY-SEVEN

Olivia waited impatiently on the platform, sighing irritably as she just missed a train. She took a deep breath of the polluted, stagnant underground air and glanced up at the arrivals board: 4 agonising minutes until the next one.

She took her phone out from deep within her pocket and eyed the unopened messages from Theo. She had purposely not read them. She steeled her resolve, and read:

> I know you don't want to hear from me. But I was selfish, and I know I have no excuses, but for what it's worth, I'm sorry.

> For some silly reason I thought you would respond to my text, but your silence is killing me. I just want to know you're okay. That you're safe. I'm sorry.

> I never meant to hurt you. Shit, the look you gave before walking away haunts me. I'm sorry.

> I'm sorry.

> I'm sorry.

I'm sorry.

I'm so fucking sorry, Livvy.

The train rumbled into the platform, a rush of people exiting the carriages before she stepped over the gap, eyes scanning the messages and noticing that there was only a grand total of two days he didn't text her those two words.

I'm taking your silence to mean you don't ever want to speak to me again, and as much as it kills me, I understand. I lied. I just want you to know a few things. It was only Tommy. He was the only one. Edward, Taylor, Mason... they were all real dates. I really did want to help you, Livvy. I wanted you to write again. After meeting you, I didn't even care about the agreement, I just wanted to know you. All of you. The good, the bad, the ugly. All of it. After your bad dates, all I wanted to do was take care of you, give you hope, make the dimples in your cheeks appear whenever you smile, hear the sound of your laugh. I never paid him. It was my mate Danny's idea and the thought of paying someone to make your date bad made my stomach ache more than the idea of setting you up with Tommy in the first place. But I was selfish. I was selfish and mean and wanted you all to myself. Somewhere during these past few weeks, I have grown to care deeply about you, Olivia. You're magic, and joy, and happiness, and just everything.

I know you'll never respond to this, but I'm going to tell you one last time, then I'll stop bothering you. I'll stop messaging. I'll take your silence as a sign you never want to talk to me ever again, and like I said, I don't blame you. You deserve so much more. A man who will be everything you need, not some selfish liar. You lost your own leading man once, and I'm not going to let you lose the chance to meet a new one. So, with all that said, I'm so sorry. I'm sorry. I'm sorry. And I wish you all the best with your writing, cause like Micah said, everything you touch is fucking magic, and I can't wait to see what you create next. I'm sorry.

With shaking hands, she typed out a response. Her first in days.

Me
Do you mean that?

She watched as her message whooshed away into the universe, making her clutch her phone tighter in her hand as the train began to move, the automated voice announcing the next stop. The car was busy, with a string of office workers and women clinging off their boyfriends' arms. Her phone buzzed in her hand and her heart thudded wildly in her chest. Unlocking her phone, she stared at the screen, feeling a steady build of tears form at the words on there.

Theo
Every single word.

Three small dots appeared but she didn't wait to respond. Her fingers rushed along the keyboard, her words forming before she even realised what she was typing.

Me

I miss you.

Theo

I miss you too. I'm sorry.

Me

I had a meeting with Hannah today about the book.

Theo

How did it go?

How did it go? She considered. It went like this: *I'm madly in love with you, and it took me writing a whole manuscript and a stupid, embarrassingly long time to realise it.* She couldn't say that though. Taking a deep breath, she typed out her response.

Me

Can I see you?

Theo

Always.

Me

Meet me at Nero in thirty.

Theo

I'll be there x

He signed it with a kiss.

Olivia pursed her lips and stepped off the crowded

underground train, squeezing her body through clusters of people and making her way up the marble steps and out onto the street.

Thirty minutes.

She had a brief, but all too long, half an hour to consider how she was going to approach this. After all, walking up to him and saying *I love you* would be completely insane.

Right?

They were sitting at the very same table where they'd had their first non-date. The familiar dark-grained wood helped Olivia gather the confidence and poise to approach this scenario with full intention and clarity.

She was going to be frank. Really frank.

She wanted to be completely transparent. She wanted to get straight to the point and kiss him. She wanted much more than they currently had. She wanted much more than he knew she wanted.

And she was scared.

Her usual confidence – the same confidence that allowed her to tell him she had unashamedly eaten over three baskets of breadsticks – disappeared as soon as she noticed Theo's tall, broad figure approaching the café door.

As he pushed open the heavy black door, Olivia couldn't help but drift her eyes down over his firm build. He was wearing a long navy trench coat, the collar of his work shirt peeking out from the top, making her inhale deeply at the way it clung to the firm muscles of his shoulders. She had almost forgotten how handsome he was, all tall and brooding, with those bright eyes and dark locks. Almost.

Flashes of his olive skin, the way she had raked her fingertips down the planes of his back, intruded into her mind. She didn't even wait for him to sit down. Get a coffee. Say hello. It just came out. As if their bad date had never happened, as though his apology had already sunk deep into her bones, in acceptance.

"I did it," Olivia announced abruptly. "I handed it in. It's all approved."

"So, you found him?" Theo grinned. He leaned down and kissed her swiftly on the corner of her temple before pulling back and finally sitting down beside her.

Not across from her. Beside her.

Olivia's heart began to thrum faster than before. Her fear no longer stemmed from the thought of telling him. Instead it buzzed from the way he was looking at her, attentive and excited for her to continue her good news.

Olivia was aware of the subtle yet electrifying jolt of his knee against hers underneath the table and the way he turned to face her, body positioned so he could easily reach a strong arm over the back of her chair, silently claiming that she was his to every person in the coffee shop. She now noticed it all. Every small gesture, movement, look. She took note and relished the fact that despite her radio silence, despite her harsh words, he still looked at her like she hung the moon.

Oh, she had found him alright.

He was sitting right in front of her. In all of his masculine beauty. Raking a hand through his hair, Theo shot her another grin. The grin she had kissed right off his face a few weeks prior when they had both given in to the buzzing attraction they'd neglected for quite some time.

The grin that spoke volumes of what was between them, of whispering sweet nothings and dirty secrets into each other's ears. It told her how he wanted to ravish her body and mind. How beautiful she looked, whether she was in a little black dress or an old, thrifted AC/DC T-shirt.

She didn't even listen to AC/DC.

"Yeah," she finally said, feeling the corners of her lips turn up into a vibrant smile. One where her cheeks ached, and the top row of her teeth showed. "Yeah. I found him."

Not once did his gaze leave her; instead, a smile, matching her own cheesy one, pulled up onto his face. *God, he's handsome*, Olivia thought. She felt her stomach tighten at the appearance of his dimples, and the daring thought of licking them made her shuffle in her seat and squeeze her thighs together at the sensual imagery.

"I knew you'd find him."

"You did?"

"I did." Theo continued grinning.

Biting her bottom lip, Olivia retrieved the crumpled, rain-sprinkled manuscript from the top of the table and pushed it towards him nervously.

Theo glanced down at the stack of white papers. "Is this it?"

"That is… it." Olivia let out a relieved laugh, watching as his eyes flickered with the same curious spark, they had during their first ever meeting. When he had seen her with her little green notebook. Knowing what he was going to ask, she pushed it further into his hands. "Go on then, curiosity must be killing you."

"You have no idea." Theo laughed, flipping open the first page, his eyes moving from hers down to the paper, and began devouring the small Times New Roman text.

As Theo began to read, it became clear.

It was just as he had expected. He knew what the book would be like long before he had opened the front page. He already knew it would be just like her.

Fucking perfect.

But it was even more brilliant than he had expected. She was brilliant. The thought made him drag his eyes across the pages even faster, the feeling of reading her words making him dizzy with pride and something else all too consuming.

Sitting there in Caffè Nero, at 5:50 in the evening on a Saturday, he hungrily devoured the first few chapters of her fourth novel, and with each chapter, each page, each word, the feeling became clearer and clearer. Until finally it was printed in bold, woven into her writing, into the way she was watching his reaction to the text in front of him so intently. Into the way she bit her lip, the way she tilted her head and licked her lips whenever he grinned at her words.

It became so clear to him, and he found himself struggling to keep his eyes on the page instead of reaching over the small space between them and kissing the living daylights out of her.

That's what he thought of this novel, of her.

Any doubts he'd had previously he now struck out in his

mind with his own black biro. The obvious streamed into the forefront of his mind: underlined and highlighted with urgency.

He loved her.

CHAPTER THIRTY-EIGHT

"Olivia."

The way he said her name made her palms sweat.

Did he notice?

She had waited patiently and watched as he had read. Ski reading certain sections, closely reading others. Frowning, smiling, blushing. Every mistake, every joke, every innuendo.

Hannah had given the stamp of approval to the manuscript, sending it off to her literary agent with her own congratulatory bias; saying it was the best book from her yet, and shedding a small tear at the thought of Olivia not only finding her leading man, but also finding him.

By the time he was on the last page, she had seen all of the grins, all of the frowns and flickers across his face, and memorised them by heart.

And once he had finished, he closed the final page and sat there for a few beats.

The silence ate away at her nerves.

Did he not like it? Was it too obvious? She kind of hoped it would be obvious. She felt her heartbeat excessively in her chest at the extended silence between them. He opened and closed his mouth multiple times, eyes still heavy and set on the three-hundred-page final draft in front of him.

She watched as his fingers toyed with the corners of the pages, his jaw set in thought.

Theo took a deep breath, and then, like a perfect symphony, said her name.

Her goddamn name with the same deep baritone she had been compelled by from the very beginning.

Looking up, Theo's eyes met hers. She watched the swirl of gold darken in his eyes, his body sitting up straight, and fully turning towards her.

Feeling her panic and nerves begin to surface, she began talking, overcompensating, excessive nattering about how it was just a draft and that she'd welcome more criticism even if it were to mean she would have to go back and edit once more. That the leading man wasn't perfect yet, that she could still improve it.

"Olivia," he said again, as though saying her name once would never be enough. She loved the way his tongue formed her name, the way he pronounced the 'l', as if he was making slow and passionate love to each letter.

"Yes?" she breathed softly.

"It's…" he started, before reaching up and messing up those stupidly perfect curls of his. He pursed his lips, glancing up at her with a look she had never seen before. His eyes mischievous, shining in a way that screamed words she had never heard. "I love your mind."

Inhaling sharply, Olivia glanced at his lips. How she'd thought her name sounded from his lips was nothing compared to the way they formed the word love. It was the nicest compliment she had received by a long shot, and it had come from him.

Her lips wobbled slightly, tears of overwhelming joy threatening to fill her eyes.

"I'm so happy for you," Theo continued. "Your writing…" He took a deep breath. "It's… you're amazing."

A flush of scarlet spread across her cheeks, the kind words taking her off guard. Theo thought she was amazing.

"I love your mind."

He thought she was brilliant.

It was as though her nerves were connected to an electric cable, a sharp spark of electricity starting her heart up once again as he smiled at her.

I love your mind too, she thought. *I love all of you. I love you*, she wanted to say, but she couldn't. Not when he had just read her novel and called her brilliant and shared that look with her.

He would think she was being polite. Thanking her for finding her leading man rather than acknowledging that it was him.

Theo was her leading man.

He might neglect to acknowledge that he was the leading man she wanted forever. Not only for three hundred pages, but for the rest of her life. For every book she would write in the future. Fiction and non-fiction.

He wasn't a fictional character she had made up.

No, he was the real thing.

And he was sitting right beside her, close enough that if she were to lean forward three inches, they would be sharing oxygen, and one inch further, and he would be tasting the latte and gingerbread biscuit she had scoffed nervously before he had finished the manuscript.

She wanted nothing more than for him to taste the hidden words on her lips, pry them out of her mind like he had when she was writing. If only he would read between the lines, he would notice.

Encoded throughout her novel, she had written him, in black and white, in technicolour.

Her eyes flicked down to his mouth, which was fighting off another smile, a smile she wanted to feel against her own. A smile she wanted to taste on her tongue. Feel on the corner of her mouth.

"Can I read it again?" Theo asked, already opening the manuscript once more.

Olivia grinned at his gleeful manner, before laughing at the way he greedily consumed the opening paragraph with such focus. He once again began to read her words, this time flicking his eyes up to hers during certain parts, winking at her whenever she caught his gaze.

Oh yeah, I definitely love this man, she thought, the thought sending silliness through her veins and setting off fireworks in her stomach.

She was suddenly quiet, nervous, unsure of how to approach the delicate subject of her feelings. She knew what she felt, and as ironic as it was for an author to say, she just didn't know how to put that feeling into words.

It was a whole other level of writer's block.

One that could only be solved by confrontation and honesty.

By admission.

It was now or never, and Olivia felt herself wanting to rip off the plaster while hoping she wouldn't bleed out.

"I guess this is the end then," Theo said, a small smile on his face. They had sat side by side, grinning and whispering like teenagers on a first date until the lights had dimmed and the coffee machine was cleaned.

"Yeah." Olivia gave a small smile, but it didn't reach her eyes. They were walking towards the station, her arm looped through his. Her manuscript had been safely stowed back in her leather side bag, the thick paper feeling lighter knowing he approved of her story.

A light drizzle had begun an hour ago, and the two were riddled with small specks of misty rainfall. The streets of London were lit with the white illumination emitting from Metro supermarkets and offices. A steady movement of workers returning home made her glad to be tucked into Theo's side, away from bumping into the rush of umbrella-laden men and high-heeled women making their way in groups downtown for the evening.

"Hey." Theo grinned, elbowing her in the side playfully. He had been noticing the small line between her brow, the gentle furrowing of her bottom lip between her teeth since they had left the café.

Olivia looked over at him and gave him a small and restrained smile. "What?"

"You found your leading man." Theo grinned smugly, tugging her forward and pulling her into his chest, his arm slinging over her shoulder as if it were the most natural thing in the world.

Over the past few months, it had almost become a natural act. As if he couldn't have her any other place but tucked firmly into his side.

Where she belongs, he thought. Hugging her close to his body, he leaned down and kissed the high point of her cheek. "I'm so proud of you."

It was a cheesy thing to say, he knew that. But little comments, ones that would make her share a small smile and roll her eyes meant a lot more to her than she communicated. After a few moments, he felt her thin arms snake around his waist, pulling him closer to her, and she burrowed her face right over his heart.

"I know. I no longer need your services," Olivia teased, her voice breaking slightly at the end.

Theo squeezed her closer for a moment. "I'm glad I could be of assistance."

"In all seriousness, Theo…" Olivia halted her steps, her chin tilting up towards him. Every time he walked by her, Theo always marvelled at how small she was. How he could easily wrap her into his side and made her feel protected and warm. As though his arms were made for her. As if his shoulder was moulded to the shape of her head, the crook oh-so-deliciously accommodating her petite figure.

"Thank you. I couldn't have done it without you."

"I don't think that's true. I think you would've written something magnificent either way—"

She was already shaking her head before he could finish his sentence. "No. You don't understand." She turned her body to face him, their lips now centimetres apart. "*I couldn't have done it without you.*"

Theo let out an uncertain laugh, a drop of rain running down the side of his temple and towards the side of his lips. "What are you saying?"

Olivia bit her own lip, glancing at the drop of water that threatened to fall onto his plump lips. "What I'm saying is…"

Theo lowered his gaze to her neck, watching as she gulped heavily, before letting his eye flicker between her blue orbs and the dusty rose-coloured lip gloss she had on.

She puckered her lips gently, before speaking once more. "What I'm saying is… what if I don't need your assistance anymore? What if… what if I want it?"

"Olivia—" he began.

"When I was writing… I realised something." He glanced down at the women standing before him. Even in the rain, even in damp clothing, her lipstick smudged slightly and a frown on her face, she was still the most beautiful thing he had ever seen.

Nothing had changed in that regard since the moment he had first laid eyes on her all those months ago. "I realised that my leading man, the one who you just read, the one who is attentive and listens, the one that is respectful, and kind. Loving and smart. Loyal and ambitious. Passionate. I realised that… my leading man is you."

Olivia took a deep breath. "I know it sounds crazy, and I didn't even believe it. It took me until I was sitting in my literary agent's office, questioning the quality of my work, that I realised I had written you. That I couldn't change it. I didn't want to. I simply refuse to, because the man I had written is you. The man who is my lead character, who I had fallen madly and deeply in love with… is you."

Theo felt the cool misty rain settle on his warm skin, her confession raining down on him and sinking deep into his bones like the rain through his coat. "You wrote me?"

"Yes." The one-word confession almost felt sacred and holy. "I wrote you. I know I shouldn't have, and I know it sounds absolutely crazy, but you're my leading man, Theo. You always have been and—"

His lips cut off her rambling, cool wet lips slanting easily with the rain over hers. The taste of gingerbread and warm coffee made him groan, before he grabbed her face with a firm hand, tilting her jaw up just enough to brush his lips more intently against hers.

Olivia sighed into his hold, lips moving against his, the soft kiss becoming more heated as she pressed her lip gloss covered lips to his firmly.

They couldn't get enough of each other, lips moving fast then slow, her hands twisting around the long collar of his navy coat and dragging him closer to her. Lifting herself up onto her tiptoes, she let out a soft moan against his lips, the taste of coffee and cool rain sending shivers down his spine, until her front was pressed up against his, and the bustling noise of the central London street was nothing but a dim hum in the background.

All he could feel was her. All he could think was her. All he could taste was her. He swore he could kiss her forever and never get bored of the soft, plump lips and the taste of purely *her*.

Each time he had allowed himself to think of her as something more, he had pulled back, cautious of both her heart and his thoughts.

But his mother was right. He could try to be careful with her, but Olivia was a tornado of love barrelling through his city and destroying everything he had ever known. She was a force to be reckoned with, leaving debris and litter of the sweetest thoughts and touches in her wake.

During their time together, he had begun to welcome her destruction, and now he craved it.

"Get a room!" someone shouted, causing the pair to break apart, their lips humming with the same electricity buzzing in the small space between them.

They both looked over at the young teenage boy biking away down the street, before turning back to each other.

Theo stared into her eyes, getting lost in their deep blue hue.

The sides of her eyes crinkled up, and before they knew it, they were standing in the middle of the London street, under the dim glow of the streetlights, laughing.

"You've got a little something—" Olivia reached up and wiped some of her lip gloss off from the corner of his mouth.

"Oh yeah? Well you've got a little something—" Theo leaned forward, capturing her lips once more, grinning into her mouth as he felt her own smile against his lips. "Come on, let's get you out of this rain," he said, pulling her back into his side, this time grasping her tightly around her waist and leaning down to whisper into her ear. "And out of these clothes."

Olivia flushed bashfully, hitting him on the arm, knowing full well when they got back to her apartment that he would follow through on his word.

ABOUT THE AUTHOR

Kate Gaskarth is a British author who studied Education at the University of Canterbury and now calls Christchurch, New Zealand home. She lives there with her partner and spends her days writing, reading, and enjoying time with family. *Love and Fiction* is her debut adult novel.

Why not keep up to date with Kate's future projects by following her on socials:

Instagram: @kategaskarth
TikTok: @kategaskarthauthor